"You aren't going to leave me to drown!"

The astonishing thought distracted Annja from the floodwaters until they rose above the tops of her waterproofed shoes. Their touch was as cold as the long-dead Emperor's.

"At least leave me my pack!" Annja shouted, jumping up and swiping ineffectually at the dangling rope-end. She only succeeded in making it swing. She fell back with a considerable splash.

"I'm afraid not," the woman called. "You have to understand, Ms. Creed. There are two ways to do things—the hard way and the *easy* way."

Annja stood for a moment with the water streaming past her ankles. The words were so ridiculous that her mind, already considerably stressed by the moment, simply refused to process them.

Then reality struck her. "Easy?" she screamed. "Not Easy Ngwenya?"

Annja stared. The chill water reached her knees. She stood, utterly overwhelmed by the realization that she had just been victimized by the world's most notorious tomb robber.

Titles in this series:

Destiny
Solomon's Jar
The Spider Stone
The Chosen
Forbidden City
The Lost Scrolls
God of Thunder
Secret of the Slaves
Warrior Spirit
Serpent's Kiss
Provenance
The Soul Stealer
Gabriel's Horn
The Golden Elephant

ROGUE Angel

Alex Archer

THE GOLDEN ELEPHANT

A GOLD EAGLE BOOK FROM

WORLDWIDE®

TORONTO • NEW YORK • LONDON
AMSTERDAM • PARIS • SYDNEY • HAMBURG
STOCKHOLM • ATHENS • TOKYO • MILAN
MADRID • WARSAW • BUDAPEST • AUCKLAND

First edition September 2008

ISBN-13: 978-0-373-62132-3
ISBN-10:   0-373-62132-9

THE GOLDEN ELEPHANT

Special thanks and acknowledgment to
Victor Milán for his contribution to this work.

Printed in U.S.A.

THe
LEGEND

...THE ENGLISH COMMANDER TOOK
JOAN'S SWORD AND RAISED IT HIGH.

The broadsword, plain and unadorned,
gleamed in the firelight. He put the tip against
the ground and his foot at the center of the blade.
The broadsword shattered, fragments falling
into the mud. The crowd surged forward,
peasant and soldier, and snatched the shards
from the trampled mud. The commander tossed
the hilt deep into the crowd.
Smoke almost obscured Joan, but she continued
praying till the end, until finally the flames climbed
her body and she sagged against the restraints.

Joan of Arc died that fateful day in France,
but her legend and sword are reborn....

1

Tomb of the Mad Emperor

"Oops," Annja Creed said as she felt something give beneath the cleated heel of her Red Wing walking shoe.

The floor of the passageway was caked inches thick in dust. Annja couldn't see the trigger. She had sensed more than heard something like a twig snapping.

Already in motion, Annja dived for the floor. She heard a grind, a rumble, a rusty creaking. Then with a hefty metallic sound something shot from the stone walls above her.

Catching herself on her hands, Annja looked around by the light of her bulky hand lantern, which lay several feet ahead of her. She spotted three bronze spears spanning the two-yard-wide corridor a yard above the floor. They were meant to impale any unwary intruder. That included her.

Annja shook her head. "Emperor Lu may or may not have been crazy," she muttered. "But he sure was paranoid."

The echoes of her words chased each other down the slanting corridor, deep into the earth's dark recesses.

CAUTIOUSLY ANNJA WIGGLED forward. As her weight came off the hidden floor plate the spears began to retract into the walls. By the time she reached her lantern they had vanished. The stone plates that covered the ports through which the spears had thrust out swung back into place.

Coughing on the dust she had stirred up doing her snake act, Annja sat up and shone her light on the walls. She could see no sign of where the spears had come from. The walls had been painted with some kind of murals, perhaps once quite colorful. They had faded to mere swirls and suggestions of faint color. They worked to camouflage the trap, though.

She shook her head and picked herself up. "Got to move," she told herself softly as she dusted off the front of her tan shirt and khaki cargo pants. This would be her only shot. With the construction of a giant dam nearby, the floodwaters were rising. By tomorrow they would make the subterranean tunnels unsafe.

With redoubled caution she made her way deeper into the lost emperor's tomb.

The corridor walls were hewed from a yellow limestone. Tests showed it had been quarried in some hills several miles away. The passageway air was cool and dry. It smelled of stone and earth.

Some indeterminate distance down, as Annja began to feel the weight, not just of years, but of millions of tons of earth pressing upon her, the corridor leveled. It had taken several bends and a couple of doglegs, and had plateaued briefly, as well. Annja wasn't sure whether the zigs and zags had some ritual significance, were meant to additionally befuddle an interloper or were simply to prevent a cart full of spoil from running all the way back down to the bottom during the digging of the corridor. She suspected it was all of the above.

Far down the hallway, in which she could just stand upright, Annja saw that something was blocking the way. Could that be the door to Lu's actual tomb? she wondered. Her heart beat quickened. According to the ground-penetrating radar scans, it could be. The last Chinese team to come down here had intended to open the bronze door to the burial chamber proper. She had no idea whether they had or not.

The Beijing University officials who had hired Annja suggested that they felt the last team had indeed made some major discoveries and had then departed by some currently unknown entrance to the great mound before vanishing. There was nothing intrinsically unlikely about that. Such huge structures often had multiple entrances. But she was being asked to play archaeology cop—to find out if the tomb had been plundered and, if possible, to trace the thieves. She was certainly willing enough. Like any real archaeologist she had an unremitting hatred of tomb robbers.

"Of course that assumes a lot of ifs," Annja said aloud. Her voice, echoing down the chamber, reassured her. Something about the place bothered her.

She flashed her light down the corridor. She thought she saw a hint of green from the obstruction. She knew that was consistent with bronze doors. The copper in the alloy turned green as it oxidized. Otherwise bronze wasn't prone to corrosion, as iron and steel were.

I wonder if I should have looked more closely for bloodstains around those spear traps, she thought. The two expeditions that had returned had warned about various booby traps.

But she wasn't here to do forensic work. Time pressed. So did the billions of tons of water that would soon be rushing to engulf the mound.

As she moved forward toward the door she became aware of a strange smell. A bad smell, and all too familiar—the stench of death.

It grew stronger as she approached the door. And then she fell right into another of Emperor Lu's little surprises.

The floor tipped abruptly beneath her. The right side pivoted up. She dropped straight down.

Without thought she formed her right hand into a fist. Obedient to her call, the hilt of the legendary blade of Joan of Arc filled her hand. Falling, she thrust the sword to her left and drove it eight inches into the pit's wall.

It was enough. Grabbing the hilt with her left hand, as well, she clung desperately and looked down.

The hint of scent had become a foul cloud that enveloped her. She choked and gagged. The floor trap was hinged longitudinally along the center. The pit was twenty feet long and sank at least twelve feet deep. Bronze spearheads jutted up from the floor like snaggled green teeth.

Entangled and impaled among them, almost directly below her, lay a number of bodies. She couldn't tell exactly how many; they had become tangled together as they fell onto the spears. The glare of her lantern, which lay tilted fortuitously up and angled in a corner, turned them into something from a nightmare.

One man hung alone to one side, bent backward. His mouth was wide open in a final scream at the spearhead that jutted two feet upward from his belly. The remnants of what looked like a stretcher of sorts, possibly improvised out of backpack-frames, lay beneath him.

At the shadow-clotted base of the pit she could just make out the dome of a skull or the multiple arch of a rib cage protruding from ages of drifted dust. The missing Chinese archaeology team were not the first victims.

She looked up. She had fallen only a couple of yards below the pit's lip. The sword had entered the wall blade-vertical. It flexed only slightly under her weight. She knew it could break—the English had done it, when they burned its former holder at the stake—but it didn't seem strained at the moment.

Unwilling to test it any longer than she had to, she swung back and forth experimentally, gaining momentum. Then she launched her legs back and up and let go.

Whatever kind of graceful landing she was hoping for didn't happen. Her legs and hips flopped up onto the floor. Her head and upper torso swung over empty space—and the waiting bronze spearheads. As her body started to topple forward she got her hands on the rim of the pit and halted herself. Her hair escaped from the clip holding it to hang about her face like a curtain.

With something like revulsion she threw herself backward. She sprawled on her butt and elbows, scraping the latter. Then she just lay like that awhile and breathed deeply.

The sword had vanished into the otherwhere.

One thing her life had taught her since she had come, unwittingly and quite unwillingly, into possession of Joan of Arc's Sword was to bounce back from the most outlandish occurrences as if they were no more significant or unusual than spilling a cup of coffee.

"That got the old heart rate going," she said.

She slowly got to her feet. The trapdoor swung over and began to settle back to the appearance of a normal, innocuous stretch of floor. As it eclipsed the beam of her lost lamp, shining up from the pit like hellfire, she reached up to switch on her headlamp. Its reassuring yellow glow sprang out as the glare was cut off.

It wasn't very powerful. The darkness seemed to flood around the narrow beam, with a palpable weight and presence. "It'll be enough," she muttered. "It has to be."

Putting her back to the left-hand wall, she edged down the corridor. The dust, which had settled in the past few weeks, hiding the doomed expedition's foot-steps, had been dumped into the pit, except for a certain quantity that still swirled in the air and rasped her lungs like sandpaper. The clean patch of floor, limned by the white light shining from below, made its end obvious.

Cautiously she moved the rest of the way down the corridor toward the green door. No more traps tried to grab her.

As she'd suspected, the door was verdigrised bronze. It had a stylized dragon embossed on it—the ancient symbol of imperial might. She hesitated. She saw no obvious knob or handle.

Reaching into her pocket for a tissue to cover her hand, she pushed on the door. It swung inward creakily. She had to put her weight behind it before it opened fully.

A great wash of cool air swept over her. Surpris-ingly, it lacked the staleness she would have expected from a tomb sealed for two and a half millennia. Bending low, she stepped inside.

The tomb of Mad Emperor Lu was almost anticli-mactic. It was a simple domed space, twenty yards in diameter, rising to ten at the apex, through which a hole about a yard wide opened through smooth-polished stone. Annja wondered if had been intended to allow the emperor's spirit to depart the burial chamber.

Dust covered the floor, a good four inches deep, so that it swamped Annja's shoes. In the midst of the dust pond stood a catafalque, four feet high and wide, eight feet long. On it lay an effigy in what appeared to be moldering robes, long cobwebbed and gone the color of the dust that had mounded over it, half obscuring it. A second mound rose suggestively by the feet.

Annja dug her digital camera from her pack. She snapped several photos. The built-in flash would have to do. Feeling time and the approaching floodwaters pressing down, Annja moved forward as cautiously as she could through the dust. Her archaeologist's reflex was to disturb things as little as possible.

But that wasn't the reason for her deliberation. Soon all this would be underwater—a great crime against history itself, but one about which she could do nothing. She still sought to do as little damage as possible, in hopes someday the artificial lake might be drained and what the water left of the tomb properly excavated. She was more worried about stirring a cloud of blinding dust.

And more traps.

Uneventfully she reached the foot of the bier. On closer inspection the reclining figure seemed to be a mummy rather than an effigy. Annja presumed it was the man himself, Emperor Lu, his madness tempered by age and desiccation and, of course, being dead. It still gave her a shiver to be in the presence of such a mythic figure.

"This isn't right," she said softly. She felt a great sorrow mixed with anger that this corpse, this priceless relic, was soon to be desecrated, and almost certainly to decay to nothing in the waters of a new lake. She thought about trying to carry it out with her.

She sighed and forced herself to let the inevitable happen. She snapped some shots of the old guy, though, from several angles, always being careful where she put her feet, lest the floor swallow her up and dump her down another awful chasm.

But Lu seemed to have no more surprises awaiting intruders upon his celestial nap. Surprisingly little did await the intrepid tomb robber, leaving aside the august but somewhat diminished imperial person. Except, perhaps, that mound by the mummy's feet.

She finished recording Lu for posterity and knelt by the foot of the bier. The mound was about as wide as a dinner plate and four or five inches high. Gently Annja brushed dust away with her hands.

In a moment she uncovered the artifact—a beautiful circular seal of milky green jade, six inches wide and a good inch thick, engraved with the figure of a sinuous dragon. It was Lu's imperial seal, beyond doubt. Annju's heart caught in her throat. Bingo, she thought. Properly displayed in some museum, it would be a worthy relic of Mad Lu's long-forgotten reign.

Reverently she reached out and touched it. The green stone was smooth as a water-polished pebble. It was hard, yet seemed to have some sort of give, as if it were a living thing and not a carved stone artifact. The workmanship was fully as exquisite as might be expected. Each of the toes on the dragon's feet was clearly visible, and the characters inscribed around it stood in clear relief. To hold such an object in her hand was itself a reward—reminding her, half-guiltily, how abundantly she would have earned her commission.

A rustle of movement tickled her ear in the stillness of the tomb—a dry creaking, a soft sound as of falling dust. A flicker of motion tugged at her peripheral vision.

She turned. Emperor Lu was sitting up on his bier. The shriveled face with its empty eye sockets looked not just mad, but angry.

Annja gasped.

For a moment she crouched there clutching the jade and staring at its moldering owner like a deer caught in the headlights. And then a great downward geyser of water shot out of the ceiling, drowning the mummy and knocking Annja sprawling.

She was washed toward the bronze door on a torrent of glutinous mud. For a moment the wildly spiraling beam of her headlamp illuminated the mummy. It sat there on its catafalque in the midst of the stream as if taking a shower. The jaw had fallen open, she could clearly see. It was as if Lu laughed at her—enjoying his final joke on the woman who had despoiled his tomb.

Then the water obscured her sight of him. She managed to get onto her feet against the rushing torrent. She scrambled out with the water sloshing around her shins.

Annja realized the corridor was only flat relative to the steep decline she had descended, for it filled with water more slowly than it would have if level. Out of options, she ran for all she was worth. The quick death of tripping some trap, previously discovered or not, and being impaled with ancient spears seemed infinitely preferable to being trapped down here to drown in the dark. The prospect woke a whole host of fears in Annja's soul, like myriad rats maddened by an ancient plague.

She vaulted the hinged-floor trap, still outlined in thin white lines of light, without hesitation. Her long jump wasn't quite good enough. The floor pivoted heart-wrenchingly beneath her feet. Adrenaline fueled a second frantic leap that carried her to safety. She raced up the steeper tunnel as the water gurgled at her heels.

It followed her right up the ramp. The place was seriously shipping water. She wondered why the passageway wasn't fatally flooded already.

That made her run the faster. Her light swung wildly before her.

But even under the direst circumstances Annja never altogether lost her presence of mind. A part of her always kept assessing, evaluating, even in the heat of passion. Or panic.

Since survival in the current situation didn't require fast thinking so much as fast legwork, she realized why the air in the tomb had not been stale and why dust had settled so deeply on the floor and upon the emperor.

That hole in the ceiling may or may not have been a celestial escape route for Lu's soul. It certainly was an air shaft. No matter how disposable labor was in his day—and she suspected that it was mighty disposable indeed—Lu had to know his tomb would never get built if the laborers kept dropping dead of asphyxiation the moment they reached the work site. Not to mention the fact that in those days skilled masons and engineers weren't disposable, and had he treated them that way, his tomb never would've been built in the first place.

No doubt an extensive network of ventilation shafts terminated at the tomb mound's sides at shallow angles. They would have been built with doglegs and baffles to prevent water getting in under normal circumstances. Otherwise the old emperor and his last bier would have been a stalagmite.

That also explained why Annja wasn't swimming hopelessly upstream right now. One peculiarity—*eccentricity* was probably the word, considering the creator—of Mad Emperor Lu's tomb was that it was entered from the top. Annja had made her way gingerly down, and was making her way a good deal less carefully back up a series of winding ramps and passages. The vent shafts were probably entirely discrete from the corridors. Perhaps Lu had contrived a way to flood his subterranean burial chamber from ground water or a buried cistern.

Screaming with friction, spears leaped from the wall to Annja's left. The green bronze heads crashed the far wall's stone behind her back. The traps were timed for a party advancing at a deliberate pace. Annja was fleeing.

Up through the tunnels Annja raced. When she dared risk a glance back over her shoulder she saw water surging after her like a monster made of froth. She was gaining, though.

That gave her cold comfort. No way was ground water, much less water stored in a buried cistern, rising this far this fast, she thought. It took serious pressure to drive this mass of water. The valley was clearly flooding a lot quicker than she had been assured it would.

So now she was racing the waters rising outside the mound, as well as those within.

If the water outside got too high, the helicopter Annja had hired to bring her here and carry her away when she emerged would simply fly away. She couldn't much blame the pilot. There'd be nothing to do for her.

Trying hard not to think about the unthinkable, Annja ran harder. A stone trigger gave beneath her feet; another spring trap she hadn't tripped on her way down thrust its spears from the wall. They missed, too.

From time to time side passages joined the main corridor. In her haste she missed the one that led to the entrance she had come in by, which was not at the mound's absolute apex. She only realized her error when she came into a hemispherical chamber at what must have been the actual top. A hole in the ceiling let in vague, milky light from an appropriately overcast sky.

Annja stopped, panting. Though she knew it was a bad way to recover she bent over to rest hands on thighs. For the first time she realized she still clutched the imperial seal in a death grip. The expedition wasn't a total write-off.

Provided I live, she thought.

Forcing herself to straighten and draw deep abdominal breaths, she looked up at the hole. It was small. She guessed she could get through. But only just. She would never pass while she wore her day pack. And she wasn't going to risk wriggling through with the seal in a cargo pocket. The fit was tight enough it would almost certainly break.

"Darn," she said. She swung off her pack. Wrapping the seal in a handkerchief, she stuck it in a Ziploc bag she had brought for protecting artifacts. She stowed it carefully in her pack and set off back down the corridor to find the real way out.

She was stopped within a few steps. The water had caught her.

"Oh, dear," she said faintly as it surged toward her. The valley was flooding fast.

She ran back up to the apex chamber. Cupping her hands around her mouth, she shouted, "Hello? Can you hear me? I need a little help here!"

She did so without much hope. The pilot and copilot would be sitting in the cockpit with both engines running. With the waters rising so fast they had to be ready for a quick getaway. In fact, Annja had no particularly good reason to believe they hadn't already flown away.

To her surprise she was answered almost at once.

"Hello down there," a voice called back through the hole. "I'll lend you a hand."

Annja stared at the hole for a moment, although she could see nothing but grey cloud. She had no idea who her rescuer was. It sure wasn't the pilot or the copilot—they weren't young women with what sounded for all the world like an Oxford accent.

"Um—hello?" Annja called out.

"I'm throwing down a rope," the young woman said. A pale blue nylon line uncoiled from the ceiling.

"I've got a pack," Annja called up, looking nervously back over her shoulder at the chamber's entrance. She could hear the slosh of rising water just outside. "It's got important artifacts in it. Extremely delicate. I'll have to ask you to pull the pack up first. I can't fit through the hole while carrying it."

She expected her unseen benefactor to argue—the primary value of human life and all that. But instead she replied, "Very well. Tie it on and I'll pull it up straightaway."

Annja did so. When she called out that it was secure, it rose rapidly toward the ceiling. She frowned, but the woman slowed it down when it neared the top. She extracted it without its synthetic fabric touching the sides of the hole.

"Thanks," Annja called. "Good job."

After an anxious moment the rope came through the ceiling again. Except not far enough.

Not *nearly* far enough. Annja reckoned she could just barely brush it with her fingertips if she jumped as high as she could. She could never get a grip on it.

"Uh, hey," she called. "I'm afraid it's not far enough. I need a little more rope here."

She heard a musical laugh. It made its owner sound about fourteen. "So sorry," the unseen voice said. "No can do."

"What do you mean?" Annja almost screamed the

words as water burst into the room to eddy around her shoes. "You aren't going to leave me to drown?"

"Of course not. In a matter of a very few minutes the water will rise enough to float you up to where you can grasp the rope and climb out. A bit damp, perhaps, but none the worse for wear."

Annja stared. The astonishing words actually distracted her from the floodwaters until they rose above the tops of her waterproofed shoes and sloshed inside them. Their touch was cold as the long-dead emperor's.

"At least leave me my pack!" Annja shouted, jumping up and swiping ineffectually at the dangling rope. She only succeeded in making it swing. She fell back with a considerable splash.

"I'm afraid not," the woman called. "You have to understand, Ms. Creed. There're two ways to do things—the hard way and the *easy* way."

Annja stood a moment with the water streaming past her ankles. The words were so ridiculous that her mind, already considerably stressed by the moment, simply refused to process them.

Then reality struck her. "Easy?" she screamed. "Not Easy Ngwenya?"

"The same. Farewell, Annja Creed!"

Annja stared. The chill water reached her knees. She stood, utterly overwhelmed by the realization that she had just been victimized by the world's most notorious tomb robber.

2

Paris, France

"You're kidding," Annja said. "Who doesn't like the Eiffel Tower?"

"It's an excrescence," Roux replied.

"Right," she said. "So you preferred it when all you had to watch for in the sky was chamber pots being emptied on your head from the upper stories?"

"You moderns. You have lost touch with your natures. Ah, back in those days we appreciated simple pleasures."

"Not including hygiene."

Roux regarded her from beneath a critically arched white brow. "You display a most remarkably crabbed attitude for an antiquarian."

"I study the period," she said. "I'm fascinated by the period. But I don't romanticize it. I know way too much about it for that. I wouldn't want to *live* in the Renaissance."

"Bah," the old man said. But he spoke without heat. "There is something to this progress, I do not deny. But often I miss the old days."

"And you've plenty of old days to miss," Annja said. Which was, if anything, an understatement. When he spoke about the Renaissance, he did so from actual experience.

Roux was dressed like what he was—an extremely wealthy old man–in an elegantly tailored dove-gray suit and a white straw hat, his white hair and beard considerably more neatly barbered than his ferocious brows.

Annja had set down her cup. She sat with her elbows on the metal mesh tabletop, fingers interlaced and chin propped on the backs of her hands. She wore a sweater with wide horizontal stripes of red, yellow and blue over her well-worn blue jeans. A pair of sunglasses was pushed up onto the front of her hair, which she wore in a ponytail.

Autumn had begun to bite. The leaves on the trees along the Seine were turning yellow around the edges, and the air was tinged with a hint of wood smoke. But Paris café society was of sterner stuff than to be discouraged by a bit of cool in the air. Instead the sidewalks and their attendant cafés seemed additionally thronged by savvy Parisians eager to absorb all the sun's heat they could before winter settled in.

She found herself falling back onto her current

favorite subject. "I'm still miffed at what happened in Ningxia," she said.

"*You're* miffed? I have had to answer to certain creditors after the shortfall in our accounts. Which was caused by your incompetence, need I remind you?"

"No. And anyway, that's not true. I got the seal. I had it in my hands."

"Unfortunately it failed to stay in your hands, dear child."

"That wasn't my fault! I trusted her," Annja said.

"You trusted a strange voice which called down to you through a hole in the ground," Roux said. "And you style yourself a skeptic, *non?*"

Annja sat back. "I was kind of up against it there. I didn't really have a choice."

"Did you not? Really? But did you not eventually save yourself by following that vexatious young lady's suggestion, and waiting until the water floated you high enough so you could climb the rest of the way out?"

"Only to find the witch had flown off in my helicopter. *My. Helicopter,*" Annja said.

"Oh, calm down," the old man said unsympathetically. "She did send a boat for you. Which she paid for herself."

Annja sat back and tightly folded her arms beneath her breasts. "That just added insult to injury," she said. The tomb robber had even left her pack. Without the seal. "Whose side are you on, anyway?"

"My own, of course," Roux said. "Why be mad at

me? I only point out things could have gone much worse. You might have seen Miss E. C. Ngwenya's famous trademark pistols, for example."

Annja slumped. "True."

"And it never occurred to you," Roux said, "simply to wait until the water lifted you high enough to climb out the hole directly, without handing over the object of your entire journey to a mysterious voice emanating from the ceiling?"

Annja blinked at him. "No," she said slowly. "I didn't think of that."

She sighed and crumpled in her metal chair. "I pride myself in being so resourceful," she said almost wonderingly. "How could it have deserted me like that?"

Roux shrugged. "Well, circumstances did press urgently upon you, one is compelled to admit."

She shook her head. "But that's what I rely on to survive in those situations. It's not the sword. It's my ability to keep my head and think of things on the spur of the moment!"

"Well, sometimes reason deserts someone like you," Roux said.

For a moment Annja sat and marinated in her misery. But prolonged self-pity annoyed her. So she sought to externalize her funk. "It's just losing such an artifact—the only trace of that tomb—to a plunderer like Easy Ngwenya. She just violates everything I stand for as an archaeologist. I've always considered her nothing better than a looter."

She frowned ferociously and jutted her chin. "Now it's personal."

Roux set down his cup and leaned forward. "Enough of this. Now, listen. Your secret career is an expensive indulgence—"

"Which I never volunteered for in the first place!" Annja said.

"Details. The fact is, you have been burning money. As I have alluded to, certain creditors grow—insistent."

Annja frowned thoughtfully. She could see his point. There was no denying her recent adventures had been costly. The rise of digital records and biometric identification hadn't made official documentation more secure—the opposite, if anything. But full-spectrum false identification was expensive. And Annja relied greatly on fake ID to avoid having her secret career exposed by official nosiness.

She leaned back and crossed her legs. "Has Bank of America been making nasty phone calls?"

"Think less modern in methods of collection, and more Medici."

"You haven't been borrowing from Garin again?" Annya asked.

His lips compressed behind his neat beard. "It's…possible."

Garin Braden was a fabulously wealthy playboy. He was also Roux's former protégé and he feared the miraculous reforging of the sword threatened his eternal life.

"I bet you've just had a bad streak at the gaming

tables," Annja said accusatorily. "Didn't you get busted out of that poker tournament in Australia last month?"

"All that aside, we must improve what you Americans charmingly call cash flow."

She sighed. "Tell me," she said.

"Somewhere in the mountainous jungles of Southeast Asia there supposedly lies a vast and ancient temple complex. Within it hides a priceless artifact—a golden elephant idol with emerald eyes. I have been approached by a wealthy collector who wants it enough to pay most handsomely."

"Who?"

"One who treasures anonymity," Roux said.

"That's a promising start," Annja said, not bothering to hide the sarcasm in her voice. "So I take it all this mystery likewise precludes your at least running a credit check?"

"Sadly," Roux said, "yes."

He spread his hands in a dismissive gesture. "However, our client—"

"Let's hold off on this *our* business until I'm actually signed on, shall we?" Annja said.

"*Our* client has offered a handsome preliminary payment, as well as an advance against expenses."

"The preliminary, at least, needs to be no-strings-attached," Annja said.

Roux raised his eyebrow again.

"What?" Annja said.

"That would require substantial faith on the client's part," Roux said.

"So? Either he-she-it has faith in me, or doesn't. If they're not willing to believe in my integrity, then to heck with it. And why come to me, anyway, if that's the case? If I'm not honest, there's ten dozen ways I could chisel, from embezzling the expense account to selling to the highest bidder whatever it is this mystery guest wants me to get. There isn't any guarantee I could give that could protect against that. If I'm a crook, what's my guarantee worth?"

Roux looked as if he were bursting to respond. She glared him into silence.

"While we're on the subject," she said, "there's not going to be any accounting for expenses incurred. For reasons I really hope you won't make me explain out loud."

He sipped his coffee and pulled a gloomy face. "You don't ask for much, my dear child," he said, "beyond the sun, the moon and perhaps the stars."

"Just a star or two," she said. "Anyway, you're the one whining the exchequer might be forced to go to bed tonight without any gruel if little Annja doesn't hie herself off to Southeast Asia and do something certainly arduous, probably dangerous and more than likely illegal. You should be happy to ask for the best no-money-back terms available."

"I don't want to scare the client off," Roux said.

"This strikes me as skirting pretty close to pot-hunting," Annja said. "The jade-seal affair already came too close."

"But you've done similar things in the past," Roux

said. "And after all, who better to ensure the Golden Elephant is recovered in a…sensitive way rather than ripped from the earth by a tomb-robber?"

He turned his splendid head of silver hair to profile so he could regard her sidelong with slitted eyes. "Or would you prefer to leave the field open to, say, the likes of Her Highness, E. C. Ngwenya?"

"Quit with the psychological manipulation," she said. But even to her ears her voice sounded less than perfectly confident.

3

London, England

"Tea, Ms. Creed?" asked the bluff and jovial old Englishman with the big pink face, a brush of white hair and a red vest straining slightly over his paunch. With an exquisitely manicured hand he held up a white porcelain teapot with flowers painted on it.

Annja smiled. "Thank you, Sir Sidney." She started to rise from the floral-upholstered chair. She would term the small round table, the flowered sofa and chairs, the eclectic bric-a-brac in Sir Sidney Hazelton's parlor as fussy Victorian.

He gestured her to stay seated. He poured the tea with a firm if liver-spotted hand protruding from a stiff white cuff with brisk precision, then brought her the cup with a great air of solicitude.

"Thank you," she said, accepting.

Sir Sidney reseated himself in his overstuffed chair. He'd offered one like it to Annja, insisting that it was more comfortable than the one she chose. She declined, fearing if she sank into it the thing would devour her. She had to admit that despite his bulk he moved with alacrity, including in and out of the treacherously yielding chair.

"Really, isn't this notion of lost cities or temples more frightfully romantic than realistic?" he asked. "I mean, what with all these satellites and surveillance aircraft and such today."

Annja pursed her lips. She had some experience with what could be seen from satellites—and also of things that could not. She chose her words carefully.

"It's a matter of who pays attention to what image," she said. She told herself she didn't need any extra complications. "Not everyone who runs across overhead imaging of, say, a lost temple has the knowledge to recognize what they're looking at. And many of the most skilled image analysts don't care. They're looking for military information, or maybe stray nuclear materials. Not ancient ruins. Although some pretty astonishing ruins have been discovered by overhead photography, just in the last couple of decades."

"So I gather," Sir Sidney said. "Well, I must say it does a body good to believe there's still some mystery left in this old world of ours. Quite bracing, actually."

She raised a brow. "Aren't you the expert in lost treasures and fabled ruins?"

He smiled. "My dear, the operative word there is *fabled*. I am, as you know, a cultural anthropologist. Specifically I am a mythologist. I study the phenomena of myths. Particularly pertaining to myths about lost treasures."

He grinned. "But there's very little more exciting than the possibility a myth turns out to be true."

She had to laugh, both at what he said and his very infectious enthusiasm. "That's how I feel about it." Usually, she thought. "And there's a very definite possibility the trail I'm on might lead to a myth being confirmed."

He waved grandly. "If I can be of any assistance to a lovely young woman such as yourself—"

He paused to pour more tea and stir in plenty of milk.

"I've got to thank you again for sharing your time with me," Annja said.

"Nonsense, nonsense. The pleasure is mine. I am retired, after all. It's not as if there are abundant claims upon my time these days. My partner of many years died last year. It was quite sudden."

"I'm sorry," Annja said.

"Don't be," her host replied. "I'm sure you had nothing to do with it, my dear. I can't say I've grown comfortable with it, or ever shall, I fancy. Doubtless I've not that long left in which to do so. On the whole I must say I'm rather glad it happened the way it did. So suddenly and all. It saved him the suffering of a long and possibly agonizing decline—saved us both, really.

And at our age it's not as if our own mortality was a tremendous surprise to us. We've seen enough old chums put into the ground to have few illusions on that score."

Annja smiled.

Sir Sidney leaned forward. "Now," he said, "suppose you tell me this myth you're trying to pin like a butterfly to reality's board."

After a moment's pause—she didn't really like thinking of it that way—Annja did. She shared such scanty information as Roux had provided, plus a few not very helpful details from a file he had subsequently e-mailed her.

Sir Sidney sat listening and nodding. Then he smiled and sat back. "The Golden Elephant," he said ruminatively. "So you've reason to believe it's real?"

Her heart jumped. "You've heard of it?"

"Yes," he said. "Please don't get your hopes up quite yet. Just let me think a moment, see what I can recall which might prove of use. Do you mind if I smoke my pipe?"

"No," Annja said. He produced a pipe from an inner pocket, took up tobacco and various arcane tools from a silver tray on the table next to him.

"I'm a little bit puzzled by one aspect of this," Annja admitted as he lit up. His pipe smoke had a sweet but not cloying smell. Annja had never particularly disliked pipe smoke, unlike cigarette smoke. She hoped the interview wasn't going to go on too long, though. The parlor was stuffy, with windows closed and heat turned up against the damp autumn London chill. In this closeness even the most agreeable smoke could quickly overwhelm her. "I thought Southeast Asia was mostly Buddhist."

"Quite," Sir Sidney said, puffing and nodding.

"Not that I know much about Asian mythology. But I'd associate elephants with the Hindu god Ganesha, rather than anything Buddhist."

He smiled. Blue-white smoke wreathed his big benign pink features. "Ah, but elephants are most significant beasts in all of Asia," he said, clearly warming to the role. "Not just big and imposing creatures, but economically important."

"Really?"

"Just so. It needn't surprise us too much that the elephant occupies a role in Buddhist symbolism. It symbolizes strength of mind. Buddhists envision what they call the Seven Jewels of Royal Power. These basically constitute the attributes of earthly kingship.

"One of these jewels is the Precious Elephant. It represents a calm, majestic mind. Useful trait in a king, although one honored more in the breach than the observance, as it were."

"If Asian history is anything like that of Renaissance Europe," Annja said, "that's probably an understatement."

He chortled around the stem of his pipe.

They spoke a while longer. Annja enjoyed the old man's conversation. But she increasingly felt restless. "Are you remembering any more about the myths regarding our fabulous Golden Elephant?" she asked.

He puffed. "It's said to have emeralds for eyes." His own pale blue eyes twinkled. His manner suggested a child telling secrets.

She leaned forward, pulse quickening. "That sounds like my elephant."

"Don't put it in your vest pocket yet, my dear," he said. "I'm not yet dredging up much from the murky depths of my poor old brain. But I recall hints of travelers' tales. Even reports from a certain scientific expedition from early this—in the twentieth century."

He shook his head. "I find it most disconcerting to refer to the twentieth century as the *last* century. It may not strike you so, of course."

She shrugged. "I don't think about it too much. It does strike me a little odd sometimes that there are people capable of holding intelligible conversations who were born in the twenty-first century." She laughed. "I guess that means I'm getting old."

He guffawed. "Not at all, my dear!" he said. "Not by a long shot. I dare say, I don't think you'll ever grow old."

She looked sharply at him.

"I'm sorry," he said quickly. "I suppose that could be misconstrued, couldn't it? I didn't mean you won't enjoy a long and happy life. What I meant to convey was that however deeply your years accumulate, I anticipate that your outlook will remain youthful. For that matter, I don't doubt the years will lie less heavily on you than me in any event. By all appearances you keep yourself far better than ever I did." He patted himself on the paunch.

Annja looked studiously down into her tea and tried hard not to read her future there.

"Ah, but I see I've gone and spoiled your mood. Forgive a clumsy old man's musings. Profuse apologies, dear child."

"Not needed," she said. She smiled. It wasn't forced. She was a thoughtful person, but had no patience for brooding. "Do you have any suggestions how I can track down this expedition you mentioned?"

His big pink face creased thoughtfully. At last he made a fretful noise and shook his head.

"It eludes me for the moment," he said. "I'll see what I can dig up. In the meantime I do have a next step to suggest to you."

"What's that?"

"Why, visit that great repository of arcane archaeological knowledge, the British Museum, and see what you can turn up."

She smiled. "I'll do that. Thank you so much."

"It's nothing. Indeed, almost literally—doubtless you've thought of the museum already. It's right down the lane and across the Tottenham Court Road, you know."

"Yes. Thank you, Sir Sidney. You've encouraged me. Really. If nothing else, I know I'm not the only one with fantasies about an emerald-eyed gold elephant."

She stood. "Don't get up, please," she said. "I can let myself out. You've got my card—please call me if you think of anything. With your permission I'll check back with you in a day or so."

He beamed. "It would be my pleasure."

On impulse, she went and kissed him on the forehead. Then, collecting her umbrella from the stand by the door—an antique elephant's foot, she noted with amusement—she walked out of his flat into the rainy street.

4

About midafternoon Annja pushed herself back from
the flat-screen monitor. She stretched, trying to do so
as unobtrusively as possible. Her upper back felt as if
it had big rocks in it.

She had spent a frustrating afternoon in the Paul
Hamlyn Library, flipping through catalogs and skim-
ming through semirandom volumes. She caught a whiff
from the digitized pages of *British Archaeology* for fall
1921, which mentioned the Colquhoun Expedition of
1899 to what was then Siam. But when she tracked
down the details, including Colquhoun's journals and his
report to the Explorers' Club, he made nary a mention
of gold elephants. With or without emerald eyes.

She shook her head. Certain needs were asserting
themselves. Not least among them the need to be up
and moving.

Checking her watch, Annja reckoned she had plenty of time for a turn through the Joseph E. Hotung Gallery, which held the Asian collections, before returning to her labors. She'd try the reading room next, and see if her luck improved.

The library jutted out to flank the main museum entrance from Great Russell Street. She emerged into the great court. It was like a time shift and somewhat jarring. The ceiling was high, translucent white, crisscrossed by what she took for a geodesic pattern of brace work, springing from a stout white cylindrical structure that dominated the center of the space. The cylinder housed the new reading room. The sterile style, which put her in mind of a seventies science-fiction movie, contrasted jarringly with the pseudo-Greek porticoed walls and their Dorian-capitaled pilasters.

The court wasn't crowded. A few sullen gaggles of schoolchildren in drab uniforms; some tourists snapping enthusiastically with digital cameras were watched by security guards more sullen than the children. She was vaguely surprised photography was allowed.

She concentrated on movement, striding purposefully through milky light filtered from the cloudy sky above. She focused on the sensations of her body in motion, on being in the moment.

A sudden flurry of movement tugged at her peripheral vision. A female figure was walking, strutting more, through the room. Annja got the impression of a rounded, muscle-taut form in a dark blue jacket and knee-length skirt. Black hair jutted out in a kinky cloud behind the woman's head, bound by an amber band.

Annja had never seen the woman in the flesh. But she had seen plenty of pictures on the Internet. Especially in the wake of her recent China adventure.

"Easy Ngwenya," she said under her breath. She felt anger start to seethe. She turned to follow.

Without looking back, the young African woman continued through the hall, into the next room, which housed Indian artifacts. She moved purposefully. More, Annja thought, she moved almost with challenge. Her head was up, her broad shoulders back. She was shorter by a head than Annja, who nonetheless found herself pressed to keep pace.

Annja felt uncharacteristically unsure how to proceed. Her rival—she tried to think of her as quarry—could not have gotten her famous twin Sphinx autopistols through the Museum metal detectors, if she had even dared bring them into Britain. Although Annja suspected Easy would have smuggled the guns in. Great respect for the law didn't seem to be one of her major traits.

So that was advantage Annja. No means known to modern science would detect her sword otherwise. Actually using it, with numerous witnesses and scarcely fewer security cameras everywhere, might prove a bit more problematic.

Easy Ngwenya made up Annja's mind for her by stopping to peer into an exhibit case a few yards ahead of her. I'm practically committed now, anyway, Annja told herself.

The younger woman studied an exquisite jade carving of an elephant in an elaborate headdress, standing with trunk raised to bedangled forehead. Annja felt a jolt. Could she be here for the same reason I am? she thought with something akin to panic.

She dismissed the idea. A collector who came to Annja, even anonymously, would know of her reputation for honesty and integrity, even if she was willing to operate under the radar. Somebody so discerning would hardly recruit a tomb robber as notorious as Ngwenya. Would they? Anyway, elephants weren't exactly an uncommon motif in Asian art, and Ngwenya might be forgiven a special interest in them, given she was named for one. Also it wasn't gold.

Annja came up on Easy's left.

"Annja Creed," the younger woman said without looking around. Annja realized Easy must have seen her approach in the glass. "What a delightful surprise to encounter you here."

"A surprise, anyway," Annja said through gritted teeth, "after the way you marooned me on that tomb mound in the middle of a rising lake."

"Did the boat I sent back for you not reach you?" Ngwenya asked. "You must have had an unpleasant swim. Not my intention, I assure you."

"The boat came," Annja admitted grudgingly. "That's not the point. I'm…placing you under citizen's arrest."

Ngwenya's laugh was musical and entirely uncon-
cerned. "Why, whatever for?"

She turned to look up at Annja. Annja was struck by
just how young the international adventuress looked.
She was in her twenties, having gotten an early start at
a life of adventure. Or crime. She looked fifteen.

Annja was also struck by just how pretty Easy was.
She had a big rounded forehead, a broad snubbed nose,
full lips, a small round chin. That should have been less
of a surprise—despite the currently unfashionable
fullness of her figure, Ngwenya occasionally did
modeling, not always fully dressed. The curves, Annja
knew from the pictures she'd seen online, did not come
from excess body fat.

"You have committed countless violations of international law regarding traffic in antiquities. As you
well know," Annja said.

The girl batted her eyes at her. Annja wished she
wouldn't. They were huge eyes, the color of dark chocolate, with long lashes. Annja suddenly suspected why
she was named "elephant calf." She had eyes like one.

"You'd already looted the seal from the feet of Mad
Emperor Lu," Ngwenya pointed out. "Congratulations
on getting past the booby traps, by the way."

"I had official permission, if you must know," Annja
said. Whether it was the Museum's cathedral atmosphere or her own desire to remain as unobtrusive as
possible, she kept her voice low. She only hoped she
wasn't hissing like a king snake having a hissy fit. "I
had all the proper paperwork."

Ngwenya laughed loudly. "And so did I! Remarkable how easy such things are to come by for those willing to be generous to underappreciated civil servants. One is tempted to ascribe that to the customary blind Communist lust for money, but honestly, I wonder if it was any different back in dear old mad Lu's day."

"It's not like it was an isolated incident. So come with me," Annja said.

"You can't be serious. There are people here. Behave yourself, Ms. Creed."

"I told you—you're under citizen's arrest."

The young woman laughed again. "Do you think such a legal archaism still has force? This is a country where someone who successfully resists a violent assault is likely to face brisker prosecution and longer jail terms than their attacker. Do you really think they'll give weight to a citizen's arrest? Especially by someone who isn't a citizen? Or were you forgetting that little dust-up of a couple of centuries past? So many of your countrymen seem to have done."

"When Scotland Yard gets your Interpol file," Annja said, "they probably won't be too concerned with the niceties of how you wound up in their custody, then, will they?"

"Oh, this is entirely absurd." To Annja's astonishment the young woman turned and walked away. Before Annja could respond, Easy had pushed through into a stairway to the upper level.

Frowning, Annja followed. She expected to find the

stairwell empty. But instead of sprinting to the second level and through the door into the Korean exhibit Easy trotted upstairs. Her pace was brisk. But it definitely wasn't flight.

You cocky little thing, Annja thought.

She caught her up just shy of the upper-floor landing. She grabbed Easy's right arm from behind. It felt impressively solid. "Not so fast, there."

Using hips and legs, Easy turned counterclockwise. She effortlessly torqued her arm out of Annja's grasp. Her left elbow came around to knock Annja's right arm away as if inadvertently. She thrust a short right spear hand straight for Annja's solar plexus.

Annja anticipated the attack. Just. She couldn't do anything about Easy fouling her right hand. But she bent forward slightly, functionally blocking the sensitive nerve junction with the notch of her rib cage while turning slightly to her right. Instead of blasting all the air from her lungs in one involuntary whoosh, the shorter woman's stiffened fingers jabbed ribs on Annja's left side.

Annja had no doubts about why they called that strike a spear hand. She felt as if she'd been stabbed for a fact. But that was just pain: she wasn't incapacitated.

Knowing the omnipresent eyes of the surveillance cameras constrained her Annja straightened, trying at the same time to deliver a short shovel hook upward with her right fist into Ngwenya's ribs. The woman's short stature defeated her. The blow bounced off the pot hunter's left elbow and sent another white spike of pain up Annja's arm.

Ngwenya frowned at her. "Really, Ms. Creed," she said primly, "this is most unseemly."

There was a short flurry of discreet short-range strikes.

After a brief, grunting exchange, barely visible to the high-mounted camera, Easy Ngwenya sidestepped a short punch, reached with her right hand and caught Annja behind the left elbow. She squeezed.

The younger woman was chunkily muscular. Annja had noticed in some of her photographs that she had short, square hands, large for her height. Practical, practiced hands. Even in glamour shots the exiled African princess disdained long nails, even paste-on fakes.

But even her exceptional hand strength couldn't account for the lightning that shot through Annja's body.

She could barely even gasp. It wasn't the pain. There was pain, to be sure; it felt as if a giant spike had been driven up her arm and at the same time right through the middle of her body. The problem was, literally, the shock. It was as if a jolt of electricity had clenched her whole body in a spasm, dropped her to her knees and left her there, lungs empty of breath and unable to draw one. Her vision swam.

"Oh, dear," Easy's voice rang, clear with false concern. "Are you quite all right, miss? I'll go and get help." She trotted away up the stairs with rapid clacks of her elegant but practical low-heeled shoes.

Annja rocked back and forth. Darkness crowded in around the edges of her vision. What's wrong with me? she wondered in near panic. It was as if she was suffering a giant whole-body cramp.

An unbreakable one.

But slowly, as if molecule by molecule, oxygen infiltrated back into her lungs and permeated her bloodstream. Slowly the awful muscle spasm began to relax. She slumped.

She was just regaining control of herself when two uniformed guards, a man and a woman in caps with little bills, came pattering down the steps for her.

"Oh, dear, miss," the man said in a lilting Jamaican accent. "Are you all right?"

She nodded and let them help her to her feet. She didn't have much choice. She still didn't have the muscular strength to stand on her own.

"I-I'm fine," she said. "I get these spells. Epilepsy. Petit mal. Had it since childhood. Really, thank you, it's passed now."

The two exchanged a look. "We don't want you suing us," said the blond woman.

"No. I'm fine. Did you see which way my friend went?"

"No," the man said. "She seemed very determined that we help you right away." He shook his head. "She was quite the little package. It was too bad we had to rush away—"

"Oi!" the woman exclaimed. "That's so sexist! I've half a mind to report you for that."

"Now, now," he said, "don't go flying off here like—"

"Like what? Were you going to make another demanding sexist statement, then?"

"Don't you mean *demeaning?*" the male guard said.

Annja set off at what she hoped was a steady-looking pace, up the stairs to the next level. She made it through the door before she wobbled and had to lean back against it for a moment to gather herself.

The Korean exhibit was nearly empty. It was totally empty of any rogue archaeologist Zulu princesses. Annja drew a deep abdominal breath. It steadied her stomach and cleared her brain. Her vision expanded slowly but steadily. She no longer felt as if she were passing through a tunnel toward a white light.

She managed to walk briskly, with barely a wobble, through a door into a wider hall. Another set of stairs led down. Annja set her jaw.

The stairs descended to the ground level, and then to the north exit. She found herself outside on broad steps with Montague Place in front of her and the colonnaded pseudoclassical facade of the White Wing behind. It was called that not because it was white, but because it was named after the benefactor whose bequest made it possible to build.

The cool air seemed to envelop her. She sucked in a deep breath. The moist draft was so refreshing she scarcely noticed the heavy diesel tang.

A light rain began to tickle Annja's face. She grunted, stamping one foot. Passersby glanced at her, then walked quickly on.

Calm down! she told herself savagely. This doesn't always happen. She's got the better of you twice. That's not statistically significant.

She walked on as fast as she dared. She didn't want some kind of behavior-monitoring software routine on the video surveillance to decide she was acting suspiciously. But she wanted to get away from the museum.

For a time she walked at random, lost in thoughts that whirled amid the noise of the city center. She stopped at a little café inside a glass front of some looming office building for a cup of hot tea.

Sitting on an uncomfortable metal chair, she gulped it as quickly as she could without scalding her lips. Outside she was surprised to see that twilight was well along. Gloom just coalesced atom by atom out of the gray that pervaded the cold heart of the city.

Setting the cup down, she strode out into the early autumn evening. The rain had abated. She headed toward Sir Sidney's, a dozen or so blocks away. Maybe he'd turned something up.

IT ALWAYS AMAZED ANNJA how many little alcoves and culs-de-sac, surprisingly quiet even in the evening rush, could be stumbled upon in downtown London. Sir Sidney lived on a little half-block street, narrow and lined with trees whose leaves had already turned gray-brown and dead. It was so tiny and insignificant, barely more than a posh alley, it didn't seem to rate its own spy cameras.

Trotting up the steps to the door of Sir Sidney's

redbrick flat, Annja wondered how his aging knees held up to them. Before she could carry the thought any further, she noticed the white door with the shiny brass knob stood slightly ajar.

She stopped in midstep. Her body seemed to lose twenty quick degrees. Foreboding numbness crept into her cheeks and belly.

"It's all right," she said softly. "He's old. He might be getting absentminded. Just nipped out and forgot to fully close the door—"

Trying not to act like a burglar, she went on up the steps. She knocked quickly. "Sir Sidney?" she called. She was trying to make herself heard if he was within earshot inside without drawing attention to herself from outside.

She did not want to be seen.

Putting a hand in the pocket of her windbreaker, she pushed the door open and stepped quickly inside.

The entrance hallway was dark. As was the sitting room to her right. Nonetheless, the last gloom of day through the door and filtering in through curtained windows showed her the shape of Sir Sidney lying on his back on the floor.

The rich burgundy of the throw rug on which he had fallen had been overtaken by a deeper, spreading stain.

5

Annja knelt briefly at the old man's side. The skin of his neck was cold. She felt no pulse.

She almost felt relief. If he was still alive with half his head battered in like that—

She shook her head and straightened. She would rather die than persist in such a state. She hoped Sir Sidney had felt the same way.

One way or another, he felt nothing now.

Moving as if through a fog that anesthetized her extremities and emotions, Annja took stock of the sitting room. The gloom was as thick as the cloying combination smell of old age, potpourri and recent death. She didn't want to turn on a light, though. She wanted to draw no attention to her presence, nor leave any more signs of her presence than she had to.

Than I already have, she thought glumly. Irrationally if unsurprisingly, she regretted the earlier carelessness with which she had handled her teacup and saucer, the careless abandon with which she had handled the objects on display. Could I have left any more fingerprints?

The floor was scattered with toppled furniture. Strewed papers mingled with artifacts. Sir Sidney had welcomed his murderer—or murderers. There was no sign of forced entry. But he had not died easily.

Not far from the body lay a two-foot-high brass statue of Shakyamuni. The screen behind the seated figure was bent. The heavy metal object was smeared with blood. Annja looked away. She had seen too much death in her short life.

An overturned swivel chair drew her attention to the rolltop writing desk. Briskly she moved to it. She had little time. She racked her brain trying to remember if there had been anybody in the short, tree-lined lane who might have seen her enter the flat. Then again, anyone, driven by nosiness, caution or simple boredom, might have been peering out through the curtains to watch a long-legged young woman approach the apartment.

On the desk an old-fashioned spiral-bound notebook lay open. Annja almost smiled. She would have been surprised if the old scholar had kept his notes on a computer. But to her chagrin the first page was blank. Frowning, she started to move on.

Then she turned back and leaned close to study the page in the poor and failing light. With quick precision she tore the page away, folded it neatly and stuck it in her pocket.

She paused by the body. She made herself look down and see what Sir Sidney had suffered. It had been because of her, she knew—the laws of coincidence could be tortured only so far.

"I'm sorry, Sir Sidney," she said in a husky voice. "I will find whoever did this."

Already a deep anger had begun to burn toward Easy Ngwenya. Could her presence in the museum that afternoon possibly have been coincidence?

"And I will punish them," Annja promised. It wasn't a politically correct thing to say, she knew. Even to a freshly murdered corpse.

But then, there was nothing politically correct about wielding a martyred saint's sword, either.

She quickly left the flat.

WHEN SHE WAS BACK in her hotel room the sorrow overtook her—suddenly but hardly unexpectedly. She didn't try to fight it. She knew she must grieve. Otherwise it would distract her; unresolved, it might create a tremor of intent that could prove lethal.

She wept bitterly for a kind and helpful old man she had barely known. And for her own role in bringing death upon his head.

When her eyes and spirit were dry again, she took out the notepaper, ruled in faint blue lines, unfolded it under the lamp on the writing desk and examined it closely. The neat curls and swoops of the old scholar's

precise hand were engraved by the pressure of the pen
that had written on the page above it.

Among the tools of the trade she carried with her
were a sketch pad and graphite pencil. Extending the
soft lead and brushing it across the sheet of paper,
Annja was pleased when the writing appeared, white
on gray.

She bit her lip. Not what I hoped, she thought. Not
at all.

THE LIGHTS INSIDE THE Channel striped the window
next to Annja in the bright and modern Eurostar passenger car. Annja placed her fingertips against the cool
glass of the window. It was still streaked on the outside
with rain from the storm that had hit London as it
moved out, well before it headed into the tunnel
beneath the English Channel.

The weather fit her mood.

The notebook page, burned in the hotel room sink
to ashes Annja had disposed of crumpled in a napkin
in a public trashcan on the street, hadn't held the key
to the mystery of the Golden Elephant as Annja hoped.
But Sir Sidney's memory, and perhaps a little research,
had unearthed what could prove to be a clue.

"The Antiquities of Indochina," Hazelton had
written. It appeared to be the title of a book or mono-
graph, since beside it he had written a name—
Duquesne.

He had either done a bit of digging on his own or
called friends. Without checking his phone records

she'd never know. Given her contacts in the cyber-underworld it was possible. But she didn't want to risk tying herself to the case.

Perhaps he'd simply remembered. In any event, after jotting down a few grocery items he had written "Sorbonne only." The word *only* was deeply outlined several times.

It was the only lead she had. But the gentle old scholar's ungentle murderers also had it.

If Sir Sidney's murder had been discovered by authorities, it hadn't made it to the news by the time she boarded the train in the St. Pancras Station—quite close, ironically, both to Sir Sidney's flat and the British Museum. She'd bought passage under the identity of a Brit headed on holiday on the Continent.

Roux was right, she thought. As usual. This business was expensive. She hoped the commission from this mysterious collector would cover it.

She grimaced then. Nothing would pay for Sir Sidney's death. No money, anyway. Her resolve to bring retribution on his killer or killers had set like concrete. And she felt, perhaps irrationally, she had a good line on who at least one of them was.

Although she was renowned for going armed, and for proficiency in the use of various weapons—neither of which Annja was inclined to hold against her—cold-blooded murder had never seemed part of Easy Ngwenya's repertoire. But perhaps greed had caused her to branch out. Annja only wondered how the South African tomb robber could have learned about her quest.

Unless their encounter in the museum—just that day, although it seemed a lifetime ago—was pure coincidence. Oxford educated, Ngwenya kept a house in London. She was known to spend a fair amount of time there. And given she really was a scholar of some repute, it wasn't at all unlikely she'd find herself in the British Museum on a semiregular basis at least.

But Annja had a hard time buying it.

She made herself put those thoughts aside. You can't condemn the woman—on no better evidence than you've got, no matter how much reason you have to be mad at her, she told herself sternly. For better or worse, from whatever source, you have the role of judge, jury and executioner. You've carried it out before. But if you get too self-righteous and indiscriminate, or even just make a mistake—how much better are you than the monsters you've set out to slay?

6

"So, you work for an American television program, Ms. Creed?" The curator was a trim, tiny Asian woman with a gray-dusted bun of dark hair piled behind her head and a very conservative gray suit. Annja guessed she must be Vietnamese.

"That's right, Madame Duval," she said. "It's called *Chasing History's Monsters.*"

The woman's already small mouth almost disappeared in a grimace of disapproval. "I'm employed as—" She started to say "devil's advocate." Taking note of the silver crucifix worn in the slightly frilled front of Madame Duval's extremely pale blue blouse, Annja changed it on the fly. "I'm the voice of reason, on a show which, I'm afraid, sometimes runs to the sensational."

Did she defrost a degree or two? Annja wondered.

"Why precisely do you seek credentialing to the University of Paris system, Ms. Creed?"

The University of Paris, commonly known as the Sorbonne after the commune's 750-year-old college, was actually a collection of thirteen autonomous but affiliated universities. Annja stood talking with the assistant curator for the whole system in the highly modernized offices of University I, Panthéon-Sorbonne, one of the four modern universities located in the actual Sorbonne complex itself. If accepted as a legitimate scholarly researcher, she would gain access to collections throughout the system, even those normally closed to the public.

Annja smiled. "Whenever possible I like to combine what I like to call my proper academic pursuits with my work for the show. As an archaeologist I specialize in medieval and Renaissance documents in Romance languages. The predominant language, of course, being French."

The woman smiled, if tightly. She was definitely warming.

"I have a particular interest in the witch trials of the Renaissance," Annja said. She knew she gained a certain credibility because she showed she knew when the real bulk of the witch prosecutions took place; most people, including way too many college professors, thought they were a phenomenon of the Middle Ages. Still, the woman stiffened again, ever so slightly.

Annja was hyperattuned to her body language—and keying on that very reaction. "As what you might call the show's revisionist," she said, "I am particularly interested in the notion that the church might have had some justification for its actions in the matter. Not their methods, necessarily, but rather the possibility there existed a sort of witch culture that posed a real and deliberate threat to the church. Instead of the whole thing being a sort of mass hysteria, as is mostly assumed these days."

Everything she said was true in the most legalistic and technical sense. There were such notions; they interested Annja.

Madame Duval smiled. "That appears to me to be a perfectly legitimate course of study," she said in her own academic French. "If you will come with me, young lady, we will begin the paperwork to provide you the proper credentials."

"Thank you," Annja said.

Four hours later Annja's vision was practically swimming. She was accustomed to deciphering fairly arcane writing. *The Antiquities of Indochina* was printed in a near-microscopic font. Unfortunately, unlike her Internet browsers, Annja's eyes didn't come with a handy zoom feature. The early-twentieth-century French itself was no problem; it was just hard to see.

Her heart jumped as she made out the words:

…the 1913 German expedition to Southeast Asia turned up many marvels indeed. Its reports included a fabulous hilltop temple complex, hidden in the reclaiming arms of the jungle, with the breathtaking golden idol of an elephant in its midst.

The passage then went on to talk about rubber production in Hanoi Province, in what was now Vietnam.

"Wait," Annja said aloud, drawing glares from other researchers in the reading room. She glared back until they dropped their eyes back to tomes and computer screens.

Of course she felt bad about it at once. It's not their fault, she reminded herself sternly.

Isn't there more? she wondered.

She returned her attention to the book.

The crisp evening air felt good and smelled of roasting chestnuts. Annja was hungry, walking the summit of Montmartre with her hands jammed in her jacket pockets and her chin sunk into the collar. Over her left shoulder loomed the white domes of the Sacré Coeur Basilica. From somewhere in the middle distance skirled North African music. From nearer at hand came the thud and clank of what she considered mediocre techno music. The days of the Moulin Rouge and other noted, or notorious, cabarets were long gone. The fashionable night spots had long since migrated down across the river to the Left Bank and city center. Nowadays the area was given over to generic discos, artists' studios and souvenir and antique shops, most of which were closed in the early evening.

Annja had found a fairly deserted section of the windy, narrow streets winding gradually down the hill. That suited her mood.

The one reference to the 1913 German expedition had been it. Not just for the book. For such as she'd been able to check of the University of Paris collection until they booted her out of the reading room at seven-thirty.

The good news was that she now knew stories of a golden elephant statue in a vast lost temple emanated from a German expedition to Southeast Asia in 1913. The bad news was that wasn't much to go on.

It hadn't been enough to lead to any more information, at least so far. The various archaeological reviews and journals from the period she had read stayed resolutely mute concerning any such expedition. She would have thought there'd be some mention.

Walking along in air just too warm for her breath to be visible, with fallen dry leaves skittering before her like small frightened mammals, she wondered if chauvinism might have come into play. The Great War, as it was then naively known—and for a few years afterward, until an even greater one happened along—broke out a year or so after the expedition. Indeed, if it set forth in 1913 the expedition might well have still been in progress when the First World War began. And in 1913 the French were still grumpy over the Franco-Prussian War.

So it struck her as possible that mention of German expeditions might've been embargoed in French journals. But scientists of the day still would have considered themselves above such political disputes, cataclysmic as they might be. Wars came and went—science endured. So the Germanophobe angle might mean much or little.

I see two main possibilities, Annja told herself as she turned down a quaintly cobbled alley between steel-shuttered storefronts that reminded her of home in Brooklyn. One, that the expedition simply got lost in the shuffle of World War I. It was easy enough to see how that would happen.

And two, she thought, the frown etching itself deeper into her forehead, that it was all just rumor.

That made her bare her teeth in dismay. It was possible. Probable, even. Scientific anthropology and archaeology were rife with such speculations in the wake of Schliemann's discovery of Troy—or a reasonable facsimile thereof.

So the whole Golden Elephant yarn could just be hyperactive imagination.

"There's a third possibility," she said quietly to herself. "Or make it a subset of the first possibility," she said with a certain deliberateness. "That there was such an expedition—and the only mention of it that still exists anywhere on Earth is the sentence you read in that book today."

She knew that was an all-too-real likelihood. The priceless ceramic relics Schliemann had sent back to Berlin had been busted in some kind of grotesque drunken Prussian marriage ritual. The Lost Dinosaurs of Egypt had been lost when the Allies bombed the museum where they were stored. Paris had famously been spared the ravages of WWII. But the expedition, of course, was German. That was not so good, from a preservation point of view. The whole country had been handled pretty roughly. And most artifacts went through Berlin—which, between relentless bombing and the Red Army's European tour, had pretty much been destroyed.

Every last journal or other scrap of writing relating to the 1913 expedition stood a really excellent chance of having been burned up, shelled to fine gray powder.

She sighed again. "Great," she said. She decided she'd give it at lest one more try in the University of Paris system. If that came up dry—

From behind she heard a masculine voice call out, "There she is!"

7

Annja stopped. She set her mouth. She sensed at least two men behind her. She braced to run. Then from the shadowed brickwork arch of an entry into a small garden courtyard she hadn't even noticed before, a third man strolled out into the starlight before her.

She'd wandered, eyes wide open, into a classic trap.

Annja scolded herself furiously. Walking around like that and not paying attention to your surroundings! she thought. Doing a perfect impression of a perfect victim. What were you thinking?

Unfortunately, *thinking* was what she had been doing. In contrast to maintaining situational awareness. It was an unfortunate propensity of hers. And what really annoyed her was that she knew better.

"What have we here?" the man who had appeared in front of her said in nasal, slangy Parisian French. He was a bit shorter than Annja, wearing a knit cap and a long dark cloth coat against the autumn chill.

Annja looked around. The other two men came up on her left and right, winging out to the side. They were positioned to catch her no matter which way she might bolt.

"Careful," one said in an Algerian accent. "She has long legs, this one. She could run fast."

She was in a tight spot, she knew. They were very smooth, very tactical, coming on her from three directions, allowing her no options to escape. They radiated hardness, both in attitude and physically. Each one of them would be stronger than she was. Her skill in martial arts, not to mention real fighting experience, gave her an edge on a single man, if he underestimated her. These men almost certainly did. To them she was another American woman, a tourist or student, spoiled, soft and foolish.

Foolish enough to wander dark, deserted city streets with head down and eyes turned inward. A perfect victim, she thought again with a wave of self-disgust.

The first man stopped two yards from her. He seemed aware of the possibility of a long-legged kick.

"Not a good thing for you, missy, being out alone like this," he said.

"Nice talking to you," she said. "Now, if you'll kindly step aside, I'll be on my way."

He pulled his head back on his neck like a turtle starting a retreat into its shell and blinked at her with slightly bulbous pale eyes. Then he laughed. "It's a spirited one we've got here."

"Yeah," said the third man. "It's a damned shame."

"Shut up," said the Algerian.

Annja's blood chilled as the men flanking her each grabbed one of her arms.

She had been caught in a dilemma. She knew many people, even self-defense consultants, advised not resisting street robbery attempts. "Your watch won't die for you," the line ran. "Why die for your watch?"

But she had a practical objection to giving violent criminals what they wanted—rewarding their behavior. If you let them succeed, they'd just do it again and again. And next time their victim might not have the option of resisting—and next time they might want more than a wallet….

She was certain this was no mugging.

Whoever these bad boys were, and they were certainly bad, they weren't common criminals. They were talent, Annja thought.

All these ideas flashed through her mind as her neuromuscular system more than her conscious mind evaluated her opponents. They were lax. They underestimated her, right enough, or they would have slammed her to the ground straightaway. They figured sheer masculinity would control her as effectively as physical techniques. Which was true of most people.

Annja waited for her moment.

The movements of the man on her right suggested he was about to press a knife to her neck to complete her submission. She sagged away from him, letting the guy on her left suddenly take almost her whole body weight.

The man on her left grunted in annoyance. The other, the Algerian, was pulled way off balance hanging on to her.

She thrust her right leg straight out behind his. With a powerful twist of her hips she swept his legs from under him. She used his own grip on her arm, still firm, as a handle to slam him to his back on the pavement.

He let go of her.

The other man was all over her, cussing her viciously in a blend of French and bad Italian. His right arm went around her neck.

He was interrupted when she jammed her right thumb straight back into his mouth. He was too dumbfounded even to try to bite. Then the opportunity was gone as her thumb started stretching out his right cheek.

Wishing she had long nails, for the first time since she'd actually grown them out when she was a teenager, Annja dug her fingers into his face with all her substantial strength. He squealed in agony.

Then she put her hip into his legs just below the hips and threw him over her shoulder.

He landed on the Parisian in the long black coat and the knit cap. Both went down in a tangle on the unyielding uneven stones. One began to screech like an angry chimp.

Both were out of the fight for the moment. But the Algerian wasn't. After lying stunned for a moment he arched his flat belly into the air and snapped himself to his feet in the classic Hong Kong movie move. That confirmed to Annja he was trouble—probably a trained, seasoned killer.

Annja concentrated. The sword became a reassuring weight in her hands. She moved so quickly she barely felt any resistance as it slashed through the man's neck.

The Parisian was back on his feet. The third man still thrashed around on the stones. Improbably and with horrific luck he had managed to impale himself on his partner's lock-back blade when Annja threw him.

The sensible thing now was for everyone to run away as fast and far as their legs would carry them. Even in this dodgy and little-tenanted part of town the wounded man's shrieking would attract attention. It was like an air-raid siren.

But the Parisian wasn't having any of that. He launched himself in a rush straight for Annja.

She watched him for the second necessary to see he was coming high, going for a front bear hug, rather than low to take her by the legs and bring her down. In his anger and stupid machismo he still underestimated her.

Or maybe he had seen the sword and figured his best shot was to immobilize her arms before she could bring the three-foot gleaming blade into play. He was too close for Annja, fast as she was, to use the sword.

But she hadn't always had the sword. Unlike a lot of people, even well-trained ones, she never forgot there were ways to fight that didn't involve a weapon.

She met the man with a front thrust kick to the

sternum. She rolled her hips to transmit maximum shock through her heel. It wasn't the strongest kick, probably wouldn't trip his switches and black out his vision the way a spinning back kick over the heart would—but it stopped him, stood him up straight. It also sent Annja back three semicontrolled steps.

It was still an outcome good for her, bad for him. She could use the sword.

His eyes widened as he noticed the broadsword she held in her hands. Most likely this was just the first time his brain was forced to actually accept the input of his eyes. It wasn't possible for Annja to have carried such a weapon concealed. So his brain didn't want to admit that she had.

Instead of doing the sensible thing—running—he jammed his hand beneath his coat, in the direction of his left armpit.

He wasn't fast enough. Annja darted forward. The sword flashed.

Blue eyes stared at her in shocked incomprehension. Blood sprayed from his left carotid artery, severed by the stroke, which had slashed though his collarbone and into his chest. He mouthed a soundless word. Then he fell to his right.

His right hand, clutching a black 9 mm Beretta pistol, fell to the street. The Beretta clacked on the stones but didn't discharge.

The man Annja had thrown was quiet, his lifeblood spreading in a pool beneath him. He didn't even acknowledge her as she walked up to stand over him.

She made the sword go away. Walking quickly down the hill, she turned into the first alley to her right, and was gone from that place.

8

Harsh half-muted voices drew Annja's attention to a tableau in the street below. Leaning over a concrete balustrade once white, now grayed and specked with city grime, she could hear no words. She made out three voices, two masculine and low, and one feminine. The woman's voice was young, contralto. Just from its pitch and flow it was clearly as educated as the men's speech was rough.

It was also very familiar. Easy Ngwenya! Annja thought.

Her heart sprang into her throat. She crouched to reduce her visibility from below. The three didn't seem to have noticed her. That was good. She left the sword where it was. It was going to be hard enough explaining hunkering down here peering over the railing like a little girl playing hide-and-seek to any random passerby without trying to account for a large and deadly weapon.

Easy stood with feet apart just more than shoulder width, toes of designer Italian shoes pointed slightly outward. She wore a long black leather coat that looked expensive.

Easy's hands were on her hips, under the tails of the long coat, hiking them up. The two men, who were dressed in a manner surprisingly reminiscent of Annja's three recent acquaintances showed no sign of awareness of what she was about.

The woman's voice rose, becoming sharp and peremptory. Annja made out an unmistakable *"Non!"*

The men's hands moved fast and decisively.

Annja was too far away to do anything about what she knew was about to happen. She didn't know whose side she'd intervene on anyway.

The man on Easy's left shouted. His partner lunged suddenly for her from what he seemed to think was her blind spot. Metal glinted in his hand in the light of a streetlamp a block away.

Easy's right hand came out. A gun fired. The man staggered and sagged as a bullet, apparently not even aimed, slammed into his midsection.

The other man tried to move. He dropped his knife and reached back in his peacoat. Easy's left hand snapped up to shoulder height at her arm's full extension. The muzzle-flash lit a feral, stubbled face.

Annja winced as a dark cloud puffed out behind the head. The man collapsed. Easy now turned her head toward the man on her right, who was still on his feet and waving what Annja took for a knife. Easy straightened her right arm, sighted quickly. Her Sphinx spoke again. The man pitched onto his face. The knife bounced on the sidewalk. His hands scrabbled at the pavement, spasmed once, went still.

Easy was walking away, briskly but not hastily, tucking her matched weapons back into their holsters.

Annja let out a long breath she hadn't realized she was keeping in. She hurried down the steps.

The confrontation had taken place at a broadening of an otherwise narrow street. A retaining wall kept bits of Montmartre from falling on passersby on one side, and on the other were two- and three-story buildings, their lower floors armored by accordion-style steel shutters. Hurrying toward the scene of a recent, and loud, double homicide—especially when spattered with blood not her own—wasn't the smartest thing to do, Annja knew. But there was something she had to know. If spotted, she could always claim she was trying to aid the victims.

No lights showed on any of the upper floors on the two nearby blocks, although Annja guessed some held residences and some were almost certainly currently inhabited, allures of Parisian nightlife notwithstanding. But this was also not the choicest neighborhood in the city. Residents might be somewhat accustomed to the sound of nearby gunfire. They were a lot more likely to lie on the floor for a spell than peer out and make possible targets of themselves.

Much less call the police.

Annja rushed to the nearest man. Easy had shot him in the face. He lay sprawled on his back with arms outflung.

She toed gingerly at the front of his peacoat. It slid aside enough to reveal a glimpse of dark metal and checked rubber. He carried a pistol in a shoulder rig.

It was all she needed to know. Sirens commenced their song, in the middle distance and getting louder fast. She picked a different direction from the one Easy had taken and walked away fast without appearing to hurry.

It was fast enough. No one stopped her.

THE CENTER OF PARIS itself is tiny, and can be walked around in a day, despite the vast and expanding dreary suburbs surrounding it. Walking to her hotel at a more leisurely pace, Annja breathed deeply into her abdomen in a basic meditation technique to soothe her heart rate and metabolism back to normal and bring her thoughts under control.

She lacked the luxury of blanking her mind for any protracted stretch, though. Nor was she sure she wanted to. She had just killed three men. No matter how justified that was, she had vowed she would never take that lightly. She had also seen two more men killed with ruthless efficiency.

Key to her mind was that she had bumped into notorious pot hunter and media personality Easy Ngwenya three times in her life in person. And twice had come in the past thirty-six hours. In that latter span six people had died in close proximity to the two of them. One, Sir Sidney, had been unquestionably and brutally murdered. The others appeared to have been making good-faith efforts to kill, in one case Annja, in the other Ngwenya.

What's going on?

One thing she felt confident dismissing out of hand—those had not been standard street muggings. Annja's had been a hired assassination from the get-go. But Easy's?

The fibers of Annja's being seemed to glow like lamp filaments with the desire to blame all this on the errant heiress. Could what Annja had witnessed at ground level below Montmartre have been a falling out among thieves or murderers?

Walking through the lights and the chattering camera-flashing throngs of the Champs-Elysées as the traffic hissed and beeped beside her in an endless stream, Annja had little doubt all five would-be assassins had been cut from the same cloth—hard men but not street-criminal hard. Pro hard. Dressed cheaply but in newish clothes. Flashing knives but carrying guns. Firearms weren't rare in European crime, and were becoming less rare all the time as social order unraveled. But they were still fairly pricy items for Parisian street toughs.

No. These were hired killers. Something in the way her own attackers moved suggested to Annja they had been ex-military. Such men didn't do such work for cheap.

Well, Easy's rich, isn't she? Annja thought.

It all came back to the Golden Elephant. Was it possible they were after the same thing? When Annja had barely learned of the thing's existence—had yet to verify it really did exist?

"Put it this way," she said out loud, attracting curious glances from a set of Japanese tourists. "Is it possible we're not?"

She didn't see how. What else could explain all the coincidences, not to mention the sudden attacks?

Wait, a dissenting part of her mind insisted. There're plenty of reasons for Easy to be here. She was a jet-setter, a noted cosmopolitan, although the paparazzi were known to give her wary distance—possibly because of those twin Sphinxes. She had gone to school at Oxford and the Sorbonne, as well as Harvard.

"Right," Annja said. "So she just happens to visit two of her almas mater just as I happen to be in the same towns and a bunch of people end up dead. Sorry." The last was addressed to a young couple with a pair of small kids clinging to their legs, staring at her in mingled horror and fascination.

"I'm a thriller writer," she said, waving a hand at them. "Plotting out loud. Don't mind me." She showed them a smile that probably looked as ghastly to them as it felt to her and walked on up the street, trying to figure out what a distracted novelist would walk like.

Now you're scaring the tourists, she told herself in annoyance. If anything's going to bring down the heat on you it's that.

She sighed. I'm really trying not to leap to conclusions based on prejudice here, she thought. Prejudice as to her rival's primary occupation—Ngwenya's nationality and skin color meant nothing to Annja.

But I keep coming back to the strong suspicion Easy Ngwenya's a conscienceless little multiple murderess.

IN HER HOTEL ROOM, a modest three-star establishment not far from the Tuileries with only moderately ruinous rates, Annja sat back and ran her hands across her face and back through her heavy chestnut hair, which hung over the shoulders of her black *Chasing History's Monsters* crew T-shirt. Her notebook computer lay open before her crossed legs, propped on a pillow so the cooling-fan exhaust wouldn't scorch her bare thighs.

She had been doing research not on the Golden Elephant—a quick check of her e-mail accounts showed no helpful responses to a number of guarded queries she'd fired off to contacts across the world—but on the Elephant Calf. Princess Easy herself.

She was a concert pianist, world-class gymnast, martial artist, model, scholar. Pot hunter. There was a quote from an interview with the German magazine *Spiegel* that jumped out at Annja: "To be sure I'm rich and multitalented. But that has nothing to do with me. Those are circumstances. I prefer to focus on my achievements."

She rocked back on the bed, frowning. She badly wanted to toss that off as spoiled-little-rich-girl arrogance. Arrogant it was. But at base it made sense.

And Elephant Calf Ngwenya had achievements.

She had even been a celebrity as a little girl. *National Geographic* had done a spread on the official celebration of the birth of a royal first child of one of Africa's most powerful tribes, and again on the party her father had thrown for her fifth birthday. At the latter Easy foreshadowed things to come, wowing the crowd playing Mozart's "Eine Kleine Nachtmusik" on a concert grand piano, then ruining her pink party dress and shoes in a fistfight with the eight-year-old son of the ambassador from Mali. She won.

Her father was technically the chief of a tribe of South Africa's Zulu nation and an outspoken critic of the ANC-dominated government. He accused them of repression and corruption, of leading the populous, resource-rich country down the same nightmare path to ruin as neighboring Zimbabwe. Repeated attempts had been made on his life. In one the then-fifteen-year-old Princess Elephant Calf had killed two would-be assassins with two shots from a colossal colonial-era double-barreled elephant gun. What got widely overlooked in the subsequent furor in the world media was the fact that the recoil from the first shot of the monstrous gun had broken Easy's shooting hand. Yet she had coolly lined up a second shot and blown a hole through the midriff of an adult male wielding a Kalashnikov.

Annja had to nod her head to that. Spoiled little rich girl she might be. But she was the real deal.

Less than a year later Elephant Calf left home for

good, propelled halfway around the world by some kind of parental explosion. She had gone on to earn multiple degrees from some of the world's toughest and most esteemed institutions.

She'd carved out a reputation as an adventuress. She was outspoken in defending what academic archaeologists dismissed as pot hunting.

"The majority of artifacts recovered go straightaway into the basements of universities and government-run museums," she had told an interviewer for a rival cable network of Annja's employer. "Where they lie gathering dust. If they're not mislabeled or lost due to incompetence. Or thrown out as a result of budget cuts. Or stolen by government officials. All of which happens far more than the academic world lets on."

Annja shook her head. What Easy said was true enough, Annja knew. But it was only part of the story. She failed to mention sites plundered by profit-driven pot hunters, priceless context destroyed and lost forever; provenance muddied and, of course, indigenous peoples robbed of the priceless heritage of their ancestors.

She's one of the bad guys, she told herself determinedly. All her clever rationalizations don't change that. Even if she believes them.

And I'm getting pretty convinced she's behind all these killings—even if they did blow up in her pretty little face.

9

Annja ran her eyes back up the page of the Italian antiquities journal she was reading. It dated from the spring of 1936, during the heart of Italy's bungled incursion into Ethiopia. Since it was an official academic publication from Axis days, it promoted Germanophilia. Scholarly content had apparently been encouraged to bring in German contributions even when peripheral. Annja's eye had skated disinterestedly over an article on discoveries by the French in the Cambodian sector of their Indochinese empire in which the author felt compelled to mention the infrequent German efforts in the region.

Suddenly her awareness snapped to the phrase, "German Southeast Asian expedition of 1913-14."

Her gaze whipped back up the column of the time-yellowed page. She was surprised the old journal hadn't been transcribed to digitized form and the original stored away; perhaps the French library system was showing residual pique at the fascists. And there it was—the phrase that had belatedly snagged in her attention, which continued, "led by Professor Rudolf von Hoiningen of the University of Berlin."

She pumped her fist in the air beside her. "Yes!" And smiled happily at the glares that earned her.

"EXCUSE ME," A VOICE said. "Aren't you Annja Creed?"

The voice was young, masculine, smoothly baritone without being oily and spiced with a Latin accent. Annja couldn't place it. That was unusual.

She looked up from her croissant. She blinked. The only thing she could think of were American beer ads, where drinking the advertised brand seemed to guarantee the drinker the company of magazine-cover models.

If women got their own beer commercials, the man standing at her little table in the library's cafeteria would be their reward for imbibing.

He was tall, lean, immaculately dressed without being overdressed. His hair was dark and slicked back on his fine, aristocratic head. His cream-colored jacket was thrown casually over one shoulder. His eyes were dark and long lashed, his features fine yet thoroughly masculine.

"I beg your pardon," she said.

"I'm a fan of yours. Both your yeoman service on *Chasing History's Monsters* and your more serious work," the man said.

She managed to avoid having either to clear her throat or gulp her coffee to speak intelligibly. "Uh, really?"

"If you'll forgive the forwardness, please allow me to introduce myself. I am Giancarlo Scarlatti Salas. A colleague, at least in the scientific realm. I am an archaeologist myself. I received my degree from the National University of Córdoba in Argentina, my homeland. I did my graduate work at the University of Padua."

"That's in the Humid Pampa, isn't it? Land of the Comechingón people?"

He laughed. It was a surprisingly easy laugh. "Spoken like an archaeologist!" he said. "The average person would no doubt have said 'land of the gauchos,' if she even recognized the word *Pampa*. May I sit?"

"Where are my manners? Sure. Yes. Please." She started to get up, for no reason she could actually identify.

He held up a perfectly manicured hand. "No. Please. I'm fine." He sat.

"You seemed a bit preoccupied when I noticed you," he said. "I'm here doing research into recent progress being made in translating the great hoard of documents from the ancient kingdom of Tombouctou in Africa, which were recently discovered."

"Oh, yes. I've heard of that. It's outside my area, but seems tremendously exciting," Annja said.

"Quite." He leaned forward. "But, if you'll forgive my noticing, you seem perhaps a bit excited yourself."

Am I that obvious? She almost blushed.

"You must have just learned something remark-able," he said.

She sat a moment. What the heck, she thought. She leaned forward and rested her elbows on the table.

"I'm trying to track down an early-twentieth-century German expedition into Indochina," she said.

"Indochina? Not the usual German stomping grounds of the day," he said.

"Not at all, as far as I can find. Then again I've had a ridiculously hard time finding any mention of it what-soever. What's got me worked up is that just minutes ago I was finally able to put a name to it—the von Hoiningen expedition of 1913."

"Congratulations," he said with a genuine smile.

"Thank you. I have yet to turn up anything more on the expedition. But at least now I know I'm on reason-ably solid ground. For a while there I wasn't sure the expedition really happened."

"I see. You must be most gratified." He sounded en-thusiastic. "Do you mind if I ask, does your interest arise from your work on the show or your own re-searches?"

"Both," she said. "I'm afraid I'd better not say anything more about it because of that. The network's legal department is a bear about their nondisclosure agreements."

"Ah! Lawyers. I understand." He sat a moment, looking distracted. His elevated foot swung slightly to and fro.

"I work mostly in Mediterranean and South American archaeology," he said at length. "But something about that name seems to tweak my memory. If I were to be able to provide you a further lead, would you be able to tell me what all this mystery is about?"

"Sure! If you're willing to wait until the show is either shot and scheduled, or the proposal gets shot down." None of which was exactly untrue.

"If I get a paper out of it, I'll be happy to credit you," she added.

"That would be most kind. And now, if you'll excuse me, I won't take up any more of your valuable research time. It's been a delight meeting you, Ms. Creed. May I offer you my card?"

"Oh, yes." She fumbled in the day pack she wore. "And here's mine, too. It's got my cell number. In case you remember anything about Rudolf von Hoiningen, you know."

"To be sure."

She extended her hand. He took it in both of his, bent over it and lightly pressed his lips to it. Then he let it go, and with a last smile turned and strode off.

She stood looking after him, goose bumps all over, wondering if this was what it felt like to be asked to the prom, and feeling like a damned fool for feeling that way.

THE SOUND OF HER cell phone trilled Annja awake.

In the darkness of her hotel room she floundered a moment. The ring continued, above the muted traffic noise from the street outside and the radiator's hiss and clank. She was crabby at being roused from sleep.

The air was thick with the smells of traffic and hot metal. She thought about turning on the light but decided against it. She could see her cell phone glowing on the nightstand, even though her eyes wouldn't focus.

She groped for it and knocked it to the floor. Fortunately it bounced on the throw rug next to the bed.

Finally she found the phone and fell back into bed, clutching her prize. I'm too stressed, she thought. Usually I snap wide-awake. It was another thing to worry about, since that facility had saved her life more times than she wanted to count.

She managed to say "Annja" instead of "Yeah?" And was instantly glad.

"Splendid." The baritone voice poured from the phone like honey with its distinct accent. "It's Giancarlo. Giancarlo Scarlatti. We met today."

"I remember," she said. "Hi, Giancarlo. What's up?"

"I may have something for you," he said. "I remembered where I heard about Professor Doktor von Hoiningen."

Annja sat up straight. "What?" she asked.

"I believe I know somebody who can help you...."

10

Out of the traffic a remarkable figure materialized. An obviously female rider, with a colorful polycarbonate mushroom of a helmet and a UV-blocking face shield, she was dressed in a dark burgundy sweater, gray culottes, stockings that matched her sweater and grey athletic shoes. She sat at ease in what appeared to be a mesh lawn chair atop two wheels, pedaling serenely with feet secured by black straps. The apparition held her arms by her sides, steering by means of handles jutting to the sides below the level of the seat. The vehicle negotiated its way deftly through the traffic to the curb. The rider disengaged her shoes from the pedal straps, clambered out of the seat, hauled the unlikely-looking bicycle up onto the sidewalk and wheeled it to the rack. She locked it in place, then took a shoulder bag from the rack behind the seat.

Unstrapping the helmet, she walked toward the door. As she pushed into the little pastry shop where Annja sat, she shook out a head full of gleaming wine-red hair. Her eyes lit on Annja. Beaming, she strode forward, helmet tucked under her arm like a medieval knight.

"But you must be Annja Creed," she said in charmingly accented English.

She was tall, Annja discovered as she stood up politely, no more than an inch or two shorter than Annja herself. She had that sort of lush tautness Annja associated with French women. At close range, as Annja shook her proffered hand, finding her grip strong and cool, she could see the woman's red hair was laced with a few silver strands.

"And you must be Dr. Gendron," Annja said. "I'm so pleased to meet you."

"Isabelle, please," the woman said. "We are not Germans, after all."

Annja laughed as they both sat. "Interesting you should mention Germans and titles," she said. "But I thought national distinctions were supposed to dissolve over time in the European Union."

The professor made a rude noise. "Many things are *supposed* to happen. I understand that in America, when children put lost teeth under their pillows the tooth fairy is supposed to bring them money. Alexander, Napoleon, Hitler—aside from being destructive monsters, what had those men in common?"

"They all tried to unify Europe?" Annja guessed.

"*Bon!* You *do* know history. Instead of just the pretty

lies that are so often told in its place. But enough of events beyond our means to affect. I'm hungry!" She picked up a menu.

Annja sipped her coffee as the professor fished a pair of reading glasses from inside her sweater and perched them on her fine, narrow nose.

The waitress came. Both women ordered pastries. I can see why the professor does it, Annja thought, riding that bike everywhere. I'll have to run around the whole city to work off the starch overload.

Gendron crossed her legs and leaned forward when the menus had been surrendered. "So. Giani tells me you've a question about some antique German expedition."

"How do you know him?" Annja asked.

"Giancarlo studied under me for a time." A slight smile flitted across her features.

Annja felt a stab of curiosity. She also felt a strong desire not to ask. It would have been intrusive, anyway.

"He must have enjoyed it," Annja said. She felt like kicking herself. Instead she drove on. "I actually read one of your books as a textbook my freshman year. *Dynamite and Dreams: A Survey of Pre-Twentieth-Century Archaeology.* I found it fascinating. A delightful surprise, I have to tell you."

"I hate it when my students fall asleep on me," Gendron said. "I'll try not to let that make me feel old, that you read my book as a schoolgirl."

"In college," Annja said. "It wasn't that long ago."

"I'm just having you on, as the English say. When

I was a student I always felt years older than my peers. Now all my students seem to be twelve, and yet my contemporaries all seem decades older than I. I appear to have become chronically unmoored. Alas, it doesn't stop age slowly taking its toll. But I refuse to let that compromise my enjoyment of life."

"Good for you," Annja said sincerely.

"Now, what was it you wanted to know?"

"Whatever you can tell me about Rudolf von Hoiningen and his expedition to Indochina."

"He came of East Prussian nobility reduced to genteel poverty by Bismarck's German unification. By what exact means I do not know. He appears to have burned up what remained of his inheritance to finance his 1913 expedition."

Gendron sipped her coffee. "Rudolf was a gay, apolitical, physical-culture buff obsessed with the mystic knowledge of the ancient Buddhists and Taoists. None of those things was particularly unusual among wellborn Prussians of the day, although not so frequently in that exact combination. He was also a premier archaeological explorer of his day, very progressive in his refusal to rely upon dynamite, a staple of the time. As the title of my textbook reminds us."

Annja felt a chill run down her spine. The destructive everyday practices of early archaeologists struck her, as they did any well-brought-up modern archaeologist, as actively obscene. At least as abhorrent as the depredations of a modern-day tomb robber like Easy Ngwenya.

"He apparently met with great success, as his letters back to the University of Berlin attest—the few that survived the bombardments of the Second World War. But when it came time to return home, he faced a difficulty."

"World War I?" Annja asked as the waitress delivered their pastries.

"But yes." Gendron picked up a fork and addressed herself to a hearty slice of chocolate cake. "Owing to British control of the Suez Canal, von Hoiningen was forced to travel an arduous, dangerous, circuitous land route. He had to travel up through China to the ancient Silk Road, then through Turkestan into Turkey."

She gestured with her fork. "Having survived all that, he loaded his specimens and journals onto a ship, the freighter *Hentzau,* and set sail from Istanbul. Whereupon a British submarine lurking in the Sea of Marmara promptly torpedoed it."

"Oh, dear," Annja said.

"The explosion killed poor Rudolf outright. The captain, thinking fast, managed to ground his ship in shallow water. Von Hoiningen's assistant, Erich Dessauer, who may or may not have been his lover, recovered a few of his artifacts and journals. The assistant made his way back to Germany with as many journals and crates of artifacts as he could, intending to send for the rest later. Instead he was promptly drafted and died in the British tank attack at Cambrai in 1918. Most of what he brought home vanished in the

Second World War. What survives remains in the Istanbul University collection."

Annja winced. "That's quite the litany of disasters," she said.

"Almost enough to make one believe the expedition was cursed," Gendron said. She smiled. "But we know there are no such things as curses, yes?"

"Sure," Annja said.

"A Turkish researcher stumbled across the bare facts of the lost von Hoiningen expedition in the middle fifties. In the seventies much of the story was pieced together by a writer for American adventure magazines. In 1997, scholars substantiated the American's account and filled in the gaps."

She shook her handsome head and smiled sadly. "In the modern archaeological world the doomed von Hoiningen expedition is remembered, to the minor extent it is at all, more as a cautionary tale about the dangers and disappointments of the archaeological life than for its science."

"I'd imagine. Thank you so much," Annja said.

Gendron sat back. Despite talking fairly steadily, she had managed to polish off her cake without chewing with her mouth open. Annja admired the feat.

"So why the interest in this most obscure of misadventures? You don't seem to have the taste for others' misfortunes," the professor said.

"Not at all. Recently I've been given hints of important cultural relics the Germans found. Perhaps even a vast temple complex which has yet to be rediscovered."

"A lost temple? In this day and age?" Gendron seemed bemused. But she shrugged. "Still, I read every now and again of such things being found around the world with the help of satellites and aircraft."

"It's a tantalizing possibility," Annja said. "Whether or not it's more than that—well, that's what I'd like to find out."

"To be sure. What archaeologist worth her whip and revolver wouldn't want to be the one to discover a grand new lost temple?"

Annja laughed out loud at the *Raiders of the Lost Ark* reference.

Gendron's own smile was brief. "Adventures are all good and well. You seem a most competent young woman, well able to take care of yourself. I was always more the scholarly type, at home in the musty stacks of the library, rather than the adventure-seeker. Still, I learn things in this old imperial capital. Southeast Asia does not currently get as much lurid press as, say, the Mideast or Afghanistan, or even Africa, but it is a most perilously unstable place these days."

"I'll be careful," Annja said. "I'm not even to Istanbul yet. I guess that's my next stop."

"Turkey is no picnic these days, either, I fear. So much unrest."

"But where's that not true?" Annja asked.

"Fewer and fewer places these days," Gendron said.

"Really, Professor," Annja said, "I'm in your debt. If there's any way I can help you, please let me know."

Gendron looked pensive. "You might do one favor

for me," she said. "There is a certain cable-television personality—if at all possible, I'd be most grateful if you could arrange for me to meet him someday. Or at least put in a good word."

"Well, I'll try. For what it's worth," Annja said.

"A most fascinating gentleman," Gendron said, "of obvious French extraction."

That didn't fit any Knowledge Channel hunk Annja could remember. "Who?"

"Anthony Bourdain."

Annja's smile was half grimace. "Wrong network." She took a sip of her drink. Seeing her companion's crestfallen expression she said, "There's kind of a Montague-Capulet thing between our network and his. Except nastier. Tell you what, though. I only know him as you do, from seeing him on television, but I get the impression he has no more patience for that sort of rivalry nonsense than I have. Should I chance to meet him, I'll tell him he has a fan. One definitely worth his while to get to know."

The professor's own smile was impish. "You'd make such a sacrifice for an old lady, for so trifling a favor?"

Annja snorted. "Old lady my foot," she said. "If I look half as good as you do at your age, I'll consider myself the luckiest woman on Earth.

"And as for sacrifice—well, while I admit he's a very attractive man, I also made a vow a couple years back not to date older men."

Gendron's eyebrows rose. "But at your age, dear child, doesn't that leave you with nothing but boys?"

Annja shrugged. "There is that."

Then she recalled recent events, and brightened. "But perhaps not always."

11

"It is with very great pleasure that I am able to place the Istanbul Archaeology Museum at the disposal of so distinguished a peer as Ms. Annja Creed," the curator said as he led her through the dimly lit exhibition hall. He was a huge, fat man with a bandit moustache, tapering shaven head and dark wiry stubble on his olive jowls. Ahmet Bahceli looked like the stereotypical evil Turk from central casting. He was in fact a cheerful, gentle-voiced scholar of enormous international repute. He was curator of special collections for the museum and overflowing with enthusiasm.

Annja looked into a case of Byzantine coins so he wouldn't see her slight grimace. Is it because I'm really such a notable archaeologist, she thought, or because I play one on TV?

Still, enough lay at stake that she needed to swallow

her ego and go with what worked. Again. She wasn't deceiving the man. She just was taking a hit to her pride. Again.

"It's so good of you to allow me access to the von Hoiningen collection, Dr. Bahceli," she said.

"Please understand," he said, "that it is meager and incomplete."

"I gathered as much from my previous research. But believe me, Doctor, anything will help. Even if it's only something to peer at through glass."

Istanbul was a modern city, so big and boisterous and full of history that a single continent wouldn't hold it. It sprawled like an unruly giant across the Bosporus Straits, which ran from the Black Sea to the Sea of Marmara, upstream of the Aegean, and separated Europe from Asia. She loved visiting there.

They city was surprisingly green. Although the green was turning rapidly sere with the onset of a chilly autumn. Winter was a ways off yet, but the autumn was damp and cool enough for her.

She didn't have time for sightseeing. She felt driven. She sensed other forces moving around her—probably including the tomb-raiding renegade Easy Ngwenya. That made it urgent to find the truth about the von Hoiningen expedition, beyond the fact of its being well and truly doomed. And if there was anything to the rumors of a fabulous temple lost in the jungle, with its appropriately fabulous treasure, she had to find and secure them before the plunderers arrived like a Biblical locust plague.

The looming, vaguely conical mass of her guide halted by a case of small artifacts displayed against a cream-silk backdrop. "Here you see such artifacts as we possess. Von Hoiningen's assistant lacked the means to carry them with him back to Germany. His misfortune proved a blessing for archaeology. No doubt you are aware the bulk of the artifacts he saved from the sunken *Hentzau* were destroyed in the Allied bombing of Berlin in World War II."

Annja nodded.

Bahceli shook his head ponderously. "Even though expeditions are notoriously prone to catastrophe, I have seldom if ever heard of such a concatenation of calamities as befell the von Hoiningen expedition. It is almost enough to make one believe in a curse."

She smiled. "But you don't, do you?"

"Of course not! Especially a curse by infidels. That would be mere superstition."

Bahceli rather grandly produced a set of keys and opened the case's glass cover. He gestured for Annja to examine what she would.

Not much to see, she thought glumly as she pulled on the pair of nonlatex medical-style gloves he had provided her. A few coins, a few small carvings and castings, a lacquer medallion.

One object caught her eye. She reached in and gingerly picked up an elephant figurine no bigger than the palm of her hand, in verdigrised bronze. Its workmanship was exquisite. It stood with trunk curled to forehead and mouth open. It almost seemed to be smiling.

"Ah," the curator said. "That catches your eye, as well? There is something to it, some...quality I cannot put my finger upon."

He shrugged. "It has been rumored since Dessauer's departure that it is the replica of a larger statue, of pure gold, to which von Hoiningen referred in his notes," he said. "Sadly, we do not have these notes. It is why we exhibit these items as relics of the tragic expedition itself, since we cannot authoritatively source them or connect them to specific sites or cultures, other than by inference."

With a sigh Annja handed the figurine back to Bahceli. "Thank you," she said. "If I could see the surviving notebooks, now, please?"

His villainous face split in a great benign grin. "Of course," he said.

ANNJA SAT IN THE dark and cool confines of a private reading room with the journal open before her. To her right lay her computer, connected to the Internet via the museum's wireless network. Despite the fact that the museum's exterior was pure faux classical, the facility itself seemed most thoroughly up-to-date. She was typing in promising-looking passages from the journal and then running them through a translation program.

The work was tedious but she plodded on. And then words jumped out at her—"the jungle a mighty temple gave up."

She stopped, reared back, barely able to believe it. She carefully studied the words surrounding the phrase.

"The climb up the plateau was hazardous. We lost two bearers to a mudslide when a rope in a sudden downpour gave way…."

A few sentences on she read more.

"The guardians of the temple were cautious. Our guide, Ba, managed to convince them we meant no harm. We only meant honor to the ancients and the Buddha to give."

There followed a matter-of-fact discussion of his dealings with the plateau's inhabitants, who were wary of them. They warmed after the expedition's physician, Dr. Kramer, set a child's broken arm. Annja got the notion the natives were capable of the feat—they just appreciated the gesture. At last the visitors got permission to climb a small peak in the center of the plateau.

"The special sanctuary, the holy of holies. The Temple of the Elephant was colossal! Our hearts were in our throats at the splendor of this marvel, this treasure, this golden elephant with emeralds for eyes.

"I made complete sketches of the temples, and the idol, in my sketchbook—"

"Oh no," Annja said softly. None of that had survived the *Hentzau*'s torpedoing.

She sighed and read on. "It can still be found where I found the map. Inscribed on the base of the statue of Avalokiteshvara in the Red Monastery outside Nakhon Sawan, in the Kingdom of Siam."

Annja sat back, frowning speculatively. On the one hand, she thought, it makes me crazy that the solution to the mystery isn't here. On the other, at least there really is a Temple and a Golden Elephant.

"Ms. Creed?"

She started and looked up. A painfully earnest young man with a mop of heavy coal-black hair stood respectfully back from her chair. "Yes?" she said.

"Curator Bahceli would like to speak with you in his office immediately, if it is convenient to you."

Bahceli had been more than kind in granting Annja access to the museum's special collection, as well as giving her a personal tour. If he wanted to see her, the polite and politic thing to do would be to respond promptly.

"Certainly," she said, rising. She felt a brief tug of concern over leaving her computer unattended. But the reading room was closed to the public. And Bahceli, for all his jovial manner, did not strike Annja as the sort who'd put up with pilferage in his department. It was a cardinal sin in such an institution, for obvious reasons. She walked briskly back to his office.

But when she rapped on the open door, then peeked around the frame, the office was empty.

A dreadful certainty she'd been tricked stuck in the base of her throat. She turned and walked back to the reading room as quickly as she could without making a scene that would raise questions she didn't want to answer—or leave hanging.

Her computer and von Hoiningen's open journal still sat on the table. Disappearing out the far door of the long, narrow room she saw a familiar, expensively clad figure whose well-schooled grace did not conceal a certain walk-through-a-wall thrustfulness to its gait.

"Easy," Annja said, as if cursing.

The figure vanished from sight. Annja sprinted after. She got all the way out into the warm daylight with nothing to show but a wisp of expensive scent and a suspicion of mocking laughter hanging in the air.

She made herself march back to the reading room, neither dashing nor slouching in defeat. Rudolf von Hoiningen's aggravating notebook was intact. A surprisingly quick diagnostic reassured her that no nasty software had been quickly and covertly installed on her computer.

"But it's not like there's no such thing as a digital camera," Annja muttered.

She was sure the little witch of a pot hunter had photographed the relevant pages to translate or digest at her leisure. Annja knew it with bitter certainty. Not that Easy didn't speak German, along, apparently, with every other known language and an alien tongue or two. She probably had a photographic memory to boot.

Cautious, here, Annja told herself. Let's not wallow too deeply in paranoia.

But even paranoids have enemies, she thought.

And once more hers had gotten the better of her.

12

"Annja! Annja Creed! What a delightful surprise."

On the steps of the museum Annja stopped and turned at the greeting.

"Giancarlo!" she exclaimed, with a rush of genuine pleasure. Then, frowning slightly, she said, "This is quite a coincidence."

His dark, lean, handsome face lit with a smile. "Some might call it kismet. As they do here, come to think of it. I might call it synchronicity."

He came forward holding out his hands to her. He was dressed in that expensively casual way that only the wealthy can pull off. His hair was slicked back seal-like.

"But really, it's not such a great coincidence after all, is it? We share a profession, and many particular interests. My researches have brought me to Istanbul.

Naturally, as a Mediterranean archaeologist, I gravitate here. I can only presume you have done the same," he said.

"Yes," she replied guardedly.

"Of course, you are a Renaissance scholar," he said, taking her hands in his firm, strong grip. Despite the humid heat off the Bosporus his palms were dry. She envied him; she herself had been outdoors less than a minute and felt as if she'd just emerged from the shower with her clothes on. Autumn or not, cold nights or not, it still got plenty warm during the day. "The Turks were the great enemy of Renaissance Europe. So naturally at some point in your studies you likewise find yourself here."

He said it with such conviction that she didn't have the heart to disabuse him. She accepted a warm hug and a peck on her cheek.

She smiled at him. "It's good to see you again," she said, "no matter the reason."

"Will you join me for a cup of coffee?" he said. "The coffee here is excellent. But what am I saying? Of course it is. It's Turkey!"

He laughed delightedly. She laughed with him. She always appreciated a man who could laugh at himself.

"SO THAT'S WHERE THINGS stand," Annja said. She sat slumped in a chair in the air-conditioned comfort of a café two blocks from the Museum. "Every clue I find seems just to add another link to the chain. I never seem to get closer."

She shook her head. "And the most substantial clue I've managed to locate I just handed to the world's most notorious pot hunter on a silver platter."

Giancarlo nodded sympathetically. He had listened raptly as she poured out her story to him—minus the details of exactly what it was she sought.

"Surely it's not so bad, Annja, my dear," he told her.

"But it is," she said, tossing back her hair. A ceiling fan swooshed overhead. Annja wasn't sure whether it was needed to circulate the refrigerated air or just there because it was an expected element of Turkish atmosphere. "I think—I think people have been killed over this already," she concluded.

"But you have the information you needed, do you not?"

"Well—I have leads to follow. And I seem to have confirmation that what I've come chasing clear across Europe is actually real. That's encouraging, anyway. But I just feel so frustrated. I keep running and running after this…thing, and I never seem to get any closer."

"But you have gotten all there is to be gained in Istanbul, yes?" he asked.

Reluctantly she nodded. "I'm afraid so."

He stood with an abruptness that belied the languid ease with which he'd sat and listened to her outpourings of woe. "Well, then! You are off duty. Is it not time to relax and put your troubles aside? This is a beautiful city, full of history that you are rarely qualified to appreciate. At least let me show some of it to you and take your mind off your troubles."

"Sure," she said, and stood to join him. "That sounds wonderful."

WITH GIANCARLO AS HER laughing, knowledgeable and attentive guide they took in the sights of the great ancient city. Annja thoroughly enjoyed being a tourist for the day.

"In 1534," Giancarlo said that evening, with candle-light dancing in his eyes, "the sultan, Suleiman, heard that the young widow of the count of Fundi was the most beautiful woman in all Europe. She was also renowned for her wit and erudition, although it is possible these mattered less to the sultan. So he sent his great corsair captain Barbarossa to kidnap her. They attacked in the middle of the night. As her family re-tainers battled to hold them off she leaped on a horse, rode down several would-be abductors and galloped off to safety in her nightgown."

The conversation of the other diners was soft susur-ration in the background. Through the great window beside the couple the fabled ancient city tumbled down to the water from seven hills almost as famous as Rome's. Its lights made jeweled streaks across the slowly rippling waters of the Golden Horn.

"A woman after my own heart," Annja said.

They'd taken in a few sights such as the Blue Mosque, and a few nondescript stubs of wall, here in-corporated into later structures, there holding up green slopes, that Annja's escort told her dated from Lygos, the first port settlement, which predated even Byzantium's founding by the Greeks of Megara. At evening they found themselves sitting in a pleasantly upscale Turkish restaurant.

Annja felt a strange vibration. She frowned, wondering if she were somehow getting dizzy. Then she noticed ice tinkling in glasses and silverware rattling. A French tourist couple across the dimly lit restaurant looked around in wild-eyed dismay; a middle-aged Japanese couple sitting near Giancarlo and Annja continued eating without paying visible attention.

Annja smiled and tried to relax back into her chair, although her hand was not altogether steady setting her lamb kabob down into its bed of rice. "I'm not used to earthquakes," she said. "I guess that comes from growing up in New Orleans and now living in New York. They're what you'd call pretty seismically stable. And I've never really experienced them much on digs."

Giancarlo grinned back over a forkful of dolma, eggplant stuffed with lamb and rice, doused with hot red pepper in olive oil and the sour yogurt Turks served with every meal and practically every course. "A tremor," he said, with a gleam in his dark eyes. The lashes were long, almost feminine. Yet they had no effect of reducing his masculine appeal. Rather the opposite—something Annja was becoming more and more uncomfortably aware of as she passed time in his company. "Hardly an earthquake by Turkish standards," he said.

He took a sip of wine. "Turkey is terribly afflicted with earthquakes, you may be aware," he said. "The great tsunami of 1509 overrode the seawall and killed ten thousand people."

She smiled wanly. "Let's hope these shocks stay more modest," she said. "At least while we're here. Oh, dear. I guess that sounds selfish."

"It sounds eminently sensible," he said. "More wine?"

"No, thanks. I'm not really much of a drinker. I am surprised to find alcohol so readily available in a Muslim country."

"The Turks have long had a reputation for their…relaxed interpretation of Islam. And of course the country's been officially secular since the 1920s, although that could change in an eye blink, the way things go these days."

"You're very knowledgeable about Turkey," Annja said.

He shrugged. "I feel great affinity for Istanbul. Much history has passed through here—passed through that great harbor out there."

"Much cruelty, too, it would seem," she said. "As much before the Ottomans conquered the city as after." She thought of her recent adventures in the city with Roux and Garin, then pushed them aside.

"You speak of the Byzantines with their blindings and other baroque punishments? To be sure. But was there ever a ruler more justly named Magnificent than

Suleiman? A cruel man, *claro*. But a scholar, a warrior, a patron of the arts."

He shook his sleek head. Annja thought she saw genuine sadness in his eyes. "There's so little of splendor in our present age, isn't there?" he said.

She sighed. "I suppose so," she said. "Maybe that's why I spend so much time burrowing into the past myself."

AS THEY WALKED A PROMENADE Annja's arm had threaded into the crook of Giancarlo's. She kept meaning to disengage it.

"That story you told me over dinner," she said. "About Suleiman sending raiders to kidnap that Italian countess. Was that real? That actually happened?"

"Ah, but yes," he said. "The woman in question was Julia Colonna, of a great and famous family. You forget I am Italian! Would I lie about such a thing—to a fellow archaeologist and historian, to boot? Not to mention a woman herself notable for both beauty and intellect!"

Annja laughed and shook her head. "Thank you. And no. I suppose not. Although it's a delightfully lurid episode I somehow managed never to hear about. It just seems too melodramatic to have taken place in reality. Like the stories I read when I was a girl. I'd get enthused about them, and then the sisters would tell me they never happened and never could happen. Since then I've kind of…collected stories like that from history. To prove to myself that adventures really are real."

Listen to yourself, her inner voice said. You carry

the sword of a martyred French saint. You find yourself fighting evil. And you need proof there's such a thing as adventure?

But Giancarlo's handsome face had set. He lifted his chin, stopped, turned to face her in the light of the crescent moon rising over the plateau behind them. He gripped her arm. Is he going to kiss me? she wondered. She carefully refrained from wondering whether she would let him.

"I fear I have a more disturbing tale for you now, Annja," he said. "I hope you will forgive me for not telling you before. But you seemed so distraught by your misadventure in the museum that I hadn't the heart until you had time to recover."

"What do you mean?" she asked.

"Professor Gendron has been murdered," he said. "She was found shot to death in her office with a .40-caliber handgun."

Annja turned to the ancient weathered parapet. She was scarcely aware of breaking free of his double grasp, strong though it was.

A .40-caliber handgun. Trademark of Easy Ngwenya.

She walked a few blind steps, stopped when the wall's rough stone rapped her knees and its sharp edge bit into her thighs. She felt as if she were encapsulated in a glass bubble, around which seethed a storm, a veritable tempest of emotions—rage, grief, fear and self-reproach.

Despite their flash acquaintance she had connected

with Isabelle Gendron. As she had with Sir Sidney Hazelton.

It was a paradox of Annja's life, or nature. She was a highly empathetic person, someone who tended to get along with others and make friends easily. Yet she led an essentially hermitic existence. She had trouble maintaining friendships. It wasn't that she fell out with friends; she kept touch with a horde of people dotted all over the globe.

But it was a desultory sort of contact, conducted almost entirely through e-mail, the odd text message or cell-phone call. Sparse and at distance.

It was Annja's gift, and curse, to make contact at a fairly deep level almost instantly. But not to keep it. Everyone she met, it seemed, touched her deeply—and went away.

Which, needless to say, contributed more than slightly to the lack of romance in her life.

Annja shook her head and forced herself back into the present moment—horrible as it had become. The news of Isabelle Gendron's murder was like an amputation in her soul.

Especially since she could not avoid the guilty certainty that she, Annja Creed, was the reason that joy- and life-filled woman had been murdered.

She found herself sobbing in Giancarlo's arms on a concrete bench. He held her and let her sorrow run its course.

Finally the tears ran dry. Such open displays of emotion were unlike her. But this atrocity had blindsided her. She sat up. Felt long, surprisingly strong fingers grip her chin and lift her face upward. His lips touched hers.

For a moment she yielded to his kiss. Then she turned away.

Giancarlo stiffened. From the corner of her eye, still tear-blurred, she could see a hurt expression on his handsome face in the amber glow of a distant street lamp.

"I'm sorry," she said.

She stood and took a few steps away. And Easy Ngwenya, she thought. There was no question—she was locked in a contest with a conscienceless murderer.

"At least let me help you!" he cried.

Annja shook her head. She avoided his dark and fervent eyes. "I wish I could, Giancarlo," she said. "But I don't want to put you in the crosshairs, too."

The main reason she couldn't look at him was her dread he would read in her face her real fear.

What if I already have?

13

Annja flew from Istanbul to Bangkok. *Have I let the little murderess get too big a lead on me?* she could not stop thinking. *If only I hadn't wasted the afternoon and evening playing tourist with Giancarlo.*

She also flew in a state of increasing stiffness. She'd been able to get an early-morning flight out of Istanbul on Turkish Airlines. Unfortunately that went no farther than the capital, Ankara; it seemed no flights left the country from Istanbul. Then for some reason the only way to Bangkok was through Germany, far to the north-west—the opposite direction from where she wanted to go. She flew to Frankfurt, where she had to hustle to catch a Royal Brunei flight leaving for Bangkok little more than an hour later. She considered herself quite fortunate to have snagged a desirable window seat directly aft of the jumbo jet's midship exit, where she could stretch her long legs instead of riding with her knees up under her chin, as she so often found herself doing.

The bad news was that she'd be in the seat for eleven hours.

She touched down just before seven the next morning. Customs was the usual drag, but no worse than what you went through anywhere in a terrorism-obsessed world. The most significant difference was that the Thai customs officers tended to treat foreign tourists with less rudeness than their English or American counterparts.

She left everything but a light daypack in a locker at the airport. A taxi to the riverfront was pricey, but nothing compared to the cost of the short-notice plane ticket. She could have bought the taxi for that. She could hear Roux complaining. They were really going to need the commission the mysterious collector was willing to pay.

But for Annja it was no longer about the money. If indeed it ever had been.

Bangkok was called "the Venice of Asia," along with a lot of less complimentary names. It was veined with canals and its whole existence centered on Chao Phraya, the great green waterway that ran through the middle of the country. Annja had the driver let her off at an open-air market a few blocks from the waterfront so she could buy some fruit and packaged snacks. She was blessed with a ferocious immune system, a vital attribute for anyone who did extensive fieldwork around the globe. But she didn't want to press her luck; getting laid out with dysentery or some kind of awful amoeba would allow her deadly rival the latitude to rob the Temple of the Elephant of whatever artifacts it held. And quite possibly she would leave more dead bodies in her wake.

The fruit was protected with rinds Annja could peel; the snacks had their plastic wrappers. Annja couldn't answer absolutely for the cleanliness of the plants where they'd been packaged, but knew standards were likely to be higher than for random street vendors. Several bottles of water also went into the pack to sustain her.

Then she found a riverboat, basically an outsized canoe with a rounded roof and an engine, and engaged passage upriver to Nakhon Sawan. The railroad had run that way for over a century, and reasonably modern highways connected the city to the national capital. But even though central Thailand was flat, Annja didn't care to trust her life to the buses any more than necessity required, which was hair-raisingly often enough. She knew the trains were likely to be overcrowded and stifling. Water travel was quicker—especially since Annja would bet both the trains and the buses stopped frequently and often at random—and were the least uncomfortable option.

Slipping under the shade of the low rounded roof, Annja slid her pack under the bench and settled against the gunwale amid a haze of smells of the river water, commingled with raw sewage. The boatman shouted, the engine snarled and the craft set out into the great sluggish flow, wallowing slightly in waves reflected from the bank. Once it got out in the stream and under way for true, the water's slow rhythms were soporific and the engine noise became white noise blocking out other sounds. Annja had slept on the flight, but that never seemed to rest her. Little bothered by the relative discomfort, she huddled in upon herself and fell sound asleep.

By midafternoon they reached their destination. The city of Nakhon Sawan, capital of the province of the same name, lay near where the rivers Nan and Ping converged to form the arterial Chao Phraya. It was a lot less modern and glossy than Bangkok—the modern and glossy parts of it, anyway. The riverfront gave her mostly the impression of stacks of huge teak logs, the region's main resource, lying or being loaded onto barges.

Shopping around, Annja found a cabbie who demonstrated some grasp of English, and hired him as guide, as well as driver. She herself couldn't understand a word of the local language.

The guide's name was Phran. He knew about the Red Monastery. He drove Annja out of town through country not a lot different from that around New Orleans to a graveled lot in the midst of a stand of tall hardwoods he told her weren't teak. He was a skinny, middle-aged man without much of a chin and a sort of loose-jointed look. He seemed cheerful but did not, blessedly, insist on chattering. He answered her questions readily enough. Mostly he seemed to go along in his own little world. Fortunately he was not so immersed in it that he drove alarmingly.

Stepping out into the slanting, mellowing light of late afternoon, Annja was once again struck by the difference even the wind of passage through the car's open windows made. Walking resembled wading through a swimming pool, but with more bugs. She scarcely felt the lack of a shower after her flight anymore; she couldn't be any more sweat-drenched and grubby, and was hardly more so than if she'd arrived in fresh-laundered clothes.

Phran followed her to the monastery doors with a head-bobbing gait like a species of wading bird. Annja saw little mystery to why this was called the Red Monastery. Rather than the massive stone piles she usually saw in pictures or documentaries about Southeast Asian temples, this place had been built out of native hardwoods. It was enameled in a scarlet that was as bright and startling as fresh blood even in light well diluted by angle and long tree shadows. Where it wasn't red it was gilded, like the heads of ceremonial guardian dragons carved into the beam ends.

The doors opened at their approach. A large-bellied monk in a scarlet robe over a saffron undershirt stood with sandaled feet splayed far apart. A gaggle of younger, thinner monks wearing yellow robes hung behind him. They gazed in seeming amazement at the tall foreign woman.

But the head monk, or at least senior monk on duty, wasn't impressed. His scowl and head shake were universal language.

"Am I too late?" Annja said. She wasn't thinking as

clearly as she should, with stress and travel. It had slipped her mind that the monastery might reasonably impose visiting hours.

"Tell him I'm not just a tourist," she said. "I'm an archaeologist—a scientist. I'd like to spend a few minutes examining some of their relics. I'll be no trouble." She began fumbling in her pack. She had come well credentialed with a letter of introduction from a prominent Columbia University professor and various documents attesting to her status as an archaeologist in good standing.

For once Phran's sunny disposition clouded. "Is not that," he said sadly, after listening to a string of grumpy grunts Annja was surprised amounted to intelligible speech.

"Please tell him I'm a consultant for *Chasing History's Monsters,*" she said. "The American television show."

To her amazement Phran shook his head. "No, missy," he said. "Problem is, no women allowed. This monastery. You see?"

Whether she did or not, she couldn't misunderstand the heavy door slammed in her face.

Annja stood before the blazing-red door with a smiling Buddha and sinuous Thai characters embossed on it in gold, feeling foolish. "Oh," she said.

She felt no outrage. Although like most modern nations Thailand made a great show of celebrating women's rights, Asia remained thoroughly patriarchal. Which, in Annja's observation and research, meant that in reality the women ran everything, albeit behind the scenes, without official or acknowledged power. Lording it over women in petty ways was the men's way of getting some of their own back.

And Annja was a foreign woman. If she stormed into town and complained to the authorities, they'd hear her out, smiling and nodding. Then they'd do nothing.

In fact Annja was scarcely even surprised, after the initial shock of having the door slammed on her. It was a monastery, after all. She'd been raised in an environment from which all males were scrupulously excluded, except the occasional visiting priest, and maintenance and repairmen squired as closely by the sisters as weasels touring a hatchery. She hadn't enjoyed it that much. But she came out of it with a conviction that people ought to be able to hang out with whomever they liked and exclude whomever they liked.

She stood a moment to take careful stock of her surroundings. This wasn't triple-canopy rainforest. The tall, thick-boled trees stood widely spaced, with plenty of undergrowth between, and they grew close by the great weeping-eaved structure.

"All right, then, Phran," she said to her guide, who stood by looking as if his pet guppy had just died. "Surely they can't object if I take some photos of the outside of their monastery with my digital camera."

Phran seemed to reinflate, his skinny shoulders rising and squaring. "No," he said slowly and guardedly. Apparently he'd had some experience with Westerners who had an exaggerated sense of their own importance.

Annja smiled encouragingly. "So now I'm going to wander around outside and snap some shots. Then do you think you can find me a nice hotel in town?"

His expression brightened. "Oh yes, Miss Annja!" he said. "For you, double nice."

CLAD HEAD TO FOOT in the darkest long clothing she'd packed, Annja lurked in the bushes forty yards from the Red Monastery. Night was in full effect. That meant prime time for the loudest, most aggressively hungry creatures, especially bugs. She particularly noticed the bugs because they acted out their aggressive hungers on her, notwithstanding the long sleeves and pants. Although she had to give some credit to the tree frogs yammering raucously as damned souls above her head and from all the trees around.

At least the noise sort of lowers the bar for stealth, she told herself. She could go in wearing wooden clogs and with bells sewn all over her and it was unlikely anybody'd notice for the nocturnal racket. Nature was a wondrous thing sometimes.

Nonetheless, when she slipped from cover she tried to move as noiselessly as possible, if for no other reason than to keep herself in the proper state of mind. There would be no striding boldly around, looking as if she belonged, which was usually less conspicuous than sneaking. She was a tall white woman who spoke not a word of Thai, out here on the verge of a great reeking swamp far away from anything but the forbidden monastery. She might as well sneak, since she was going to be suspicious as hell to anyone who spotted her no matter what she did.

With Phran's help she had gotten rapidly ensconced in a reasonably clean and reasonably cheap hotel. Nakhon Sawan lay far off the paths beaten for Thailand's infamous sex trade, and its swamps were not a mad tourist draw even with the monsoon petering out. She showered and changed and treated herself to a very good dinner. Having downloaded her photos of the monastery to her notebook computer and reviewed them while sitting cross-legged on the bed making a token gesture at drying out, by the time dinner was finished she had worked out what she thought was a decent plan of attack.

The doors all looked forbiddingly solid behind their frequently replenished lacquer coats. However, like many Thai roofs, the one on the main temple structure was compound. Between the upper roof, steeply slanted, of red fired-clay tiles, and a second tier ran a row of windows. These looked to be about two feet by three and were clearly opened for ventilation. As far as Annja could tell they weren't screened.

As was to be expected, given its function as a residence, as well as a place of prayer, the monastery comprised a whole cluster of buildings, including dorms and storage structures. Some butted right up against the tall main building.

That made her smile. There's my way in.

Back in her room she dressed in her best stealth outfit, went out and putted away into the hot tropical night on the little Honda scooter she'd rented with the help of a well-tipped hotel clerk after Phran dropped her off. The monastery lay half a mile or so up a dirt turnoff from the river highway. Annja hid her bike in dense undergrowth a hundred yards off the main road and hiked up the dirt path. A fair amount of traffic ran along the main route, noisily enough she felt confident it had covered the sound of her little engine, but nobody seemed to be driving up to the Red Monastery after hours. She figured if anyone did turn up the cutoff, between the engine sound and the headlights she should get ample warning.

At first glimpse of the few pale lights from the monastery Annja ditched off into the underbrush. The monastery had been built on a slight rise, probably just high enough to keep it from flooding when the Chao Phraya got frisky. The ground around it was mostly solid. That was a relief—wading through swamps wasn't her favorite thing to do in the world.

Of course, crouching in humid darkness with thorns sticking into her right thigh and something sucking the blood out of her left earlobe, preparing to commit criminal trespass didn't exactly top her favorites playlist, either.

She drew a deep breath and tried not to notice she'd sucked in at least one unfortunate gnat. If it was just for the commission, she told herself, I wouldn't do this. But it's gone beyond that now. And it's not as if I'm going to steal anything….

"Oh, stop it," she said softly. "Quit making excuses and go."

She went. Bent almost double, she slipped from the saw-edged foliage as quietly as she could. She half ran to a structure protruding from the backside of the main hall like some sort of growth, away from view from the road. Climbing up a tree growing right alongside it, she walked along a big branch, using smaller ones for handholds, right onto the substructure's roof.

Its steeply pitched tiles were glazed ceramic and slick as wet glass. But their flared, knobby ends provided traction of a sort.

From there she proceeded up onto the main roof's lower course and began to work her way gingerly around. She held on to the upper-course tiles, although they provided more the illusion of a purchase than anything that was actually going to stop her from falling a dozen feet onto hard-packed clay if she lost her footing. Thanks to Google she knew the statue she sought stood in a side chamber toward the back, near the main altar with its traditional larger-than-life seated Buddha.

At what she hoped was the right spot she hunkered down and peered inside. She saw a wide space lit dimly with the wavering yellow glow of oil lamps. She slid inside, being careful to keep her feet on the base of the window frame. Shutters to keep out the rain hung beneath, presumably to be pushed shut with long poles when necessary. The last thing she needed was to put weight on one, have it give way, and have the whole monastery come running to the racket to find her lying on the floor of their sanctum with her leg broken.

It was farther to the floor than she expected. Perhaps ten feet. She let herself hang from a lower corner of the window frame by one hand and drop. Her long, strong legs flexed, easily taking up the shock. She put a hand on the floor to help support her in a crouch and listened.

Her rubber-soled shoes hadn't made much noise hitting the polished hardwood floor. Straining her senses, Annja heard nothing, felt no vibration transmitted through the wood to her fingertips. She seemed to have the hall to herself.

Outside the monastery the insects trilled and tree frogs screamed. The air within hung thick and still as a swamp backwater. Keen incense sliced the humid air; she smelled the pungent oil used on the floors and mustiness lingering from sweaty monks' robes.

A quick survey took in an altar with its big golden Buddha to her right, illuminated from beneath by brass lamps whose tiny, flickering yellow glows made the seated figure's plump, benign face seem disconcertingly alive. Alcoves lined the walls, each containing its own figure and lit by a single lamp.

Annja doubted any of them was her guy Avalokiteshvara. None was wider than her palm. Not for the first time she wondered why anyone would bother, or how anyone would even come to, scrawling a map on the bottom of a statue in some obscure monastery in a swamp in the Thai central plains.

No doubt von Hoiningen had explained how that came to pass in his journals, which were meticulous to the point of stereotypical Prussian anal retentiveness. Perhaps an earlier explorer, seeking a more permanent form in which to transcribe details fading from memory or a scrap of paper decomposing in the inevitable constant dampness? Some refugee, perhaps from one of the wars that had constantly racked this region throughout known history? Maybe the archaeologist even explained how he happened to find out about it. She was sure either in itself would prove a tale worthy of a modern action film or two.

But either those journals had gone to the bottom of the Bosporus, like von Hoiningen himself, or succumbed to water damage after the torpedo attack. Also like von Hoiningen, she supposed.

She straightened and moved forward. She walked carefully, placing the lead foot fully on the floor before beginning to transfer weight to it. It not only stilled her footfalls but also made it far less likely a loose or humidity-warped floorboard would creak more than with normal walking. She stood upright; it made balancing easier, and any monk chancing in was not going to be any less likely to spot her in the middle of the open floor if she scuttled like a spider.

Stopping at the intersection, she leaned forward to look left for three seconds, drew back, then took a peek right. To her left ran a hallway, lit by a faint gleam from somewhere. Its steadiness betrayed its electronic origin. A short step led up; a door opened beside it, presumably to a rectory or some other kind of office.

To Annja's right lay a small chamber. In the midst of it, upon a waist-high pedestal of gleaming polished teak, danced the many-armed figure she recognized from her research as Avalokiteshvara.

She entered the chamber, stepping quickly to the side so that anyone walking through the hall wouldn't spot her. She studied the statue. It was about two feet high and gleamed gold in the light of a small overhead electric light in a recessed niche, as well as eight oil lamps placed on the octagonal pedestal around it. The statue's base was the size of a dinner plate, sufficient for a respectable if compressed treasure map. Of course if the statute were solid gold it could weigh fifty or sixty pounds or more; Annja wasn't sure, but she knew gold was heavy.

She tried it. As she hoped and expected it was hollow. Likely it was also some other metal, possibly bronze, cast as thin as feasible and then gold-washed. It was still very heavy. But Annja was strong. She found the weight manageable.

She tipped the object to the side. She was able to hold it in the crook of her right arm as she crouched to examine the base. To her exhilarated surprise the map was clearly visible. A quick inspection by the light of her digital camera, held in her left hand, suggested the inscription had been gouged with some kind of fine, sharp tool, then inked. The ink had aged and fallen out in places, but the map seemed mostly legible. Her quick examination showed a legend in, of all things, French.

She snapped a couple of images. Then she tucked her camera away in a cargo pocket of her long pants so she could lower the icon from its pedestal to the floor. She intended to examine it carefully, to memorize the details, then replace it. It wouldn't take more than five minutes, and then she'd be gone.

A squawk of outrage made her start and look up.

At the entry to the alcove a wizened, bent man in scarlet stood holding a flashlight. Flanking him were four younger acolytes in saffron robes. They carried staffs in their hard brown hands.

14

"Just leaving," Annja said, smiling and nodding in what she hoped was harmless affability but suspected made her look like a deranged clown, especially in the dodgy light. Oh, well. She started to tip the heavy statue back onto its plinth.

The wizened little monk uttered a screech of surprising volume. Somewhere a bell began to ring. This is all getting rapidly out of hand, Annja thought.

The yellow-robed acolytes came for her. She noticed that while none of them were what she'd call burly, they were certainly wiry and moved with a grace that suggested something other than a life of peaceful contemplation. She knew there was lots of hard physical work to do around a monastery.

One of the monks whacked her on the shoulder

with his staff. Annja yelped, more from astonishment than pain.

"Ow! Hey! I thought you Buddhists were pacifists!"

The young man grinned at her. The expression suggested he understood her meaning perfectly, even if he didn't grasp the words. The young man's expression did not suggest contemplative serenity.

She rolled the heavy statue toward him. "Catch."

His staff clattered to the hardwood floor as he dropped it to catch the relic. I am so going to archaeologist Hell for that, she thought as she darted past him. Even though all she'd wanted was for him to grab it and do something with his arms other than whack her again.

His partner held his staff horizontally to bar her way. Annja kicked up, caught the hardwood staff painfully on her shin, knocked it into the air right out of the startled monk's grasp. He blinked and drew back. She shouldered him out of the way. Surprise had rocked him off balance onto the heels of his sandals, and she knew she likely outweighed him. She was a head taller than he was.

As she ran out into the main nave another of the saffron-robed quartet cracked her sharply on the shins with his staff.

She tripped but managed to tuck a shoulder and roll without doing any more damage than the staff had, much less doing a face plant on the hardwood floor.

It wasn't exactly a neat and graceful roll. She landed heavily on her back, blasting the air out of her as she skidded clear across the floor to fetch up against the wall on the far side beneath a statue of a figure she didn't recognize.

The bell still tolled. She didn't need to guess for whom. The great hall's imposing double front doors had been flung open. More monks poured in. They clutched not only staffs but nasty curved swords.

Annja managed to snap to her feet, quickly if not quite gracefully.

Sandals slapped wood behind her. Apparently still more monks were pouring into the hall from the corridor across from Avalokiteshvara's alcove.

"Yikes," she said. "This is not good."

She spun. A monk was rushing her from behind with his staff raised in both hands. She side-kicked him in the gut. It was a maneuver she'd picked up from an archaeologist she'd been on a dig with in Colorado and involved her turning away from her opponent and rolling her hips so that the kick shot straight out like a back kick. It was very powerful, especially when you added in the energy of an onrushing target. The monk went flying back with his robes, limbs and staff colliding with the half a dozen monks behind him.

She used the momentum the kick imparted to dash right at the monks streaming in the doors. Charging into the faces of the greater concentration of foes might not have seemed the best idea. Then again a foreigner trespassing on hallowed ground in the middle of the boondocks in a reasonably repressive Southeast Asian country wasn't the brightest idea, either. Thinking fast,

Annja had formed a plan—disorganize the more threatening group with a whirlwind attack and thereby gain
breathing room to form a better plan.

The charging monks raised staffs to smite the
infidel. Annja dropped and slid into them sideways. It
was a risk—but a calculated one. She expected sheer
unexpectedness to work in her favor.

It did. The monks faltered, blinking in confusion
with staffs wound up and nothing to whack as the tall,
strong American woman slid across the slick floor into
the shins of three of them.

Since they kept charging, they obligingly tripped right
over her. She came upright nose to nose with a startled
acolyte. She plucked the staff out of his shock-weakened
grasp and rapped him across the nose with it. He
promptly fell down clutching his face and keening,
probably more in shocked outrage than actual pain. Two
of his buddies tripped over him. Annja sidestepped them
neatly.

It was too good to last. But her sneak attack had trans-
formed a concerted surge of angry monks as if by magic
into a milling mob of confused monks. They were all
around, now, so she held the purloined quarterstaff by one
end, like a bat. She was mainly trying to make it whistle
menacingly and keep the mob back, but she wasn't afraid
to bounce it off a saffron-clad shoulder or shaved pate.

The monks duly gave way. Of course now Annja
formed her own special island in the midst of the mob.
The momentary disorder was quickly transforming to
focused anger.

She tucked the staff under an armpit and turned, holding her other hand out stiffly. It was a move she'd seen in Hong Kong martial arts flicks. It did seem to have the effect of encouraging the monks to keep a respectful distance. For the moment.

Turning to face the main door, she saw through the crowd the ferociously scowling face of the abbot who had turned her away in the first place. She toyed with the notion of taking him hostage then discarded completely the notion of heading that way.

It was time for plan B. Mooting the fact there was never a plan A.

A monk stepped forward. He wore a red robe over a saffron T-shirt. This suggested things Annja didn't want suggested, such as a greater resolve than the juniors, none of whom seemed eager to get a knot on the crown from a mere foreign woman who couldn't even receive enlightenment. And greater levels of skill, which he quickly displayed. With a stern expression over his iron-colored mustache he closed with her, crossed staffs and wound one end of his stick around the inside of hers between her hands. A nasty-quick twist of his hips and the stick torqued right out of her hand. It was as irresistible and inexorable as if some kind of giant machine had snatched it away.

Instead of pressing his advantage, the man paused. Annja kicked him in the groin.

As he doubled over, she realized she needed to start pressing back. Hard.

She formed her right hand into a fist and reached with her will.

The sword responded to her summons and materialized in her hands.

With a gasp the monks jumped back. Even the abbot's eyes flew wide in amazement.

Annja wheeled toward the altar with its seated golden Buddha. The statue smirked as if enjoying the show. Annja raised the sword high and brought it whistling down toward the first monk to bar her path.

The acolyte, a skinny kid with zits and ears like amphora handles, screeched, closed his eyes, ducked his head down between his narrow shoulders and threw his staff up horizontally to protect his earthly shell.

The sword came down on the middle of the staff. The tough Thai hardwood parted like twine.

The sword's tip whistled harmlessly inches from the acolyte's nose as Annja had aimed it. The acolyte dropped both halves of his stick from stinging palms, fell to the floor, curled into a fetal position and began to cry.

Annja jumped over him to deliver a very credible flying front kick to the chest of the next man in line. He was so taken aback by what had happened to his compatriot that he was not only wide open but also unmindful of balance. He fell immediately.

Sparks flew in Annja's eyes from a stinging savage impact from her left. Things weren't going to go all her way after all. Blinking at the tears that suddenly filled her eyes and trying to ignore the ominous ringing in her ears, she wheeled counterclockwise.

But she did not lash out with her sword.

Like it or not, she knew the monks were innocent. *She* was the trespasser. And they were doing nothing to her she wouldn't have done to intruders in her Brooklyn loft.

Unwilling to risk killing a monk defending his home and place of worship, or even nick one if she could help it, Annja raised the sword in a horizontal overhead block to meet the staff rapidly descending toward her skull.

The staff parted as readily as the first had. The liberated end bounced right off the crown of her head. It probably didn't even cut the scalp—her eyes didn't instantly flood with blood—but it still hurt a lot. The monk meanwhile did nothing to the control the downward sweep of his truncated stick. He left himself wide open and Annja caught him on the chin with a somewhat more enthusiastic high kick than she otherwise might have delivered.

His teeth clacked and he went down. She doubted he'd get up shy of a ten count.

Violent motion tore at her peripheral vision. She spun right. A monk was swinging a sword for her neck in a decapitation stroke.

She hacked desperately across her body, aiming for the blade. It flew from his hands with a musical twang as she struck it an inch from the hilt. She let her momentum carry her into the erstwhile swordsman and slammed him with shoulder and hip. It knocked him sprawling, not off his feet but staggering drunkenly into his comrades behind.

More by instinct than anything else, Annja ducked sideways beneath another horizontal swipe from behind. Its wind of passage kissed her left earlobe. She kicked straight back with her left foot, felt her heel connect with meat and bone, heard the sound of expelled breath.

Her training and experience were sufficient that her body could fight by itself; she blocked and struck without conscious intent. Indeed she had to in a swirling fight like this. Her mind raced, trying to spin out a plan. Because no one was skilled enough to survive long against these odds.

Apparently her subconscious was already on the job. She found herself rushing at the man whose sword she'd knocked away. She parried left and right. One cut slashed sparks, bright orange in the gloom, from the sword reaching for her, along with a sliver of steel. The other chopped another blade off just below the tip and barely missed the top of the wielder's head.

The man's eyes opened wide in horror. His arms flew up to protect his face. The voluminous yellow sleeves of his cloak billowed before him like wings.

It cleared Annja to boot him hard in the crotch.

She felt bad about that—additionally bad, since after all, these men were blameless, if perhaps a little zealous in their pursuit of somebody wandering the grounds after hours. All she needed from him was that he double over. She just didn't see a way to ask nicely.

Double up the hapless monk did. Annja sprang. Her foot came down on his bent-over back between the shoulder blades. With all her momentum and the steel-spring strength of leg muscles she drove herself upward.

As she did she released the sword. Soundlessly it returned to the otherwhere.

She caught the top of the open transom. Never designed to support the weight of a woman as tall and well muscled as Annja, its support chains instantly began to rip free from the wall. But her walking-shoe soles slammed into the wall beneath it. She pushed off instantly, pulling hard with her arms, and half scrambled, half slithered through the opening into the warm, moist embrace of the night.

She did a somersault on her way over the lower course of the roof to the ground below. By good fortune as much as acrobatic skill she got her legs under her. She even had the presence of mind to let them cushion her shock of landing, then let go. She went into a forward roll and wound up flat on her back dazed and breathless from the impact.

Annja lay still for the duration of an inhalation deep into her abdomen. From inside the temple a furious clamor rose to a crescendo. She heard a bellow she took to be the head monk himself, presumably commanding the pursuit.

She jackknifed, snapping herself to her feet from flat on her back, and sprinted for the woods.

As she did, something registered on her subconscious—a glint from the underbrush to her left, beyond an outbuilding behind the great hall that looked suspiciously like a garage.

Making no attempt at stealth, Annja crashed into the brush of the nearest treeline. Ten feet in she drastically slowed. Moving cautiously, she breathed through her nose in long, slow breaths from the diaphragm despite the sheer effort of will it cost her, because it was the best way to rapidly reoxygenate her adrenaline-pumped body. She angled off to the right.

She picked her way carefully, circling around to the left, about thirty yards back in the woods. The moon had risen. Between that and backlighting from the now wide-awake monastery she was able to find paths that brought her into least contact with crackly twigs and rustly boughs.

The racket from the buildings helped. She could probably have tramped around like a Shriner two days into a Bourbon Street binge without being heard, as the abbot hollered orders she couldn't understand. The monks and acolytes darted this way and that, uttering shrill cries to show their zeal and waving swords and staffs menacingly but not venturing too far into the woods. Nobody, it seemed, wanted to run into that magically appearing sword.

Annja slipped back toward the monastery. Sooner or later the abbot would herd a search party into the woods, and they knew their home ground far better than she did. Besides, she had at least a measure of payback in mind. She suspected her detection by the monks hadn't totally been a stroke of bad luck.

She paused beside a thick trunk with shaggy bark peeling off in long strips. Not fifteen yards ahead and to her right crouched a familiar, emphatically female figure. Even from behind there was no mistaking Easy Ngwenya.

Annja looked around. Bending a little lower, she found a broken branch. It was well on its way to decomposing back into the jungle floor, but plenty solid for her purposes. Rising, she threw it end over end.

It hit the tree to the crouching figure's left. Annja winced—she had been aiming at the tree to the right. But it had the desired effect—it produced a satisfying thunk.

Instantly it seemed ten million birds and some poodle-size fruit bats erupted from the branches above the lurker, all complaining at the top of their lungs.

Instantly the beams of a dozen flashlights converged on the figure's hiding place. With a triumphant roar the monks charged.

Annja ran lightly away, back toward the road and her hidden Honda.

My work here is done, she thought.

15

"Excuse me, miss?" A stout Chinese businessman in a blue business suit with sweat streaming down his face behind his knockoff Armani shades stood over her.

"You're Annja?" a wiry woman with blue-lensed sunglasses pushed up onto her frizz of red hair asked.

"Miss?" the Chinese man said.

Continuing to ignore him, Annja rose from her table in the little tea shop in Bangkok's Phra Ram 2 district. Outside the window all around the little shop, giant crane-topped buildings rose into the sky. Between the nascent skyscrapers she could see the skinny cone of an ancient *wat,* or temple, across the Chao Phraya.

"You're Patricia Ruhle?" she asked as the redhead approached. Annja knew from reading her curriculum vitae online that her guest was in her early forties. As the woman approached between the mostly empty afternoon tables Annja saw that while she looked her age, and had probably never been conventionally pretty in her youth, experience and activity, and probably attitude had given her a rugged exuberance that neither years nor mileage seemed likely to erode any time soon.

The woman nodded. "That's right. And you're Annja, yes?"

"Miss, if I may intrude," the Chinese man said. "I may be able to make a proposition which would be of benefit—"

His English was excellent. But his intent would've been way too transparent to Annja even if he hadn't spoken a word. Since returning to the Thai capital to muster resources for the last leg of her journey to the fabled and elusive Temple of the Elephant she'd learned the hard way that the famed Bangkok sex trade wasn't just all about rich Westerners purchasing the services of young Thai girls and boys. Well-heeled Japanese and Indian tourists, as well as the Chinese, proved to be anything but averse to leggy russet-haired American girls. This wasn't the first allegedly lucrative invitation she'd been tendered. She doubted it'd be one of the most peculiar, either.

"Buzz off, Jack," the red-haired woman said. To Annja's complete astonishment Ruhle then snarled at him in what Annja could only guess was Mandarin. Whatever she said made his eyes go wide and his features ashen before he turned and practically scuttled from the tea shop.

The woman came up to Annja shaking her red head. "I'm Ruhle. Call me Patty, please."

She stuck out her hand. Annja shook it, unsurprised to find the grip dry and firm as a man's. Patty had square, well-used hands. They suited the rough-and-ready rest of her.

Patty wore cargo shorts like Annja's, red Converse knockoffs, and the mark of her profession: a tan photographer's vest of many pockets and a camera over a short-sleeved shirt printed in flowers of red and pink on white. Annja was similarly dressed in adventure-ready tropic fashion.

"Not that there was anything wrong with that guy's concept," Patty said as they sat, "if you edit him out of it."

It took Annja a beat to realize she'd just been propositioned. She smiled and shook her head. "Not that I'm not flattered—"

"Say no more," Patty said. Her grin never slipped. Annja had the impression it seldom did. "It's usually best to keep professional relationships about business anyway."

If the older woman felt any resentment about being turned down, Annja could detect no sign of it.

Annja nodded. "I agree."

The server, a tiny Thai woman with round cheeks who seemed to be the proprietor, came and took Patty's order for green tea. Then the red-haired American woman leaned forward onto an elbow on the table.

"So," she said. "You're mounting an expedition. Tell me about it."

"Oh, you know," Annja said with a smile, "a perilous trek through jungle and mountain in search of a lost temple. The usual."

She anticipated skepticism, possibly snark. She spoke lightly to defuse that, figuring it might make it easier to overcome resistance. Instead Ruhle arched her brows and rounded her eyes.

"No shit?" she said.

"None whatsoever," Annja said, still smiling.

"But I thought, with satellites and aircraft and all, there wouldn't be any lost sites left."

"There probably aren't. But they're still finding them, one or two a year," Annja replied. "Most satellites have higher-ticket tasks than hunting archaeological sites," she said. "The discoveries are usually made by accident when third parties analyze imaging for other purposes. And in this part of the world the jungle can still do a lot to conceal structures."

"If you say so," Ruhle said, less dubiously than Annja expected. "You're willing to pay even if this turns out to be a wild-goose chase?"

Annja nodded. "I'm paying for the expedition," she said, "not its outcome. Although I hope—and think— the outcome will mean a lot for all of us."

Any shots Ruhle took of artifacts would belong to Annja. But Patty was free to snap incidental pictures of the expedition and the country they passed through along the way. She could sell those at a profit. Possibly to her usual employer. If Annja really turned up some amazing new discovery, even incidental pictures would skyrocket in value.

Ruhle stuck out her chin and nodded. "Sounds good so far," she admitted.

The server brought tea and bowls of soup. Annja smelled pungent spices in the steam. She smiled. It seemed that she spent half her life in tea shops, coffee shops and sidewalk cafés. Almost as much time as she spent being pursued through the brush in remote countries, in fact. Of course both were a product of the life she led—the uniquely doubled life. Or tripled, if she considered her job on *Chasing History's Monsters* as distinct from her field archaeology.

Annja had occasion to meet with all kinds of people in the course of her tangled skein of pursuits. Since she drank little and disliked bars, coffee and tea establishments provided nice neutral locations to do so. Nice public locations, where the presence of witnesses provided constraints on certain kinds of behavior. Not all of Annja's contacts were either reliable or safe.

"It was good of Rickard to recommend you," Annja said, "since I work for a rival network and all." A Dutch archaeologist she'd met on a dig in upstate New York had gone to work for the National Geographic Channel; Ruhle was a regular contributor to both the magazine and the television network. That made her technically an enemy of Annja's television employer, the Knowledge Channel.

Obviously that sort of thing mattered little more to Patricia, or their mutual acquaintance, than it did to Annja.

"How is old Rickard, anyway?" Patty asked. "I haven't seen him in donkey's years."

"No idea," Annja said. "I haven't seen him since the Patroon dig. We sometimes get into amiable debates on alt.archaeology."

"That makes you the only two on that newsgroup," Patty said with a laugh.

Annja laughed, as well.

"So where is this lost temple of yours?" Patty asked.

"How do you feel about crossing into Myanmar?" Annja asked.

"You know the Burmese-Thai border's closed." Like a lot of old-timers Patty didn't feel obligated to use Burma's newer, state-decreed name. "Been a lot of political unrest going on that side of the Mekong. More than usual, that is."

"I realize that," Annja said evenly. She had checked the CIA *World Fact Book* online. It mentioned the border closure in a traveler's advisory, as an aside to advising Americans to stay out of Myanmar altogether. The government was even more autocratic and repressive than Thailand's.

"Why not just fly right into Yangon?" Patty asked, "Save yourself a hike and a lot of Indiana Jones stuff?"

Annja laughed at the reference. "Because the central government is likely to take too keen an interest in me," she said, "especially as someone they're going to think of as a journalist."

She held up a hand. "I'm not claiming to *be* one, you understand," she said. "But I know from experience that because I'm something of a TV personality, foreign governments don't tend to see much distinction."

The photographer nodded. "Got it."

Of course, the Burmese didn't have to know she was connected with *Chasing History's Monsters*. She could arrange to enter the country under an identity other than Annja Creed. She didn't think Ruhle needed to know that much about her, especially on such short acquaintance, with no commitments either way as yet.

But a little more explanation was in order. "The Myanmar secret police are pretty aggressive with tourists right now, my contacts tell me," she said. "They're facing a lot of unrest. And of course the 'war on terror' covers a multitude of sins. Frankly, I don't want to lead a bunch of government thugs to what could prove a trove of priceless cultural artifacts."

Patty cocked her head like a curious bird. "What, you don't trust the government of Myanmar to safeguard its people's priceless cultural heritage?"

"Not on your life," Annja said. "A lot of my fellow anthropologists and archaeologists would find that heretical—way beyond political incorrectness. But no. Not Myanmar's government."

Ruhle barked a laugh. "Good call." She studied Annja for a moment. Her eyes were blue. They narrowed in a grin that rumpled the older woman's face all up and made it frankly ugly and delightful at the same time. "You're not going to be put off by a little border-busting, are you?"

"I haven't before," Annja said.

Patty laughed. "Well, one thing's for sure," she said, "you may just be a consultant and a talking head on that stupid show, but you've got the makings of a true crisis photojournalist. But is your disregard for danger on par with your lack of concern for the, ah, legal formalities?"

For a moment Annja sat returning the woman's unblinking gaze. It was not unfriendly. Neither was it particularly yielding.

"I don't know how to answer that," she said at last with a smile. "But I can honestly say…it has been so far."

The creases in Patty's brow deepened. "There's more here than meets the eye, isn't there, Ms. Creed?"

"Annja, please. And isn't there always?"

Ruhle guffawed and slapped the table as if she were killing an especially annoying mosquito. Heads turned at the few other tables occupied this time of day. "What I see I definitely like—and please rest easy I mean that in a professional sense."

Shortly they agreed on a price. It was steep but not ruinous—notwithstanding what Roux was going to say—but Annja figured that if she was going to hire somebody, she might as well get the best available. Patty seemed to be that, so Annja was willing to pony up.

"All right, then," Patty said when they settled. "You have yourself an official photographer. How about the rest of the team?"

"At the minimum," Annja said, "and I want to keep this minimal, for reasons I'm sure you understand—"

Patty nodded. Annja took the risks attendant to crossing a sealed border between two overmilitarized and adrenalized Southeast Asian states very seriously, even if Ruhle didn't believe she did. In this case it was the world-wise veteran who didn't know what she was dealing with, not the fresh-faced newbie.

"I want an area specialist, an anthropologist who knows the people and cultures of the ground we're going to cover. And we need a guide. Preferably somebody who's not a stranger to border crossing himself. Or herself," Annja said.

Ruhle nodded. "The guide I can't help you with— the best man I know for this region died two years ago of acute lead poisoning because he got a little fly around an ethnic army in Myanmar. The second best is doing hard time since the Thais caught him being a little too familiar with informal border crossing, if you get my drift. But as for an anthropologist with regional cred, I have just the man for you. He's got all the integrity in the world, he's on a first-name basis with half the tribes between here and the Himalayas and he's got an A-1 international rep. Plus he's available and in the area, as of a couple days ago."

It was Annja's turn to narrow her eyes. "Do I hear an unspoken 'but' here, Patty?"

"With two *t*s," Ruhle said. "He is the best. But he can be, well, a total asshole. Not to put too fine an edge on it."

16

"Are you sure this guy is the best?" Annja asked. She wore a cheap straw tourist hat. When she wore hats she generally wore cheap ones. They never seemed to last with her.

Patty nodded resolutely. She didn't have a hat. "And anyway, if anyone's gonna be able to find us a halfway decent guide, he's it."

Annja peered dubiously into the shade of the hut. It was hard to penetrate with eyes accustomed to the noonday sun's blaze.

"He looks," she said, "stoned."

"Probably," Ruhle said.

A bus had brought them most of the way to this village in the Chao Phraya swamps half a day's journey outside Bangkok. It was a yellow bus with twisty Thai characters painted all over it in maroon and blue. It was also perilously tall for the narrow wheelbase. The balance issues weren't addressed—or not in any favorable way—by the crates and hampers all lashed on top.

It was nothing too unusual for Annja. Local accents differentiated it from other buses she'd ridden in around the world, such as the distinctive, somewhat astringent Thai music tinkling from tinny speakers hung from the ceiling on brightly colored ribbons. But on the whole it was much like other Third World buses. Including the fact that the driver drove as fast as road conditions would allow, and usually a bit faster.

Since their destination lay well and truly out in the boonies, away from Thailand's more or less modern highway system, Annja wound up with a sore butt and a feeling as if her spine had been pounded shorter by eight inches from the bad road and worse shocks.

They stood several hundred yards from a stream meandering to join the Chao Phraya a few miles away. The hut was raised up on stilts about three feet off the ground. That didn't suggest a great deal of confidence in the creek keeping to its banks if the rains came, though fortunately the monsoon proper was over, tailing off into occasional slamming rains.

The hut stood open to a thatch roof supported by joists lashed together with tight rope windings. Long rolled screens were hung just below it to keep the weather out in storms. Annja didn't have much confidence in them, either, but she had to reckon the locals knew best. Probably they were as fatalistic about their weather as she was about their rural public transport. Anyway it didn't look like rain anytime soon.

In the hut eight men sat cross-legged, naked to the waist. She thought one of them was paler and taller than the rest, but it wasn't easy to tell. As she was standing in the sun, her eyes weren't going to get any more adjusted to the shade inside. The men swayed side to side, crooning in low, nasally, melodic tones as they passed a bowl from hand to hand.

"You're kidding, right?" Annja said optimistically.

Patty shook her head. "Nope. That's one of the reasons Phil gets along so well with the tribal types— he joins in their rituals."

"Which tend to involve consuming mind-altering substances," Annja said.

"Don't they all?"

As with a lot of such rituals, Annja suspected this was really all just another dodge for the men to get away from the womenfolk for a while, in default of bars.

Not that these village men had gone to any great lengths to escape their women. The hut stood on the out-skirts of the tiny village. But a number of women sat on the steps up to other huts and on mats on the ground nearby, smoking pipes and chopping vegetables or weaving more mats from long river grasses. They showed no more interest in the men than they did the lines of ants flowing everywhere like rivers of tiny gleaming bodies.

The day wore on. The heat pressed down on Annja like an anvil. Lizards rustled in the roof thatch, hunting bugs. Birds chirped and fussed in the forest nearby. Chickens strutted about importantly, pecking at the ants. Little children, naked or half-naked, peered wide eyed at the funny-looking foreign women from behind the struts holding up huts nearby, and fled giggling when either glanced their way.

The gathering broke up. The men ceased their ritualistic moaning. They began talking in normal tones, punctuated with bursts of high-pitched, tittery laughter. Annja didn't know if that was an effect of whatever herbal decoction they had been passing around or just the way people laughed hereabouts.

Several stood unsteadily. One unfolded himself to a greater height than the rest. Annja could now see his narrow torso was noticeably paler than the other men's. He took a shirt from a peg where it hung, pulled it on as he turned and came unsteadily down the wooden stairs to the ground.

He had dark brown receding hair, sharply handsome features behind a neat beard, blue eyes that under other circumstances might have pierced but were now notably muddy. He swayed on reaching the level earth, packed hard by many bare feet since the last rain. He noticed the Western women and walked toward them with immense dignity.

"Ladies," he said. Then he turned aside, doubled over and vomited into the black dirt.

"So," ANNJA SAID, WALKING along the grassy bank beside a stream black with tannin from decomposing plants, "fill me in a bit on your background, if you will."

She kept a part of her consciousness cocked for some of Southeast Asia's many noted species of venomous serpents. She'd heard they could get pretty aggressive.

For a man who'd been barfing not fifteen minutes before, and still wore his white shirt with tan vertical stripes open over a washboard chest, Dr. Philip Kennedy walked beside her with great dignity. It spoke well for his presence of mind, anyway, Annja thought.

"I was born in a whitebread suburb north of Boston," he said. "My father was a dentist. My mother was a terribly socially conscious housewife."

For a man who wore his leftist political views on his sleeves, and not infrequently let them fall off onto his academic publications, he didn't seem respectful of his mother's liberal activism, or so it seemed to Annja. She had researched him online in her hotel room before heading out before dawn on the hair-raising bus ride. She wanted to hear his account in his own words, and make sure it squared with his published bio. Also she had some questions.

Maybe his famed disdain for all things Western was coming out. Or maybe he was working through some other issues, she thought.

"I got an academic scholarship to Harvard—a terrible waste of resources, given my upper-middle-class background. Typical. My undergrad was in Southeast Asian social anthropology through the East

Asia center. I received my Ph.D. from the University of Hawaii."

"I understand you spent some time here in Southeast Asia as an undergrad," she said. He must have known Patty Ruhle would have told Annja something about him. They had left the red-haired woman snapping photos of the village. To keep her hand in, she said—and also because there was no telling what a professional with her contacts could sell somewhere along the line. Annja was not going to lie to him and pretend she hadn't looked him up. But she wasn't going to volunteer it, either.

Philip nodded. His beard was streaked gray down both sides. His temples were also silvered. The gray and even the way his hair was getting a little thin to the sides of his forehead only made him look distinguished. Annja couldn't see Kennedy coloring his hair or using any of those baldness cures they advertised on television. She suspected the very fierceness of his disdain for such vanities was part of an attitudinal package that helped him pull the whole thing off.

He was actually a fairly handsome man in a weather-beaten way.

"I did," he said. "In fact I worked with tribes in the very area of Burma you say you're interested in. I became fascinated with the region because of an early interest in Hinduism and Buddhism."

What Annja had read indicated he had established a reputation as an utterly intrepid field researcher with a gift for the difficult Thai family of languages spoken throughout Thailand and Burma. He had also made a name for himself for the ease with which he won the confidence of tribesfolk. Centuries of threats and oppression by heavy-handed neighbors, European colonialists and the Japanese, followed in many places by virtually continuous guerrilla warfare at varying levels of intensity, had given little reason to trust outsiders of any flavor.

"That's good," she said. "So, uh, what was going on back there with the chanting and the puking?"

"Oh, we were simply sharing a local entheogen."

"A what?" Annja asked.

"It's a psychoactive compound used in shamanic rituals. This one's an alkaloid derived from plants. Probably fly agaric."

That made her miss a step. "Fly agaric? You mean—"

"*Amanita muscaria,* yes. The mushroom. It's the most common source for such compounds. Unfortunately, various other herbs used in the decoction tend to produce a marked emetic effect. That accounts for what you termed the *puking.* As for the rest—"

He shrugged. "In this case what you witnessed was nothing quite so formal as shamanic ritual. Merely a means of bonding and socializing."

"I see," she said. "So, how did you get interested in ethnobotany?"

He looked at her with a glint in his eyes. "You sound skeptical. I assure you it's a highly legitimate field."

"All right," she said neutrally.

"I encountered entheogen use with some frequency

during my undergraduate work on the Shan Plateau in Burma," he said.

"And since then I've both actively researched entheogenic compounds and their uses, and employed them myself as an aid to harmonizing with and understanding indigenous cultures."

"Great," Annja said. "But can you keep a lid on it?"

He stopped with a low-hanging limb endangering an unruly cowlick. "What do you mean?"

"If you sign on with this expedition I need you focused and on track," she said. "That means no getting stoned on duty."

She had little enough against recreational chemistry—if you screened out the dope smokers and the drinkers, you'd pretty well screen out field archaeologists and anthropologists.

He scowled at her in outrage. "I'm not talking about *recreation* here. I engage in serious research!"

She nodded. "I'm sure you do. I just can't have you engaged in *research* that'll interfere with what I need you to do."

He frowned at her a moment longer, then looked away. "As I say," he said, for the first time not speaking forthrightly, "use of psychoactives is something I do for professional reasons. I don't let things interfere with my fieldwork."

"All right," she said a little more confidently.

He looked at her. "And speaking of this expedition, what exactly is it you have in mind? You said you had a line on an undiscovered site in Myanmar. What do you intend? To uncover it, exploit it, rape what time and nature have hidden away?"

She frowned and set her jaw at his use of the word *rape*. She thought that was an offensive use of the word. Let it go, she commanded herself. That's not what you're here for.

"I intend to do research of my own, yes," she said as evenly as she could. "But my main intention is to prevent what could be a trove of unique artifacts from being plundered by one of the world's worst tomb robbers."

He allowed himself something resembling a smile at that. "So you're a treasure preserver," he said.

"I'm looking to preserve it, yes. And see it properly conserved."

He smiled openly. "Well, well," he said. "I find I might actually have something in common with you after all."

He stuck out his hand. "I'm in," he said.

17

"Going to Burma, hah," the plump man in the red-tasseled pillbox hat said. He might have been muttering to himself, but his use of heavily Chinese-accented English suggested he spoke for the benefit of his guests. "Bad business, go to Burma. Very bad." He shook his head.

Chinese music played low in the background.

Philip Kennedy fixed the shopkeeper with a lofty look. "We're not interested in *business,*" he said, inflecting the word as a curse. "What we're doing may be bad enough. But at least we're not grubbing after profits."

A fly buzzed past Annja's nose. One or more of the various forms of incense alight in the crowded, stuffy shop was threatening to bring on a major allergic reaction.

Annja cast her other companion a look. Patty Ruhle rolled her eyes toward the roof beams of the crowded little shop in a particularly decrepit and disreputable section of the long sprawl of the Bangkok waterfront district.

It was an interaction that had taken place many times in the day since they'd collected the Harvard-trained anthropologist.

Kennedy was laser straight today. It didn't exactly make him easier to deal with.

Kennedy said something in an Asian language. It was singsong, tonal. It didn't sound to Annja's ears—and she had a definite ear for languages, even if she knew no useful amount of any East Asian tongue—like what she heard slung on the crowded streets and in the bright-bannered kiosks outside. She wondered if Kennedy had also picked up a usable amount of Mandarin along the way. Supercilious he may have been, but he was a keenly intelligent man, and ingesting all those entheogens didn't seem to have dulled him appreciably.

Annja found herself grinning at Ruhle as the two men became engrossed in singing and gesticulating at one another. Having spent time in the ethnic enclaves of New Orleans the tourists never saw, in the back streets and on the docks, she had always known that the movie version of Third World haggling was not only truthful but somewhat understated.

Then again, the people who haggled seriously were people who were often seriously poor—usually on both sides of the transaction. It was a Darwinian proposition, and sometimes the party who got the better of the deal was the party that survived.

Of course Master Chen didn't seem to have missed many meals. Skinny though he was, Kennedy wasn't hanging on the raw edge of starvation, either.

"Boys enjoy this too much, don't they?" said Patty sotto voce, putting her curly red head near Annja's. Annja laughed. She thought the same thing.

She wandered among crowded shelves and counters. She moved with extreme caution to avoid brushing anything for fear high-piled goods would tumble down on her. She suspected Master Chen strictly enforced a "you break it, you buy it" policy. And in any dispute she had few doubts as to whose side the Bangkok cops would come down on. If anything, Bangkok was more adept even than most of the Third World at the fine art of shaking down wealthy Westerners.

"See anything you like?" Patty asked.

"I hardly know," Annja said, shaking her head.

Chen's shop appeared to be a combination of modern sporting-goods store, old-time general store and combination apothecary and magic shop. Nylon rope lay wound in gleaming coils between spoils of hairy natural-fiber line. Coleman lanterns vied for shelf space with pink Hello Kitty purses, above jars full of colorful herbs and bins of fleshy roots of doubtful virtue, Joss sticks, road maps, CDs and octagonal feng shui mirrors. "I wouldn't know where to begin," she said.

Patty held up a piece of wood carved to look like a short sheathed sword with Chinese characters and unfamiliar symbols. "How about a seven-star sword for luck?"

Annja laughed. "If only it were that easy to get luck."

"Lots of Asians think you can buy it," the photographer said. "They look set to take over the world in a few years. Maybe they're onto something."

Kennedy walked up to them. He looked grave. Even on short acquaintance Annja had learned not to take that too seriously.

"Master Chen says he can supply us," he said. "He ought to have everything we need. Of course, he'd have a better idea if he knew precisely where we were going. But then so would I."

Patty laughed. "Just get used to being a mushroom, Phil," she said. "Ms. Annja has her reasons for keeping us in the dark. She's a girl who's always got reasons for what she does."

"What kind of price?" Annja asked.

Kennedy's look of disapproval deepened to a frown. He named a figure in baht, the local currency, which he quickly translated to dollars. "I know it's high," he said. "But I think you're looking at carrying along a great deal too much prepared food." He said *prepared* as he might say *tainted*.

"We can't all live on grubs and roots," Patty said. She smiled as she always did.

Kennedy sniffed. "The indigenous peoples do," he

said. "I don't see why their diet, which has served them well for years, won't serve Westerners as well. And you see far less obesity among the inland tribes than in the West."

"You calling me fat, Phil?" Patty asked. "Because our esteemed employer sure isn't carrying any excess baggage. Truth to tell, I wouldn't mind seeing her fatten up a bit before we set out—she's got no reserves."

Kennedy flushed.

"Leaving aside the relative merits of the indigenous diet versus the Western one," Annja said, putting on her best professional tone, which she used when her *Chasing History's Monsters* producer Doug Morrell tried to steamroller her, "speed is vital on this expedition. We can't afford the time to forage for food en route."

"Well," said Kennedy, with the air of a man who knows he's lost but is trying to cover his retreat, "we can obtain food from villages we encounter."

Annja nodded. "And if we do, the fresh food will be a welcome break," she said. "I'm not looking forward to a steady diet of dried foods any more than you are. But I'm unwilling to totally rely on haggling to feed us."

For one thing, she thought, we're going to want to avoid attracting any more attention than absolutely necessary. She knew their chances of completely avoiding detection by the inhabitants of villages they passed near was slight, but the more exposure they got the greater the risk of attracting the attention of the Myanmar government. Obvious Westerners bargaining loudly in the village square were hardly low profile.

"One question," Annja asked. "Why did you, as an anticapitalist, bargain Master Chen down so vigorously?"

"I wasn't going to let the fat capitalist bastard exploit us," Phil said with a set in his bearded jaw and a gleam in his eye, "any more than I had to."

Annja smiled. She couldn't shake the impression that despite their ferocious haggling the two men seemed to like each other enough to have a hard time hiding it.

"How about a guide, Phil?" Patty said. "Can old Chen set us up there?"

Kennedy turned back toward the counter. The proprietor perched behind it on a stool. He held something to his ear and spoke earnestly, if inaudibly over the music.

"He says that he can," Kennedy said.

"Wait," Annja said, "is he talking on an iPhone?"

"He is," Patty said with a nod. "Isn't that a hoot? He looks like he should be balancing his books with an abacus behind the counter. He might really use an abacus."

Kennedy strode back toward the counter as if to join the conversation. Patty put her face close to Annja's ear.

"Don't sweat the MREs too much," Patty said. "I don't know Chen, but if he's half as well connected as he looks to be, he gets 'em dog cheap by the carload from crooked quartermasters in Iraq and Afghanistan. My son tells me it's pretty common."

"You have children?" Annja asked.

"One," she said. "Army Ranger. He's in Afghanistan. He can't tell me where. But the censors let him say it's where the Soviets really lost it."

She grinned. "I reckon that makes it the Panjsher Valley. The censors don't know what his mama does for a living. I was in the Panjsher, when Jeremy was less than a year old."

Quickly her mood shifted. She lowered her head. "I wish he wasn't," she said in a muted tone. "He does, too. Says whatever they're fighting for, it's not what they were told it would be. Not what they tell the folks back home. But as long as his buddies are there, he says he'll keep going back. For them."

Annja listened mutely, unsure of what to say. Ruhle shook her kinky hair, raised her head and mustered a brave smile. "Ah, well," she said. "What's a mother to do?"

Kennedy was walking back to them. "So," Annja called to him, "any word on a guide?"

The back door opened. Annja hadn't thought the shop was particularly dimly lit. Nor cool for that matter. But the sunshine that poured in on a blast of loud Thai music and diesel fumes was blinding and so hot she flinched away.

What she took for a young boy walked in, bandy-legged, a shadow featureless against the glare from outside. She could tell he wore a baseball-type cap and shorts, but no more. The door swung shut behind him.

When the eye-frying glare shut off she could make out a young Chinese man with a round, open face and a big grin.

"Ah," Master Chen said. "Your guide."

"Our guide?" Annja and Patty echoed.

The newcomer nodded cheerily to the foreigners, then looked past them. "Hi, Dad," he called.

18

It was the most prosaic transportation to begin a headlong plunge into the unknown Annja could imagine—Eddie Chen's venerable Subaru, which was blue sunburned to gray and silver at various points. But it ran reliably and had all-wheel drive. Eddie claimed it had made the run before. At least, as far as they could safely take a car.

The drive from Bangkok north to Nakhon Sawan and beyond offered little by way of adventure. Except, of course, for the ever-present hazards of traffic, including unexpected vehicle-swallowing potholes in the middle of what looked like a modern superhighway, errant livestock, peasants in pursuit of errant livestock, big rigs and brightly colored Thai buses piloted by drivers with lead feet, loud horns and unshakable faith in reincarnation. All were real enough as dangers went.

The green woods and swamps of the central plains scrolled past outside the windows. These were rolled up; for a wonder, the air-conditioning worked. The cargo space was stuffed to the ceiling with supplies.

Patty Ruhle was the ringleader of a sing-along. She was to have appointed herself tour director for the voyage. She seemed able to pull it off, so Annja wasn't complaining.

Besides, it was better than brooding. Eddie, negotiating the traffic on the modern superhighway, pounded the heel of his palm on the steering wheel. "'The bastard king of England!'" he half sang. "How cool is that?"

"It was supposedly written by Rudyard Kipling," Patty said. "His literary partisans deny it. Of course, they all have sticks up their butts. Like all academics."

Annja took no offense; studious as she was, she'd always been more comfortable in the field or a collection in some exotic and remote location than safely at home on campus. Phil Kennedy stiffened. It only made Ruhle laugh.

"Don't even bother, Phil," she said. "You already pulled the rug out from under your own feet."

He looked out the window. Annja suspected it was to hide something very like a grin. "You're incorrigible," he said.

"And you do such a good job of incorriging me," Patty said.

Eddie laughed and pounded his hand on the wheel some more. Although in his early thirties, he had the appearance and general manner of what Annja took him for at the outset—a big schoolboy. Nonetheless, both his father and Phil vouched for his extensive experience penetrating Myanmar. He spoke several local dialects and could fill in gaps in Kennedy's knowledge.

She presumed that all added up to smuggling. Eddie and his father both disavowed involvement with drugs. They admitted they feared the drug armies, usually ethnic based, that dominated the trade in Southeast Asia. They were too big, well armed and ruthless. And they had powerful friends. Annja figured Eddie and his father were probably involved in running goods that themselves weren't controversial to avoid customs.

That wasn't the sort of thing she was bound to fight. Besides, the whole point of the expedition entailed violating innumerable laws in furtherance of what was right, as opposed to merely legal. Busting the border into Myanmar was going to be a crime, as would be everything she did afterward.

If I'm going to be a criminal, she thought, I might as well have good accomplices.

Patty was telling another joke to Eddie, who laughed uproariously. He seemed to be a perfect audience, endlessly appreciative of her rough-edged and often foulmouthed humor. It was possible those behaviors would start to wear. Still—

Annja glanced back at the supplies. "Quit fretting," Patty said.

Annja looked quickly around. The red-haired photographer regarded her calmly. She hadn't seemed to be paying any attention to Annja at all a heartbeat before.

It occurred to Annja that it might behoove a professional photographer to miss very little of what went on around her. Especially one who specialized in working innumerable crisis zones.

"Don't worry," Patty said. "We'll be fine."

Annja shook her head. She was not negating what the woman said, just expressing her own doubt and internal turmoil. "I can't seem to help myself," she said. "We need to travel as light as possible. We can't hire porters for security reasons. So I keep running everything over in my mind wondering if we'll really be able to carry enough."

"The biggest burden in any expedition like this is water," Kennedy said. "With the purification tabs we have, keeping ourselves supplied shouldn't be a problem at the tag end of the monsoons. Even on the plateau, water is not particularly hard to find."

Annja glanced at him. He gazed out the window at a passing algae-grown pond. White-bodied water birds with black heads and tails waded through it. Annja was somewhat surprised. Kennedy didn't seem the sort to say encouraging things. That in itself encouraged her—he was definitely not going to offer up empty positive thoughts.

"You said it's quick in, quick out," Eddie said. He had what Annja thought was a Southern California accent. "Should be no problem."

He switched on the radio. "No comment intended on the dirty folk songs," he said. "I just want to give my vocal cords a rest."

FROM BANGKOK IT WAS less than two hundred miles to Nakhon Sawan. Given the frequent delays, despite the breakneck pace of traffic when it did flow, the journey took them the better part of the day. The others were surprised when Annja insisted they press on to Kamphaeng Phet.

"Had a bad experience in Nakhon Sawan," she explained.

"Sweetie," Patty said, "you knock around Asia long, you'll wind up having bad experiences everywhere. Still, you're the boss."

Shadows stretched long across the land when they finally approached the small city of Kamphaeng Phet. With girlish excitement Annja saw her first elephants since entering the country, a pair bathing in the Ping River amid a flock of frolicking children.

Traffic started to clot well short of town. It was dark when they entered the city proper. The streets were full of celebrants, waving banners, playing music cranked up into indistinguishable, vaguely modulated screeches of distortion, hopping around in gaudy costumes and setting off fireworks. Annja winced whenever a string cracked off; it not only sounded too close to full-auto gunfire for comfort, but also these festivities were likely as not, in her experience, to feature *real* automatic-weapons fire. Sometimes in the spirit of the celebration.

And sometimes not.

The car had long since started to overheat with the stop-and-go of getting into Kamphaeng Phet. Eddie turned off the air-conditioning. He gave off regaling his companions with tales of Malibu surfing to roll down the window and shout in Chinese to some passersby with faces painted in dramatic winglike swoops of scarlet and blue and wearing pointy golden head-dresses. They answered back.

"What's going on?" Patty Ruhle asked. She didn't respond quite as jumpily as Annja did to the sporadic outbursts of firecrackers, but her eyes had narrowed and her voice held an unaccustomed edge. Only Philip Kennedy seemed serenely indifferent to the proceedings. Presumably he found them no more distasteful than any other manifestations of the modern, urban world.

Eddie pulled his head back in the car. "Banana festival."

"Banana festival?" Annja said.

"It's nutritionally sound, anyway," Patty said.

Eddie shrugged. "They grow a lot of them around here. What can I say?"

"We're not going to find any room at the inn tonight," Patty said. "That's for sure."

Anxiety jabbed at Annja. That was silly, she knew. She'd spent nights in low dives, half-flooded ditches, tents in howling dust storms, interrogation rooms and on the run from people eager to kill her. Yet she always felt a little uneasy when she didn't have some secure, known base to go to ground in. Even if it were literally that: a hideout under some bush somewhere. She just felt better knowing it was *her* bush.

Eddie turned a big toothy grin back over his shoulder. "No worries," he said. "I got it all under control."

He turned the car around, almost knocking over a kiosk selling *satays* on sticks plucked sizzling from oil. By leaning on the horn and shouting—mostly good-naturedly—out the window in what Annja guessed were four different languages including occasional profane English, he managed to get them out of the great crush of pedestrians and into less-crowded side streets headed toward the outskirts.

They found themselves in a tenement of dire tum-bledown shacks. Annja kept looking around nervously, concerned she might be called upon to use her sword to protect them. As far as she knew, none of the others carried a weapon of any kind. She was pretty sure Kennedy would scoff at the notion. She was much less sure about either Patty or Eddie. But she didn't know.

But they saw scarcely a soul or even a light. It seemed the slum dwellers had all piled into the joyous, raucous crush of humanity in the middle of town to celebrate the glorious banana. Meanwhile the shantytown around them tumbled straight along the riverfront so that the boundary between water and land was impossible to detect, what with hovels on stilts and sagging makeshift piers and houseboats with curved roofs all crowded together.

Eddie drove with more confidence than Annja thought could possibly be justified through alleys so narrow the haphazardly leaning fronts of the shacks seemed to threaten both sides of the little car at once. The smell of the river and all that decayed in it was overwhelming. The shacks were redolent of mildew, stale cooking oil and sewage.

Lights suddenly blazed before them. Rising right out of the midst of the shantytown was what looked to be almost a medieval Thai fortress, with swooping dagger-eaved roofs rising above high stone walls topped with thoroughly, and depressingly, modern razor-tape coils. Eddie pulled out his cell phone, hit a quick-dial number and spoke quickly.

A heavy gate slid to the side ahead of them. A small but sturdy-looking little man in a dark uniform gestured them forward. He carried an M-16 slung muzzle down and wore a turban. As Eddie drove into the compound, more men, similarly attired, came into view on either side.

"Karens," Eddie said. "Refugees from Burma. They get used as mercenaries a lot this close to the border."

Reflexively Patty raised her camera. Then she caught herself and reluctantly lowered it. "I guess I'd better get permission from our host first," she said sheepishly.

"It might not be that good an idea to go firing off your flash in the faces of armed men, either," Phil said.

None of Annja's companions showed any more sign of being disturbed by the presence of heavily armed men than she felt herself. Then again, none of them would have strayed so far off Southeast Asia's tourist paths if that sort of thing got to them. As long as they weren't pointing the things at you, Annja had long ago learned, it wasn't worth worrying about. If they were pointing them at you—well, you did what you had to do, in the full understanding that you weren't in very much less danger if they were friendly than if they were actively hostile.

"Who is our host, Eddie?" Annja asked.

"Ma Shunru," he said, "factor of the North Wind Trading Company. They're—they're, ah, based in China."

"China," Patty said. "That's People's Republic?"

"That's right." Eddie pulled in beside an outbuilding where a turbaned man gestured him to go. "We do a lot of business with them. They know me."

Kennedy, currently sitting in the front passenger seat, turned to give Annja a sharp look.

"Hey," Patty said, "what's with that? You're the one who set us up with him."

"I think this is kind of what we hired you for," Annja said. "Good job, Eddie."

The look he gave her as he got out into the muggy night air gratified her. She only hoped he really had done well by bringing them here. It struck her uncomfortably as the sort of place you could all too easily come in by the front gate and leave by the water gate—facedown floating on the Ping, waiting for the local crocodiles to drag you under. If they had big crocodiles around here. She wasn't sure.

When the double front doors opened, permitting even more light to spill out of the manor house into the grounds, the master's apparition did little to reassure Annja. That he was the master she had no doubt. He carried himself with obvious authority.

"Is it just me," Patty whispered to Annja, "or does he look just like the bad guy in *Enter the Dragon?*"

"I was just thinking the same thing," Annja said, swallowing hard. "Let's just try thinking of him as the guy who hosted the original *Iron Chef* from Japan, shall we?"

"I'm not sure that's such a huge improvement," Patty said. "He was pretty scary, too. He looked like just the sort to have a basement full of kidnapped hookers, just like Master Han in the movie."

The man in question, having shaken Eddie Chen's hand, embraced him. The apparent fervor of the gesture was belied by the extreme stiffness with which the master held his tunic-clad upper body. Annja later learned he had three fused vertebrae in his back, the legacy of a car accident two years before. But out here in the yard, surrounded by high walls and razor tangles and with what sounded like a pitched battle going on for downtown Kamphaeng Phet, it did nothing to diminish his sinister air.

Then he turned toward the three waiting Americans and approached with a big smile on his narrow face. His iron-gray hair swept back from aquiline features. His eyes were curved slits.

"If he unscrews his hand," Patty whispered, "I'm bolting."

19

"I trust you slept well," Master Ma said, entering the breakfast nook, lit up by morning sunlight streaming over the rooftops of Kamphaeng Phet and the walls of the compound. The strains of a Vivaldi concerto floated on cool jasmine-scented air.

The previous night they had dined to Rachmaninoff and candlelight, on local delicacies exquisitely prepared by Ma's silent, assiduous staff. It made Annja privately wish she had the suave, vivacious Giancarlo Scarlatti with her instead of her current companions. Not that they didn't each have an individual and peculiar appeal. Even the dour Dr. Kennedy, almost puritanical in his disapproval of the modern age, the West and just about everything Annja did for a living.

I wonder what he'd make of what I really do? she

thought. But she had no intention of allowing him, or anyone else, to learn of the Sword and of her uncomfortable and unsolicited destiny.

As for Giancarlo…she felt guilty about wishing him beside her in such impossibly romantic settings. She was trying hard not to let loneliness draw her into any more complications or entanglements for at least a while.

His ominous appearance notwithstanding, the soft-spoken Ma could not have been a more pleasant-gracious dinner host. As they ate he had asked after their recent travels and their backgrounds in flawless upper-class British English, then asked each in turn informed questions about his or her interests. He spoke with Patty Ruhle on technical points of photography in risky, fast-developing situations, Philip Kennedy on tribal shamanism in Myanmar, and Annja on the Italian Renaissance. In each case he had masterfully established having some grounding in the subject without in any way challenging his guest's superior knowledge.

He may have been no more than a good little student of Dale Carnegie, and nipped into his office while the staff were squiring the newcomers to their well-appointed and comfortable rooms on the second floor of the fortified manor for a quick Google search, but the effect still put Annja at her ease.

"I slept great," Eddie Chen said. "Like a little kid. Dreamed I was back in California."

Annja ate smoked salmon and scrambled eggs, with

fresh-cut melon, blueberries and bananas. Patty and, to Annja's surprise, Phil had opted for bacon instead of salmon, which was duly provided and on the evidence, delicious. Even Phil was forgetting to bemoan the nonlocal repast as a sign of rampant globalization this morning. Between bites she and the others murmured acknowledgment that they, too, had slept well.

"Splendid," Ma said. "Edward, I do wish you had informed me in advance of your coming. I would have prepared properly to receive you and your friends."

"Oh, thanks, Sifu Ma," Eddie said. "But it was kind of a short-notice thing."

"It pleases me you decided to honor me with your presence," Ma said. "I would not have heard of you staying elsewhere while you were in Kamphaeng Phet. I trust you will bear my best wishes back to your esteemed father."

"You bet."

If the boyish guide's informality offended him, their host showed no sign. Instead he said, "I regret that I must default upon my duties as host and withdraw. The recent border closure by the State Peace and Development Council has rather complicated my firm's affairs. I fear my commitments to my principals must in this case outweigh even the demands of hospitality. I can only pray my guests forgive this unworthy one, and permit me perhaps to make amends at some future time."

"It's we who're in your debt, *sifu,*" Annja said. "Thank you so much."

"It is nothing. I wish you a safe and harmonious journey. Should you require anything at all, please inform my servants. They will be delighted in tending to your needs."

He bowed and withdrew. A gong didn't really sound, but Annja thought it should have. Feeling slightly overwhelmed, she turned to Eddie.

"All right," Annja said, "what's the State Peace and Development Council?"

"Myanmar government," Eddie said, still shoveling in the chow. "SPDC."

"Totalitarian thugs," Patty said.

"Indeed," Phil said.

Annja glanced around to make sure their departed host had left. She sighed. "I'm sorry," she said. "But he still reminds me of Master Han."

Eddie shrugged. "To get any kind of money or power in Asia," he said, "much less hang on to it, you pretty much have to have a little Master Han in you."

"Which only makes Asia about the same as everywhere else," Patty said dryly.

"Master Han?" Kennedy asked.

"Never mind," Patty said. She reached to pat his bearded cheek. He looked annoyed.

Annja looked at Eddie with fresh appraisal. He looked and acted like a goofy adolescent—protracted adolescent, given his age. Yet she was tempted to say he'd already earned a big chunk of the money she'd laid out for his services by sparing them a night locked in some sweatbox storage room that smelled like a thousand armpits while the celebration raged joyously outside in honor of the almighty banana.

She also had to wonder at his father's exact relationship to Ma and North Wind Trading Company. Was he an investor? Or were his ties upstream in China?

She shook off the speculation. None of that mattered. A fresh sense of unease and urgency crept over her, like a thousand ants crawling out of the pit of her stomach and making their way to her skin, biting with tiny insistent jaws.

I wonder what Easy Ngwenya's doing now? she thought. She could as easily envision the remittance woman and adventuress spending the night in settings that would put these to shame, or sleeping under a bush somewhere.

Annja was convinced Ngwenya would waste no time on her way to despoil the Temple of the Elephant of its fabulous treasures. In the very best case she could not be far behind Annja, possibly no more than hours. At the worst—

Annja shook her head. At worst it was already too late.

I can't afford to consider that possibility. It could only sap her will for the trials she knew lay ahead. And despite the cheery comfort of their current surroundings she expected them to be as severe as any she had faced, even in these past few years, fraught with discomfort, danger and sheer terror as they had been.

"If only I didn't feel like Frodo eating his last meal at Rivendell before setting off to sunny Mordor," Patty said.

Phil Kennedy halted a forkful of melon halfway to

his mouth. "For someone who's always making jokes, you seem remarkably pessimistic."

"And this is inconsistent how? One laughs to keep from going bat-shit crazy, Philip dear."

"WE HAVE TO LEAVE the car here," Eddie said. "We gotta hump it for a while. At least through the pass. Then I think we can get a ride on a truck."

He had pulled the car off the main highway, such as it was—paved, at least, if not particularly well maintained—onto a dirt siding that ran a mile or so into steep, forest-clad northern Thailand hills. The station wagon sat parked off the track in the shade of a grove of saplings. A little village was nestled in a fold of the hills not far away.

Eddie nodded toward it. "I know these people. They'll watch the car for me."

"The road continues into the mountains," Phil Kennedy said. He didn't sound querulous, merely curious. It might have surprised Annja, given his usual sour take on things. But she had picked up a feeling for her companions and considered herself either good or lucky in her choices.

They started unloading the car and packing up the stores into their backpacks. From the very outset when she had e-mailed and texted the queries to friends and contacts throughout the archaeological and anthropological worlds, as well as to other adventure-oriented types she'd bumped up against on digs and with the show, she'd made it clear she wanted seasoned field types only. Not just physically fit for a demanding expedition, though that was vital. But ones who weren't illness or accident prone. There were never any guarantees on a trip like this, especially one that would likely involve hiding from bands of well-armed strangers with bad intentions.

Almost as important as physical and academic qualifications was attitude. From gruesome experience Annja knew how a whiner or chronic complainer could demoralize and factionalize even a low-stress dig, where everyone slept in air-conditioned hotel rooms or even their own beds.

So far, for all their foibles Annja's companions seemed to fit the bill. Foibles didn't faze her—people without quirky personalities did not wind up on lengthy expeditions. Much less ones that involved illegal border crossings.

It made her wonder about herself sometimes. In her own eyes she was a boringly normal, modern young American woman.

None of her three companions showed signs of excessive complaining. Phil wasn't shy about showing his many disapprovals. None arose from inconvenience or physical discomfort. To the contrary—those were things he *did* approve of.

Little frictions happened, such as the way Patty and Phil ground against each other, despite the fact that the photographer had recommended Kennedy in the first place on the basis of long acquaintance. Or perhaps despite long acquaintance. That didn't bother Annja.

You didn't get far against adversity with companions who lacked strong personalities. Of course, there were people with strong *silent* personalities.

Then again, Annja had never run into that many of those.

"There's a refugee camp up ahead," Eddie explained, stuffing food packets into his bag. They hadn't had to dip into their stores yet. Master Ma's chief servant had pressed upon them a whole cooler full of food and drink when they set out the day before. "We want to give it a miss."

Their route had taken them through Chiang Mai, largest city in the north of the kingdom, with impressive *wats* and gracious streets following tree-shaded canals. They forged on. As the land rose around them they left the major arteries behind for dicier back-country roads. They also parted company with the Ping. They had found a fairly remote and suitably rustic mountain inn to pass the night.

"They're Karens," Eddie went on. "Out of Myanmar. Supposedly the Tatmadaw Kyee has been suppressing rebels. But it's starting to look like full-on ethnic cleansing."

"What's Tatmadaw Kyee?" Annja asked.

"Burmese army," Eddie said. For once his chipper nature didn't show.

"Yangon's squatting on so many of their ethnic minorities," Patty said, "it takes less time to say who they're not picking on than who they are." She paused. "If that's anybody."

"They oppress their own people, the Burmans, as much as they do their other ethnic groups," Phil said.

"Lovely," Annja said.

"Nice people," Eddie said, "to stay well away from."

Patty patted him on the shoulder. "That's your job, junior."

"So why avoid the camp?" Phil asked, hefting a pack experimentally. Despite his narrow frame he showed no sign of being overloaded by the well-stuffed pack.

"They're full of Thai government representatives, media and solicitous NGO types," Patty said. "Do-gooder busybodies. Not so good for avoiding attention on a clandestine kind of mission like this one."

Annja half expected Phil to leap to the defense of nongovernmental organizations engaged in refugee relief. Instead he curled a bearded lip.

"Ego-tripping dilettantes and corporate tools," he said. "Worse, they keep the refugees bunched up—the worst possible thing to do. It prevents them doing anything to help themselves, keeps them dependent on aid. The only thing it makes easier is the spread of disease."

Annja had heard the latter complaint before, not infrequently from former aid workers.

"More to the point," Eddie said, "camps like this are crawling with Burmese spies. They think some of the refugees are running guerrilla ops back across the border. Which they totally are. We sure don't want them wondering what we're up to, out here in the back of beyond."

"Amen," Patty said.

She strapped on a web belt laden with sundry survival and photographer's gear. Prominent was a sheath holding a sizable Ka-Bar style knife. "A gift from the brat," she said in response to Annja's querying look. Annja wondered if her son, Jeremy, had offered her a few pointers in its use in combat.

She laughed to herself. Just as likely the lifelong combat and crisis photographer could have given her son a tip or two.

Patty squatted to heft her own pack dead-lift style. It looked almost as big as her. Annja raised her eyebrows in surprise.

"Sturdy legs and a good core," Patty said. "Pilates helps."

Annja's own burden seemed to be driving her sturdy walking shoes into the black soil. She decided she wasn't going to be the one to gripe about it.

Eddie shouldered his own pack and slammed the car's rear hatch. "All righty, then," he said, puppy-eager as always. "I'll check in with my dudes in the village. Then it's off on a nice mountain hike!"

20

"Admit it, Annja Creed," Patty said from behind her. "This is what life's all about."

From a distance the elephant Annja shared with the photographer had looked disappointingly small. Swaying side to side with her long legs straddling the broad gray back, the beast seemed immense, its power incalculable. It was a female, perhaps seven feet high at the shoulder; Annja was told she weighed about three tons.

Her heavy trunk wagged in time to her paces. Her ears, small in comparison to an African elephant's but still big as beach towels, flapped against the insistent attentions of the flies and other swarming bugs. The mahout, a man not much larger than a child to Annja's eyes, was dressed in a grubby white blouse and a white turban loosely wound around his head.

The Salween River, its water almost reddish-brown

with runoff from rains in the north, slogged and sloshed and gurgled around the animal's churning legs, and the sun began to spill its radiance above the dark mass of the Taunggyi Range behind.

Perhaps a quarter mile ahead of the three elephants stretched bare roan mudflat. Beyond and on a shore imperceptibly higher at this range sprouted palm trees with fronds beginning to stir lazily in the sunrise breeze. Beyond them the brush closed in, forming a lower rampart to a green wall of hardwood forest.

Over all loomed another mass dark with remnant night—the Shan Plateau, on whose heights their destination awaited.

Annja drew in a deep breath. In the middle of the river it mostly drew in the smell of the muddy water, not decaying vegetation. As she drew in another lungful of the fragrant morning air, Annja thought Patty was right.

This was almost perfect.

"HERE COMES EDDIE," Patty called.

Annja paced up and down on the grass alongside the impressive set of ruts currently baked into the yellow clay of the nominal road. Small peaks poked up sharply on three sides of them. The fourth was the way back to the wide, slow river. She had her arms folded tightly beneath her breasts and a crumpled boonie hat was crammed tightly down on the tight French braid into which she often wound her long hair in the field. She felt anxiety crawl along her nerves. She was so distracted she didn't notice the real bugs that swarmed around her.

They were in hostile territory. The Shan elephant drovers had wasted no time mounting up to head back across the Salween after depositing them. Somewhere ahead were the Tatmadaw Kyee, angry and active as roused-up wasps.

Though of a different ethnicity and no great friends of the Karen, the Shan mahouts hadn't seemed comforted by the fact the Tatmadaw was not hunting for them. Myanmar's army had a vivid reputation for shooting first.

Fortunately none of Annja's companions harbored the futile illusion their American passports would stop bullets or shell fragments. Of course, that awareness wouldn't turn away hostile fire, either.

Eddie smiled as he came down the path. As usual he bobbed his head up and down between hunched shoulders as he walked. But now his L.A. Dodgers baseball cap bobbed more energetically than usual. Even fifty yards off Annja could see a big grin on his face.

"Got it," he called. "There's a stake-bed truck coming from the village down the lane. They can get us to the base of the plateau, no problem."

Patty grunted. "I'd say the 'no problem' part is more up to the Tatmadaw. And the goddess."

Phil Kennedy squatted in the shade of a palm tree just outside the transition zone where the underbrush of a hardwood forest gave way to the long green roadside grass. He rose like a stork departing her nest. He cleared his throat.

"Ms. Creed," he said, with unusual formality. "If I could talk to you a moment in private, please?"

Annja sighed. It wasn't as if she had anything better to do except fret about everything that could go wrong before the truck arrived. Which was everything. But then, wasn't that always true?

I knew this was coming, she told herself.

"Let's go in the woods a ways," she said. "Get some shade. For what it's worth." Actually, anything that kept the stinging sunlight off exposed skin helped. Even if the shade did little to diminish the humid heat. It was noticeably less wet and hot at this altitude. But not enough to come near comfort.

They walked along an animal trail through thick green brush to a tiny clearing twenty yards uphill from the road cut. It was far enough to keep voices from carrying unless voices were raised. Which she didn't intend to have happen. Despite what she was sure was on the verge of being said.

"As you know," Kennedy said, "I am the most experienced person in our group, both as an academic and a field researcher. I have more experience in this region than even Eddie Chen does. And of course, ah, there's the matter of my doctoral degree…."

Annja turned and faced him, smiling. Little birds, yellow and gray and black and crimson, trilled in the trees and hopped and jittered in the brush around them. "Let's cut to the chase, Doctor," she said. "I run this show. It was my idea. It's my quest, you might say. And of course, I'm paying."

His face had frozen. Now it mobilized to the extent his bearded, slightly full lips gave an even greater impression he detected a bad smell than usual. "So you're telling me that on this expedition—"

"We follow the golden rule," Annja said, still smiling, but with nothing in her voice to suggest the least degree of give. "Who has the gold, makes the rules. If you find the arrangement unsatisfactory we'll reluctantly part ways right here. You should be able to catch the elephant guys in time to hitch a lift back across the Salween."

Phil glared at her. She held his gaze. She kept smiling.

Trained anthropologists as they both were, both knew a smile is often a form of submission in a primate.

Kennedy dropped his eyes and shook his head. "Very well," he said. "I find myself in no position to argue. But—"

None of that, she thought. "Great, Dr. Kennedy," she said, chipper as an undergraduate who thinks she might be able to flirt her way out of arduous digging on a field trip. "I'm glad we could get that cleared up."

She started to walk back toward the road. From somewhere along it came the sounds of a driver grinding through the gears of a heavy vehicle. Their ride was on its way. If it makes it this far, she thought.

"Ms. Creed," Kennedy called after her.

She stopped and turned. She continued to maintain her centered, cheerful expression. To the extent it was false, it was plastered over her fears and anxieties about the risks that awaited them and the terrible possibility that the rapacious and utterly ruthless Easy Ngwenya would reach and ravage the Temple of the Elephant before Annja could stop her.

As for Kennedy—she had faced down men berserk with rage, men armed with knives and swords and automatic weapons. She had on occasion killed foes. Even before all that she had been hard to intimidate.

There was nothing Phil Kennedy could do to intimidate her. Not if he weighed twice as much and had black belts in five kinds of sudden death.

But his manner was troubled. Almost contrite, she thought. Whoa! I didn't look for that out of such an arrogant kind of guy.

"I need this assignment," he said, his voice quieter than she had heard him use before. "I need the success bonus."

She stopped and looked back at him with brow raised questioningly. The sensation of desire, of the need to be moving forward toward her goal was pressing.

But since Kennedy had opted to remain a member of her team, she needed to be responsive to his morale. If he feels a need to talk, I need to listen. So long as she didn't have to do it too long.

"I have a daughter," he said slowly, as if it cost great effort to speak. "Back in the United States. Her mother was a Shan tribeswoman. She—my wife, by tribal ceremony—died in childbirth. I smuggled the child out of the country and got her to Hawaii."

He paused. He breathed heavily, as if he'd just run a mile. Annja didn't press.

"I set my daughter up with foster parents," the anthropologist went on. "It costs money to maintain her. Also I ran up debts to some rough characters getting her out from under the noses of the State Peace and Development Council. Not to mention into the United States. So I *need* this job."

Annja stood a moment, almost fidgeting with her need to go. Yet his admission was so naked, had left him so vulnerable, she knew she owed him something. Especially after backing him down on the issue of heading the expedition. Her innate decency as much as practicality forbade her crushing the spirit of someone upon whom her life and the lives of the other two might soon depend.

"I understand," she said truthfully. "I'll tell you what. If you think I show myself unfit to lead in any way, tell me. Now or at any time in the future. If you really, honestly can say that I have, I'll reconsider."

He nodded. A faint smile crept through his gray-dusted beard. "I'll do that. But I have to admit you've done a perfectly adequate job so far."

"Thanks," she said, through a smile that had set slightly. "Now let's go back and I'll tell you and the others exactly what we're doing in this hellhole."

THEY DANCED IN THE pouring rain. Beer helped.

At the village they had passed through before

camping for the night in an abandoned hut, Eddie Chen bought them thirteen bottles with colorful labels printed in squirmy Burmese characters.

"Hope nobody here's superstitious," he had said as he lugged them in the yellow plastic crate.

Phil frowned. "It isn't wise to dismiss folk wisdom out of hand," he said. "It's got a lot longer track record than Western materialism and rationalism."

"Ah, but is it a better one?" Patty Ruhle asked.

Phil smiled thinly. "How many people died through the use of modern technology in the twentieth century?"

"Well," Patty said, "you've got a point."

Eddie, if anything even more indefatigably cheerful than Patty, deflected the conversation by commencing to pop open bottles with a church key he carried on his belt. It had what seemed like dozens of pockets on it, more than Patty's, sealed by snaps, zippers or Velcro. He called it his utility belt. "Just like Batman's," he said.

The rain started shortly after Eddie returned. A thunderclap announced it as they sat on the edge of the elevated hut, dangling their legs and eating their MREs. The sudden noise made Annja and Patty duck their heads. Eddie did, too. Only Phil Kennedy failed to react, other than giving his comrades a look as if to say he'd expected no better of them than to fear natural phenomena.

What it suggested to Annja was that the anthropologist had never come under fire.

The rain came down in sheets in the gathering dark. They pulled their legs in under the thatch overhang and watched it out of the hut's open side. Annja didn't know how it came to be vacant. Phil dismissed risk of disease; if anybody had died in it, the hut would have been burned down. For that matter, had the occupants been arrested, the government forces would probably have burned it down, as well. Eddie had confirmed no one in the nearby village cared if they occupied it for the night. It offered a welcome change from sleeping in the open the past two nights, although this was the first night it had rained since they'd set out from Bangkok.

They all polished off their first beers during dinner. Afterward even Annja was amenable to opening a second. Eddie had gotten out an iPod and a slim set of portable speakers with a slot in the middle to accommodate the player. It wasn't anything Annja would have chosen to bring, given how little they could carry. But if Eddie was willing to carry the excess without complaint, she had no objection.

The rain slackened. They made torches from dry straw pulled from inside the roof. They sputtered but burned in the falling droplets. Eddie started playing pop songs that were bouncy, happy. You could dance to the music, and overall it made it seem natural to be out dancing in the warm rain. Which they soon were.

They had something to celebrate. They'd reached the top of the Shan Plateau. If the Red Monastery map was correct they had a two-day march left before reaching the smaller mesa where the lost temple complex stood.

So they danced and drank their third beer each. That left one beer remaining. Annja, already sensing she was fuzzed, passed. She hated losing control; it was why she didn't drink more, or do recreational drugs. She didn't know who got the last beer. She thought it was Patty.

The rain stopped. The clouds seemed to snap apart overhead, leaving the sky above clear in minutes. The stars stood out through the fresh-cleansed air like tiny spotlights focused down on them.

Annja found herself thinking about Giancarlo Scarlatti.

Phil and Patty got into a sort of free-form limbo contest. Each would lean back and try to dance as low as possible. The round ended when one—or occasionally both—fell on his or her butt in the mud. Then they got up and started over, cackling like lunatics.

Annja sat on the steps with Eddie. She felt mellow, notwithstanding a certain unease at the core of her being. Out there in the startlingly black night was Easy Ngwenya. And Annja was just sure she wasn't passing the time yucking it up and dancing.

Eddie was enthusing again about California. "I'll go back one of these days," he said. "Finish up my E.E. at CalTech."

"You're an electrical engineer?"

"Well, not yet." He held up two fingers as if to pinch. "But I'm that close."

Annja nodded.

"I've got a girl back in Cali," he said, voice dropped low and confidential. "Woman, I guess I should say."

"Really," Annja said.

"Would you like to see a picture?"

"Sure."

He opened a flap on a belt pouch, drew out a stiff cardboard jacket. From it he slid a photo and handed it to Annja. It was a three-by-five, professionally posed shot of a woman with long, wavy blond hair and blue eyes, smiling over her shoulder at the camera. She was startlingly beautiful.

"Nice," Annja said. "Is she a model or something?"

Eddie laughed. "Aeronautical engineer," he said. "She's got a job with JPL now."

Annja blinked. It all seemed pretty damned incongruous to her. "What are you *doing* here, Eddie?" she asked. "You seem to love it back in California. And if I had a girlfriend like that waiting for me back home I wouldn't stay here in Southeast Asia. And I'm straight."

He smiled shyly. For once reserve overcame his usual ebullience.

"It's Dad, see," he said. "I'm eldest. So I kind of have to look out for him."

"He seems pretty able to look out for himself, from what I saw," Annja said.

"It's a Chinese thing. A family-obligation thing."

She tipped her head sideways and looked at him in the torchlight. "Is that everything? Really? I mean, you act totally homesick. And you seem pretty American to throw over your whole life—not to mention a cover-girl of a girlfriend who happens to be an aerospace engineer—for traditional Chinese familial piety."

"Well, Dad says if I hang on over the winter, he's planning to sell everything and retire next year. Then he'll go live with my sister in Singapore."

It seemed as if there was more so Annja said, "And…?"

Eddie shrugged. "Well—I guess I kind of like the excitement. You know. Making the run across the border. Up into China and back. I—well, let's just say, no matter how much I miss Cali, there's nothing back there that compares to the rush. Not surfing, not sky-diving."

Annja wondered if he and his dad were running arms to Myanmar resistance groups. He seemed to know much about the Karen rebels. She didn't ask. It wasn't any of her business, and it was the sort of thing that, since she didn't need to know it, she reckoned she needed *not* to know. That way if the authorities scooped them up, she could truthfully say she had no information whatever about such activities on Eddie's part.

If that would do any good. She suspected it would not. She had a cold suspicion that if the Myanmar army caught them skulking around out here the only way they'd make it to Yangon for trial was if the SPDC wanted the publicity.

"Hey," Phil Kennedy called from out in front of the hut. "What's that?"

He was pointing away to the south. In the guttering, failing light of their torches he and Patty looked like a pair of golems from the slick, pale mud smeared all up and down them.

The southern horizon flickered with dull yellow flashes like distant lightning. A mutter reached Annja's ears, like thunder from a distant storm.

Streaks of yellow light, thread thin, arced up and across and down. When they vanished light really flared up, white now.

"Fireworks?" Phil asked. He sounded puzzled.

"Rockets," Patty said. "Big ones. Government's pounding rebel positions down there."

She put hands on her hips and stood gazing at the display. "Multiple Launch Rocket Systems," she said. "MLRS. During World War II the Germans called theirs fog throwers. The Americans called them Screamin' Meemies. My boy says they raise a howl like all the damned souls in Hell."

"I didn't think you believed in Hell," Phil said.

"Sometimes," she said.

Annja felt cold all over. "That's some pretty heavy-weight repression," she said.

"That's what makes Myanmar the garden spot it is," Patty said. "Its government's charming propensity to settle domestic disputes with barrage rockets."

Eddie squinted and scratched the front of his crown beneath his ball cap. "I got news for you," he said. "They could be 240 mm rockets. Made in North Korea."

"Two hundred forty *millimeters?*" Annja asked in astonishment. It was almost nine and a half inches, if her math was up to the task.

"Uh-huh."

"North Korea," Patty said, for once without her usual humor. "Jesus Christ."

Phil said nothing. He just looked at the flicker of yellow in the sky. But Annja thought his manner, rather than disapproving, seemed sad.

For once she felt in complete agreement with him. And if he was disgusted with the whole modern world—for the moment, so was she.

21

"Annja," Eddie Chen called. "Come take a look at this."

She pushed herself forward through the brush. Wait-a-bit thorns tugged at her sleeves. She wished she could summon up the Sword and chop them all back and be done with it. It didn't exactly seem appropriate. But, darn, it'd be gratifying.

They were getting close to their destination. Sporadic rain, last gasp of the monsoon, had made the forest footing mushy even though today was fair and hot. Annja's sense of urgency was a constant neural buzz.

They had come upon what looked like a road through the woods. The hardwood trees were widely spaced. It looked almost as if a path had been bulldozed through brush and a stand of saplings, transversely to their own course. But even Annja, no tracker, could see no signs of the tearing and gouging a track-laying vehicle did to such soft ground.

"What's this?" she asked. "An elephant trail?"

"Too wide," Patty said. "It'd take a herd to do this."

The women looked at Eddie, the guide, and Phil Kennedy, who had lived and worked among the tribes in this region. They looked at each other.

"Men," Eddie said. "Men made this."

He took off his Dodgers cap and wiped sweat from his forehead with the back of a hand. His normal ebullience had definitely flattened.

"Are you a tracker?" Phil asked superciliously. But Annja sensed it was pro forma.

Eddie shook his crew-cut head. "No way. But I do know what a path made by a bunch of guys on foot who don't much care what kind of a mark they leave on the environment looks like."

"Wouldn't elephants leave signs like knocked-over trees?" Patty asked.

Eddie nodded. "And their feet'd mush up the ground more."

"So who were they?" Annja asked, taking off her sunglasses and putting them up on the front of her boonie hat.

Eddie shrugged. "Like I say, I'm not a tracker."

"Tribal people move carefully," Phil said. "They leave few marks."

Eddie nodded. "I'd say it's an army. Or a militia. Whatever."

"Militia?" Annja asked.

He shrugged. "Ethnic army, drug army, bandit gang. Any of the above, all of the above. Take your pick."

"To the extent there's a difference," Patty said.

Eddie nodded crisply. "Exactly."

Annja felt her cheeks draw up and turn her eyes to unhappy slits. "Great. I'm guessing these are people we don't want to cross paths with."

"Whether they're worse than the government forces is kind of an open question," Eddie said. He seemed to be sweating more than before, even though he wasn't exerting himself. "The important thing is we don't want to find out."

"Well." Annja stood a moment with hands on her hips. She noticed some trash trodden into the pathway, little plastic wrappers from snacks or cigarettes. "At least they're going a different way."

"They were when they passed by here, anyway," Patty said. "Do we know where they were going?"

Everybody looked to Eddie, even Phil. He was, after all, the man with the best line on Myanmar's famously large and cantankerous ethnic armies. His eyes were big.

"You got me," he said. "Wouldn't I have to be, like, psychic to know?"

"This could've been just part of a larger group, too," Patty said, "headed out on patrol, or maybe coming back."

"How do you reckon that?" Phil asked. His tone held no challenge—he seemed just to want to know. As did Annja.

Patty jerked her head at the trail. "No tire tracks," she said. "Any self-respecting gang of thugs is at least going to have a pickup or a Land Cruiser or something for their big boss to ride around in."

"Maybe," Annja said.

"We need information," Phil Kennedy said decisively.

"We need out of this area," Annja said. "We can move faster than a big mob of men on foot, can't we?"

"If they're not real elite or moving with real purpose, like as not," Patty said.

"But we don't know for sure," Phil said, nodding as if he had it all worked out. "Do we really want to risk blundering into them? Or their main force, if Patty's right and this was just a patrol?"

"Or their enemies, for that matter," Eddie said.

"Maybe we should find out who's who, then," Phil said. "Don't the Arabs say, 'the enemy of my enemy is my friend'?"

"Maybe that works for Arabs," Eddie said slowly. "Around here—not so much."

"Not so much in the Muslim world, either," Patty said. "I think the proverb was meant to apply to temporary alliances."

"Yeah, and what if these guys' enemies are the Myanmar army?" Annja said. "They're not our friends, for sure."

Phil spread his hands and smiled knowingly. "You're all making my case for me," he said. "We need to find a village and find out what we can."

"OKAY, NOW WHAT?"

It was Patty who asked the question. The four crouched in the brush behind a fallen tree trunk. Beyond it a small cultivated vegetable patch was visible. Annja could make out the sharply peaked roof of a small wooden temple above the trees a couple of hundred yards away. A village lay nearby.

"I guess we might as well talk to them," Annja said. She had to admit she found Phil Kennedy's logic compelling—they vitally needed information.

"That would be me," Phil said smugly. He gave a covert side glance to Eddie Chen that Annja caught.

"Why you?" Eddie demanded a bit sullenly.

"I know this area," the anthropologist said. "These people are De'ang. They speak a Mon-Khmer dialect related to Cambodian. I speak it, as well. Do you?"

Eddie scowled. He didn't, Annja already knew.

For the past couple of days a mostly friendly rivalry had developed between Phil and Eddie. Phil, Annja suspected, felt challenged by Eddie's superior knowledge of the Tibeto-Burman languages used in some places they'd passed through. Under other circumstances the irony might have amused her. He had been behind Eddie's hiring, after all.

Annja didn't care; she mainly wanted Kennedy for the cultural work necessary to document and start in motion proper preservation measures for the Temple of the Elephant. His relationships with certain groups whose territory they had to pass through on the way were a potential plus, not the reason for hiring him. Eddie was their guide and main liaison.

Flies swarmed around them like biplanes buzzing King Kong. The smell of the human excrement that was the main fertilizer for the little garden over-whelmed the usual jungle odors. It was no improvement.

They all looked to her. Even Patty's face was paler than normal and taut beneath her sunscreen and the brim of her floppy hat. Her mouth was set in a line. No wisecracks for the moment.

The joys of being in charge, Annja thought. She drew a breath down into her belly, which did little to calm either pulse or misgivings and said, "Okay, Phil. But for God's sake be careful."

He frowned. "What's there to be afraid of? These people are peaceful. You Westerners regard all prein-dustrial people as savages."

He straightened and stepped over the log. The brush crackled as he swept through it. Annja winced. He called out across the little garden space in a warbling tonal tongue.

Fire stabbed from the brush on the far side. Even as a terrible crack assailed Annja's eardrums she heard the moist chunk of projectiles hitting flesh and bone.

Phil staggered and sat down. His head started to loll. Blood ran from the side of his mouth.

With unspoken accord Eddie and Annja grabbed him under the arms and dashed back into the brush with him. He was deadweight. His long legs dangled behind, boot heels plowing up musk and catching on things. Eddie was sturdy as a pack mule and Annja pro-athlete strong; their blood now sang the adrenal song of fear. Annja had spent much of her life successfully learning how to master the fight-or-flight reflex. Now she gave herself to it and did her best to really fly.

Annja knew what they faced. Around the world, the firearm of choice of the poor villager and farmer wasn't the notorious Kalashnikov. They were too heavy, and despite the world being flooded with them, too expensive. Also they ate up ammo too quickly. Even when the weapons themselves weren't dear, the ammunition was.

Instead the universal weapon was what Annja thought of as the monkey gun—the single-shot, break-action shotgun, simple, sturdy and cheap. Their rudimentary mechanisms could survive more abuse than even the famously durable AK. They could work without cleaning or other maintenance; their useful service life could be extended almost indefinitely by jury rigs, from binding split stocks with cord to wrapping a weakened barrel with wire. Inevitably they'd burst, if abused long enough, possibly doing crippling or fatal damage to the shooter.

The guns were even prevalent, so Annja's farm-belt college acquaintances assured her, among farmers in the American hinterland, if usually better maintained. It meant they were functionally immortal.

Monkey guns lacked glamour. But they did the job—killing pests that threatened the crops, putting meat on the table. And a good blast of buck would kill you every bit as dead as a burst from an AK-47—or a multimillion-dollar laser-guided missile, for that matter.

As Phil Kennedy had just learned.

They stumbled and bulled through brush for fifty yards, a hundred. Patty ran before them. She could easily have outdistanced her burdened comrades, left them far behind. Instead she'd dart ahead a few yards, then stop and wait, panting and quivering visibly like a frightened fawn. Annja wasn't sure whether to feel gratitude at her not abandoning them or shout for the red-haired photographer to do just that—save herself.

Patty had stopped with hands on thighs and was staring back past Annja. *"Voices,"* she hissed. "They're chasing us!"

"Put him down," Annja told Eddie. Phil continued to breathe, raggedly, with an unpleasant bubbling gurgle that made it audible above the crash of brush and the drum of their feet and above all the jackhammer solo of her pulse in her ears. They eased the stricken anthropologist down beneath a bush. She didn't hold much hope for his survival if he'd sucked a whole charge of shot to the chest. But she didn't want to finish him off herself. She started back at an angle to the direction they had come.

"Annja, wait!" Patty called in a tight voice, trying to be heard only by her companion but not their pursuers. They way they came crashing it might have been. "You're not a trained commando."

If she had anything more to say, the green brush closing behind Annja, and her pounding pulse, swallowed it.

She had simply taken for granted that if the SPDC caught up with them, its agents would either shoot them out of hand or scoop them up and interrogate them. The only real difference was that the latter would be a longer, less comfortable route to the same fate—decomposing in deep woods somewhere.

She had often heard and read that when severely outnumbered, fighting back was no option anyway, so there was no point going armed into enemy country. She had never really believed that. Her experience had certainly not borne that out. The main reason she'd brought no guns was concern they'd make her companions uncomfortable. And yet here it came again—lacking firearms, they could only flee from those who had them. Only the dense brush kept them from facing the impossible task of trying to outrun shotgun pellets.

But Annja had an edge. The last thing her pursuers would ever expect was that their fleeing quarry might double back to ambush them.

With a deliberately held coldness of heart intended to keep her from flashing over into an inferno of rage and grief, Annja was determined it would indeed be the last thing.

PATTY LOOKED UP FROM where she knelt over Phil Kennedy as Annja emerged from the brush. The anthropologist lay stretched out full length with his head propped on his own backpack. The pallor of his face, the gleam of his eyeballs beneath half-lowered lids, the stillness with which he lay told Annja all there was to know before the photographer spoke.

"He's gone," Patty said.

Annja knelt and placed two monkey guns on the grass. Patty's eyes went wide when she saw the two long, slender black objects.

"What about—?" Eddie began.

"They won't chase us anymore," Annja said flatly, grateful they'd been pursued by only two men. She bent close to feel Phil's neck. The skin was clammy, no more elastic than putty, cool despite the late-afternoon heat. There was no pulse.

"We'll divide up what we can of his load," Annja said, rising.

"What about those?" Patty said, nodding to the two shotguns Annja had laid down. One had a swirly pattern, incorporating something like a mandala, picked out in its shoulder stock with hammered-in brads or tacks. As a piece of folk art it was rather pretty. The other was wound with brass wire, holding together a broken stock and attaching the barrel to it.

Annja shrugged. She reached in a pocket of her khaki cargo pants and held four cylinders, finger length and half again as thick, out in her palm. They were brown greased paper, smudged and stained, with faded black printing on the sides and tarnished brass bases.

"The guns are loaded," she said. "I've got these shells. They're French. They're old—you can tell from the wax-paper hulls. I won't swear they're not black powder. I won't swear the guns won't blow up in your face the next time they go off, either. But the charges and the guns work."

"What good'll they do us against Tatmadaw rockets?" Eddie asked. "Or even ethnic-army AKs, for that matter?"

"How much good did bare hands do us?" Annja asked. Her voice was harsh and Eddie jerked back as if she had slapped him. She didn't care.

"Did you like the feeling of utter helplessness, getting chased through the woods like that?" Annja said. "Those were a couple of farmers. They probably thought they'd got lucky, bagging spies to sell to the chief of whatever bandit gang's working the area. Or the SPDC. Will you feel better if we get ambushed again and all we get to do is throw rocks?"

"Guns don't make us bulletproof," Patty said. She didn't seem to be denying Annja so much as talking. Possibly just to reassure herself that she could.

"Hold that thought. What they might do is give us a chance we wouldn't have without them. But they are a burden, and could be as dangerous to you as anybody you're shooting at. Your choice."

"What about you, Annja?" Eddie asked.

She knelt and began teasing the pack slowly from beneath Phil's head. If the apparent callousness shocked the others, again, she could care just now. A corpse was no novelty to her, sadly. And it wasn't as if poor Phil was going to mind.

"I don't need them," she said. "I've got other options."

22

Two things hit them halfway up the hundred-foot cliff to the mesa where the lost temple complex awaited.

One was torrential rain, the drops exploding like little mortar shells on the red rocks around them.

The other was a patrol from the Grand Shan State Army, opening fire from the jungle floor a hundred yards away.

"Shit," Patty said in a voice that sounded more annoyed than scared. She was the lead climber. Annja was poised ten yards beneath Patty. Eddie was a few feet below her, perched on relatively large and stable outcrops while the red-headed photographer hammered in pitons to belay their safety lines. Despite her years Patty Ruhle climbed like a monkey.

The burst hit somewhere too far to be visible. Patty

shook her head wearily, glanced at the jungle, then looked down at the others.

"I am *definitely* getting too old for this," she said. Then she turned her face resolutely from the danger on the ground and began to climb swiftly and purposefully. More cautiously Eddie and Annja, neither a seasoned climber, followed her.

Annja never knew what happened next. She had too little rock-climbing experience to know whether it was the torrential rains that caused the slippage, or the impact of Patty's piton going into a fissure in the yellow rock, or the photographer's weight. Or even just evil luck that caused several hundred pounds of boulder to suddenly split off the face with Patty clinging to it.

"Rock!" she bellowed as she fell. Annja felt an impulse to grab for her. She restrained it. The combined mass of Patty and the rock to which she was already bound by the rope was far too great for Annja to make any difference. In fact it ripped the pitons above Annja right out of the cliff face as it plummeted.

Annja flattened and threw herself to her right. As she did the corrugated rubber soles of her walking shoes lost their purchase. She dropped a foot to slam and then hang spinning helplessly from her own safety rope.

Patty fell past. She caught Annja's eye. For a moment time seemed to slow. Annja's frantic brain formed the impression the older woman winked at her. And she saw even in the overcast and the rain the wink of bare steel in the photographer's left hand. Her son's knife.

Time resumed. Patty and the fatal rock plunged

away with sickening speed. Whipping above them like a festive stream was a cut end of the white-and-blue rope—severed by Patty in a final act of incredible sacrifice and presence of mind.

Instead of being torn from the rock face to her own destruction, with Eddie Chen following an eye blink later, Annja hung, still turning, watching in helpless horror as Patty struck bottom. If the fall wasn't enough to kill her—as it almost certainly was—the seven-hundred-pound boulder fragment landed on her.

Tears streamed from Annja's eyes, mingling with the rain. She sought for and found a purchase for her shoes. When she no longer swung freely she secured the rope. As safety backups, both she and Eddie carried rock hammers and pitons.

There was no help for her friend. Already men in dark clothing and blue headbands had begun to filter out of the brush, cautiously approaching the crushed body of the photojournalist as if suspecting it was bait in an elaborate trap. Turning her face away from her fallen friend Annja blinked away the tears and rain. She began to climb.

"WE MADE IT," Eddie said in a tone of frank amazement.

Annja could hardly believe it herself. They stood atop the mesa that rose from the Shan Plateau. As if by cosmic irony the rain had ceased. In front of them rose a green wall of jungle. Several miles farther on jutted a fang of bare red rock. On its top stood an unmistakable weathered structure, possibly carved from the peak itself.

She sucked in a deep breath. "The Temple of the Elephant," she breathed.

"It's real!" Eddie said. "I can't believe it."

She grinned at him. Despite the exhaustion she should have felt from the desperate climb—almost a vertical run—the rest of the way up the cliff, she was totally buzzed with triumph.

At their feet lay their backpacks, including Patty's. They had hauled them up on ropes after reaching the top.

Voices floated up over the lip of the cliff. Men were shouting excitedly at each other. Annja frowned. Ignoring Eddie's warning, she walked to the edge and looked down.

A knot of dark-clad men had gathered at the cliff base. They surrounded Patty's body. One of them stepped cautiously forward and prodded an outflung hand with a boot. The hand flopped as if attached to a rubber hose.

The men closed in and began to tug at the body. Clearly they were grubbing for loot.

Rage filled Annja. They had not caused Patty's death directly, unless a stray shot had somehow caused the boulder to split from the cliff, which she knew to be unlikely. But they had shot at them, without reason, and if that additional hurrying hadn't caused misjudgment that led to Patty's death, it had contributed.

Chunks of rock lay near the cliff edge, weather-split

from an outcropping. Annja's eye lit on one about the size of her torso. She bowed her back, pushing her stomach forward and sucking a breath deep to press her internal organs against her spine and stabilize it. Grasping the rock by the ends she deadlifted it, driving upward with her legs. It almost felt easy. Anger was engorging body and mind with a fresh blast of adrenaline.

She straightened her back and heaved, pushing with her thighs. The rock rolled outward from the cliff top and then dropped toward the knot of men swarming over Patty's corpse.

From back in the brush a comrade called a warning. One man looked up and screamed.

The rock hit him in the head. It must have snapped his neck like a toothpick. Deflected slightly, it struck a second bandit in the lower back, smashing spine and pelvis. He fell screaming.

His comrades scattered like roaches from the light. Annja stood looking down upon them, flexing and unflexing her hands. She retained enough self-control not to make the gesture to summon her sword.

Her companion stared at her with jaw hanging so slack it might have come disjointed.

"You meant to do that?" Eddie asked.

Annja nodded.

His eyes were saucers. "You're not just an archaeologist, are you?"

She stooped to the packs. Her mind had already returned to the urgency of the situation at hand. They'd take any supplies they'd really need from Patty's pack, any documents or small personal effects. Then they'd cache the rest, as they had Phil's—along with his body, lacking time or energy to bury him. Although he'd doubtless prefer returning his stuff to the jungle he loved, whatever the jungle left of him Annja had vowed to herself to see recovered and returned to his family. Silently she made the same promise to Patty.

If she survived, of course. Death canceled all debts, zeroed out every promise. An archaeologist, whose study was, after all, the dead, knew that better than most.

"NO WAY," EDDIE BREATHED.

A partial wall of red stone and exposed brick filler a good fifteen feet high stood before them. It was so vine twined and overgrown, with full-blown bushes sprouting from hollows in its irregular upper surface where soil had accreted over centuries of ruin, that it looked not as if the brush had grown up around it, but as if it had itself sprung up from the earth, grown up as part of the living jungle itself.

For a moment Annja didn't understand her companion's exclamation. Then she realized he was still astonished to discover that the legendary giant temple complex, swallowed by the jungle centuries before, really existed.

Of course it does, she felt an urge to say, with a touch of irritation.

But she knew the modernist-skeptic reflex well. She shared it—or, now, clung with increasing desperation to the shreds and fragments real-world experience had left to her. Eddie was an engineer by training and inclination, although filial piety and a half-denied lust for adventure conspired to make him a Chinese Indiana Jones. Lost temples and fabulous treasure hoards were only myths in this modern world of satellites and cell phones. Confronted by one impossibility made undeniably real—the temple on its crag—he was still struggling to accept it.

Annja realized she was unprepared to document their find. She had one of Patty's cameras in her pack and went to dig it out.

"This is just the beginning," she said.

"You mean there's more?" Eddie asked.

"That's what von Hoiningen claimed. I think we kind of have to believe him now, don't we?"

"I have got to see this!"

The relief here was relatively flat. The obvious choice for a quick vantage point was to scale the ruined wall. Eddie quickly shed his pack and clambered up with his usual agility.

Annja frowned. "That might not be a good idea," she said, concerned from a preservation standpoint.

It was a bad idea. For a reason Annja never anticipated.

Ignoring her, Eddie reached a high point on the wall, where the stone outer sheathing was still intact. He stood upright. "My God, Annja!" he exclaimed. "You're right! It's like it goes for miles—"

A burst of gunfire spun him around and down to the ground.

23

Choking back an exclamation that could only risk drawing the eyes of the unseen shooter, Annja darted around the wall stub. Eddie lay on his back with his knees and forearms up. His eyes were wide behind askew glasses.

Probably more from his bad luck than the shooter's good marksmanship the burst had taken him right across the chest. Kneeling over him, Annja could see at least four entry holes in his blue polo shirt with the thin horizontal white stripes, surrounded by spreading patches of darker fabric.

He caught her hand. "Annja," he croaked, and the blood gurgled up from the back of his throat and ran out his mouth and down his cheeks. "Tell my father I'm—sorry—"

There seemed to be more. But it would have to wait.

Eddie jackknifed in a terrible coughing spasm. His glasses flew from his face. He emitted a rasping croak and fell back dead.

Squeezing his hand in both of hers, she dropped her forehead to it. The tears streamed hot down her cheeks. She had not yet had time to grieve for Patty, or even Phil—

And now she had three times the grieving to do, and no time to do it. She dragged Eddie's body under some brush; it was the best she could do for him. Then she ran hunched over around the rock, brought his pack and shoved it next to the body. A feeble gesture at concealment, it would work or it wouldn't.

Behind her a flight of crows burst raucously skyward. Someone was approaching from the cliffs.

She had to move. *Now.*

Her choice of direction was obvious. She fled deeper into the mesa, into the overgrown temple complex and toward the red peak on which the Temple of the Elephant stood. Eddie had been turning when he got hit; Annja didn't know which direction the shots came from. Parties unknown closing in were the immediate threat.

Moving as quickly as she could with some degree of quiet, she became aware of more ruins around her. Some were wall stubs like the one Eddie had incautiously climbed. Others were segments of walls of larger blocks, fallen into jumbles. She saw apparently intact small buildings or perhaps surviving rooms, some mounded with overgrown earth, inviting with blank black windows or low doors.

Annja passed these by, recognizing them for what they were—not bolt-holes but traps. She had no way of knowing which, if any, had other exits. Giving in to the siren song of a hiding place might get her caught, to be finished by gunfire, a grenade or literally smoked out.

She darted through a gap between walls. On her left a second stump of wall joined the other, a corner turned buttress when the rest of the chamber fell away. She stepped into the niche thus created. It gave her not just concealment, meaning she couldn't be seen, but cover, meaning it shielded her from gunfire, from two directions, including the way she had come. It was neither a safe nor a satisfactory position. Just the best available chance to breathe deeply, calm her wild-running emotions and try to grasp some sense of her tactical situation.

Cautiously she peered back through the gap. She could see nothing but forest with occasional glimpses of stonework. She heard nothing but the normal jungle sounds. She could almost believe she had the mesa to herself.

But someone had shot Eddie Chen. Someone close by. Very few shooters were skilled enough to keep full-auto bursts on target at any range at all. Muzzle jump and parallax usually meant so many shots from one brief burst couldn't hit a target even from a hundred yards or less. They would have dispersed too widely.

If Annja were very, very lucky, whoever killed Eddie had no idea of her presence. "Yeah," she said softly. "As if I'm ever that lucky."

"Annja!" a voice whispered from behind her. "Annja Creed."

The phrase "almost jumped out of her skin" took on a whole new meaning for her. Her heart felt as if it hit the front of her rib cage as if shot from a cannon, and she jumped a foot straight up, twisting in midair like a cat. She landed trembling violently and gasping for air.

A dark, shiny face peered at her from a stand of green bamboo ten yards behind her.

"Annja, thank God you're here," Easy Ngwenya said. "I've been hoping against hope—"

Fury filled Annja with a force to equal the fright that had picked her up and whipped her around a few jackhammer heartbeats before. "You murdering little witch!" she shouted.

Annja charged.

Easy's face creased in a frown. "Good Lord, please be quiet—" she began, obviously reacting more to the volume of Annja's exclamation than its content. Her dark eyes widened. She only just managed to duck and roll away as Annja swung for her head.

Easy rolled and snapped to her feet with the practiced grace of the gymnast she was. "What on Earth do you think you're—?"

"You killed them!" Annja screamed, berserk with anger, grief and the successive shocks of seeing three comrades die in such a short period of time.

She aimed a kick at the crouching woman. Easy flung herself to the right.

"Who?" Easy yelped as she sprang up.

"All of them!" Annja cried, running toward her. Easy darted behind a tree with a six-inch bole.

"All who?" she shouted, then ducked as Annja swung and missed again.

"Sir Sidney," Annja panted. "Isabelle Gendron. My friends. Who knows how many others?"

"I never did!" Easy said. "I never touched a hair on Professor Hazelton's dear old head. I've no idea who Isabelle Gendron is. And I—*holy shit!*"

The uncharacteristically vulgar exclamation burst from the young woman when the upper half of the tree she hid behind toppled abruptly to her right, crashing into some brush as unhappy monkeys bailed in all directions.

"How did you do that? And will you kindly quit trying to chop me in two with that bloody cleaver?"

Annja had summoned her sword when Easy had ducked behind the tree.

Annja hacked at her again. Easy dodged around the tall stump. Annja was as astonished as Easy was by the fact she'd cut through the tree with a single stroke. Now that she was trying she couldn't do it again. The blade went in halfway and stuck fast.

"Maybe you'll listen to reason now," Easy said, still keeping the trunk between herself and Annja. "I've killed people, yes. I've killed some today, as it happens. But I sincerely doubt any of them were remotely friends of yours—hey!"

After two ferocious tugs Annja had dislodged the blade from the grip of the green wood.

Annja raised the sword above her head, preparing for a mighty stroke. As she did Easy rolled into view on Annja's right, lying on her back on the short clumpy grass.

The muzzles of her twin Sphinx .40-caliber autopistols were like unwinking black eyes staring into Annja's.

"Now we've arrived at the standoff phase of our program," Easy said conversationally in her upper-class Brit accent. "You know no handgun bullet really has any such thing as stopping power—they won't prevent you splitting me like kindling with that bloody great pig sticker. But it will be a dead or dying hand that splits me, I assure you. So for the love of God, can we talk?"

Annja frowned as she considered. "That might be," she said deliberately, "a worthwhile idea."

Easy's right hand weapon flashed orange fire. Annja never heard the shot, nor the one that immediately followed. She did feel the heat of muzzle flares, and stings as bits of unburned propellant struck the exposed skin of her arm and cheek.

She did not launch a dying stroke. Because a pre-conscious part of her mind had registered how the young woman who held the purple-and-gold firearm with such unwavering steadiness had twitched a few degrees aside before the paling of the skin over a knuckle betrayed that Easy's body was preparing to fire.

Annja spun. As she did she heard a scream.

A small man dressed in dark green clothes and a blue turban was falling in the gap between wall fragments through which Annja had run in what now seemed another lifetime. His bare forearms were twined with tattoos. As he went down a dying reflex triggered a burst toward the slate-colored sky from his AK-47. The muzzle-flash was enormous. It lit the little clearing like a bonfire.

A storm of fire burst through the gap from the wall's far side. Annja couldn't see the shooters. Bullets clipped branches from trees and mowed down bamboo stalks thirty feet from the two women.

"That's torn it," Easy said. "Run!"

She took off on a course that led into deep brush, straight toward the mesa's center. Annja saw no choice but to follow. Unless she wanted to stand and fight at least one patrol of heavily-armed thugs. Or wander strange territory at random with night coming fast.

Even following a mortal enemy looked more attractive.

Easy seemed to slip between the branches and her boots landed lightly on the forest-floor mulch. Annja was acutely conscious of blundering like a rhino. Everything raked her face, legs and forearms. Everything made loud crackling and swishing sounds. The earth crunched and drummed beneath her feet.

But it made little difference. Annja had fired Kalashnikovs full-auto. She knew a person doing that didn't hear much else short of an artillery barrage landing right nearby. Stealth was no issue; speed might well mean life.

Easy turned sideways as she ran between trunks flanking the faint game trail she followed. When she passed through she almost casually extended her left arm to its full extent at an angle from her path.

As Annja squeezed after her, feeling the rough bark squeeze her boobs, Easy's Sphinx cracked off twice.

A figure collapsed forward out of a scrim of brush, a rifle falling from limp brown hands. This one wore a ratty nondescript shirt that was stained and a faded blue-checked sarong. His head was wound with a yellow turban.

That surprised Annja. She was pretty sure all the goons she had seen so far wore dark green uniforms or pseudouniforms, and definitely blue headgear.

She wasn't going to ask many questions right now nor get answers to them. The reconnaissance-by-fire had calmed down behind them, probably because the shooters had blazed off their whole 30-round magazines and were reloading. Occasional random bursts still ripped the heavy evening air, drowning out confused shouts from behind. All Annja could think to do was stick as close to Easy as possible. At least she seemed to know where she was going.

Without visible effort Easy vaulted a fallen log arching three feet from the forest floor. She kept running. Two men suddenly appeared behind her from a bush full of yellow flowers that seemed to be opening as night descended. They wore yellow headbands.

They carried M-16s, black and almost as long as they were tall. They raised them after the running

24

Not five minutes earlier Annja had been doing her furious best to harm Easy Ngwenya. Now she raised her right hand and summoned the Sword to save her.

Sensing something amiss, the closer man turned to look over his shoulder. She slashed backhand, descending left to right, diagonally right between wide shocked eyes staring from a mustached face.

He dropped as if his bones had instantly dissolved. Annja didn't break stride. A running horizontal forehand cut took the second gunman, totally unaware, right at the back of his sweaty neck beneath a yellow turban.

Annja ran past never glancing his way.

ANNJA PUT HER BACK to a tree and slid down. The rough bark of the bole rasped her skin through the light shirt she wore. She paid no attention.

woman, who hadn't noticed them. At this range Annja knew the gunmen could hardly miss by dumping their whole magazines after Easy.

They had not run that far—no more than a quarter mile, she guessed. But it had been across broken, blocked terrain, the lushly undergrown forest of the mesa top between increasingly sizable spills of masonry. And it had been high stress—nothing sucked energy out of your body as fast as combat.

Even though they had seen no sign of actual enemies since Annja had cut down the unsuspecting pair getting set to shoot Easy, her body had stayed on alert the whole way, jumping over tangles and bouncing off trees. Now she felt as if she'd kickboxed ten rounds and run a marathon.

Easy squatted on her haunches. Annja almost felt relieved to note the younger woman was panting like a dog, as well. Easy mopped at the sweat streaming freely down her high round forehead with a rag. It mostly redistributed the wetness. She took a canteen from her belt, drank deep, then tossed it to Annja without asking if the other woman wanted it.

She didn't have to. Annja needed it. She upended the bottle and drank greedily.

She threw the canteen back to Easy. "What the hell is going on?" she asked through gasping breaths. She was trying to control her breathing, channel it into the deep, slow respiration that would most efficiently re-oxygenate her fatigued muscles and calm her swirling thoughts and emotions. But it took huge force of even her strong and well-practiced will.

Easy drank again. She seemed to have her own panting under control already.

"Blue turbans," she said. "Grand Shan State Army. Marshal Qiangsha, proprietor. Self-proclaimed marshal, unquestioned warlord. Ethnic resistance army but mostly gangs. Qiangsha likes walks at sunset, Irish whiskey and sticking his enemies' heads on poles.

"Yellow turbans are Lord's Wa Army. Recruited from a tribe of backward, inbred Wa. It's politically incorrect to call them headhunters. That's exactly what this bunch were. Until they got converted from animism to fundamentalist Christianity by their current spiritual and military leader, Jerry Cromwell."

As they had fled, the sounds of a firefight broke out behind them. They died away to nothing before the two women halted to rest. Annja guessed the contestants had mainly wanted to back away and break contact with each other. Nobody was eager to get shot, and a couple of hostile patrols that happened to bump into each other had no real motivation to hang and bang to a conclusion.

"Jerry Cromwell?" Annja asked.

"Foreign name because he's a foreign bloke. A Yank, as it happens. Former cable television preacher sort of chap. Apparently made carloads of money off the faithful in his day. Big on Armageddon. I understand he left the States in rather a hurry, ahead of a slew of charges."

"Great," Annja said. She breathed almost normally now. Her lungs felt as if she'd been inhaling superheated sand. But at least she wasn't gasping anymore. "Another disgraced televangelist."

She sat with her knees up and her wrists draped

across them. She looked at the other woman. "He converted this Wa group from being headhunters?"

"I didn't say that," Easy said with a faint grin. "It was animism he got them to give up. The headhunting—maybe not."

"I'm not so sure the modern Shan bunch are much better. Heads on poles. Nice," Annja said.

"Oh, they're not," Easy said, "of course. But I suppose they'd argue that their headtaking is intended to send a message. Politics of meaning and all that. Whereas the Wa's is recreational. Much more civilized, don't you know?"

Annja grinned. She found herself liking this brash, brave young woman.

Whom, she recalled with a force like a kick to the gut, she had been trying to kill a few minutes ago. Whom she had accused of multiple murders herself.

She tried to recoup that righteous, avenging rage. She couldn't. Maybe it was just the fact she was so drained physically and emotionally—by so much more than the frenzied activities of the past few minutes. Maybe it had something to do with the fact she had just killed two men who had been trying to kill Easy Ngwenya. Then again, Annja didn't doubt for a nanosecond that they'd have killed her as quickly.

The young black woman looked at her with her head angled to one side. "Not so eager to vivisect me anymore, then?" she asked cheerfully.

Annja shook her head. "I don't know *what's* going on."

Easy let herself sit all the way down on her rump,

round and taut inside khaki cargo shorts not so different from the ones Annja wore.

"I have a bit of a line on local news," she said, "having been on the ground, as it were, these two days past. And wondering, I'll admit, what was keeping you."

She grinned. Annja felt a stab of irritation. But she could still muster no more than that. She was as befuddled as she was worn-out.

"But I admit I'm in a bit of a bother over why you were hollering about my murdering a lot of strangers while trying to reduce me to my component parts. If you'd care to elucidate—"

She waved a dark hand invitingly. Annja nodded.

"All right." She explained quickly and tersely the trail of corpses she thought Easy had left behind her on her search for the Temple of the Elephant.

"Oh, dear," Easy said. Her eyes were huge and round. It made her look fourteen. "I can see why you'd feel murderously inclined toward me."

She tightened her lips and tipped her head to the right again. "So why did you stop trying to kill me? Or not simply let that pair shoot me? Yes, I sensed something was going on and glanced back. And by that time one was down and the other's body was falling, so I put it from my mind and concentrated on flight."

Annja looked at her a moment. Too bad I didn't get the gift of reading a person's thoughts along with my magic sword, she thought. She hung her head loosely between her raised knees for a moment before answering.

"I'm not sure," she said. "You could have shot me

back there if you wanted to. I know you're fast enough to have got a couple of rounds into me. For that matter you told me to come along with you when we ran. You let me follow. It would have been easy for you to have left me behind in the meat grinder back there."

"Right," Easy said. "I admit I'm still a bit unclear on the concept of why you leaped to the conclusion that I was guilty of all that sordid homicide."

"Well, we're after the same thing, aren't we?"

Easy grinned at her again. "As we were in China," she said, "and I didn't notice either of us strewing corpses in our wake like a plague ship."

Annja shrugged. "Well. You're a criminal, frankly. You're the world's most notorious pot hunter—tomb robber. Given your disrespect for the law, how was I to know what was beyond you? Especially since you make such a show of going everywhere armed."

"You're a fine one to talk about that," Easy said. "But as for my being a criminal—is Yangon officially apprised of your presence in the happy land of Myanmar, by any chance?"

Annja said nothing.

"Thought so. Do I need to point out how copiously you're in violation of the SPDC's laws? I doubt you've reported the deaths of your comrades, even poor Dr. Kennedy. That's another slew of violations right there."

Annja shook her head. "But the SPDC's a brutal dictatorship," she said, "and its laws are unjust."

"Meaning, not to your liking," Easy said. "You're quick to condemn me for flouting laws I disagree with. Yet here you are, blithely doing the exact same thing."

Annja, cheeks flushing hot, started to refute her. The words caught in her throat. She couldn't say anything to that. Not without sounding like a jackass.

"But you're desecrating valuable archaeological sites," she said, "destroying context and stealing the priceless heritage of the local peoples."

"Exactly what claims of ownership local peoples have to these artifacts are tenuous at best," Easy said, "especially given that the artifacts were in the vast majority of cases left behind by some other group altogether. As often as not the local people's contribution to the relics' provenance was to move in and slaughter their creators wholesale. And how often do these local groups get to keep their relics, actually ancestral or not? Doesn't the government almost always swoop in and carry them off?"

"Yes, but they're official caretakers—"

Easy snorted. "So's the Tatmadaw Kyee," she said, "and you seem to have a firm grip on the kind of care they take. Are you really that sheltered, that you don't know how often the artifacts you see in the museums, or even in crates in the basement, are replicas—often not even good replicas—of objects sold to government-favored private collectors?"

Annja said nothing. It was one of those things archaeologists weren't supposed to talk or even think about. Just as abundant, irrefutable evidence of Mayan human sacrifice had been an open secret for at least a generation of anthropologists, at the price of ostracism and early-onset career death if they spoke aloud what they knew.

"And haven't you read any of the documentation I've written? I've never disrupted context, Annja—you should know that if you've done your homework."

"Well—" Annja sighed and shook her head. She knew she was right. But somehow she couldn't muster the arguments to demonstrate the facts so that Easy would have to face them.

Somehow they didn't seem to matter, right here, right now.

"Does anybody ever win an argument with you, Easy?" she asked wearily.

"You know, my father took to asking that very question, in the final few years before we stopped speaking to one another altogether."

"So what now?" Annja asked after a few moments. The evening had congealed nearly to night. The sky was indigo with streaks of sullen red and green, and the evening chorus of bugs and birds and monkeys was just tuning up.

"If you're on for a bit more of a hike," her companion said, standing, "then let's go along and meet the folks."

"The folks?"

Easy nodded. "The Protectors of the Precious Elephant, who've guarded this mesa since the Bagan Empire fell to the Mongols seven centuries ago."

25

"Many ages ago, the Kingdom of Bagan ruled over Burma."

The speaker was a man severely shrunken by the decades, who probably hadn't been big to start with. His face was full of seams and wrinkles. His white beard, though silky and growing to his navel, seemed to consist of about a dozen hairs.

Firelight danced on the faces of towering blocks of stone, and on the faces of the people clustered between them. These were anything but stoney—the assembled villagers were alive with eager curiosity and anticipation.

"In those years, many were the temples they built, and glorious. And none more glorious than the Temple of the Precious Wheel, and above it the crowning glory of the Temple of the Precious Elephant!"

The onlookers gasped and murmured in appreciation. They had to have heard this story a hundred times before. But Annja knew that, just as few people ever got tired of talking about themselves, fewer still got tired of hearing about themselves. And this was the story of the people of this lost jungle-clad mesa rising from the Shan Plateau.

The old man spoke in a nasal singsong—Mandarin, in fact. That appeared to be for the benefit of the outsiders—specifically Easy, who translated for Annja. The Protectors, as the people of the mesa called themselves, spoke a Burmese dialect. But either they all also knew Chinese, or they knew the story enough to know what was being said.

"For centuries Bagan ruled wisely and well. Then came the people from the north—the Mongols who ruled China. The princes and the leaders and the monks went away to fight with them. So great was the arrogant pride of Narathihapate the Great King that he led his armies into Yunnan to meet the enemy.

"That pride was the downfall of Bagan. The Mongols defeated the forces of the king. His own son murdered him. The Mongols invaded and conquered the land."

He paused as if to draw breath, shaking his silver-topknotted head as if in weary regret of the follies of the past. And, if Annja was any judge, for dramatic effect. The old guy was a master storyteller.

"Those of the nobles and monks who had not left to fight, and fall, alongside King Narathihapate fled to the capital, where in due time the Mongols crushed them. Before leaving here our masters charged us to guard the holy places. Not against wood, nor wind, nor water—these things would work what they would work, and their working would in time help to hide this sanctum from the wicked.

"We were left behind to defend the sacred things from the hands of desecrators. And so we have—no Mongol who set foot upon the plateau lived to take the tale back to his khan. Nor has any foe since.

"Yet now we are beset from two directions at once. And so we face the most bitter fight of our history or the dishonor of defeat."

The people rose to their feet shouting and waving their fists. I wonder what Phil would've made of them? Annja wondered. They were certainly isolated, simple tribal folk, to all appearances—preindustrial enough even for a purist like Dr. Kennedy. Yet far from being pacifists, they seemed eager to confront their lowland enemies. And not with protest songs and garlands of flowers, unless she misjudged their mood badly.

The village lay two or three miles in from the edge of the steep-sided mesa, and about half a mile from the jut of rock on which the Temple of the Elephant perched. The ruins beside the plaza rose to a *wat* of impressive dimensions. It was so thoroughly shrouded in jungle vegetation that from any distance, or even from the air, it would seem nothing more than a natural hill. Annja knew that was probably why the ruin had escaped detection for so long.

The dwellings were perfectly integrated into the tangle of worked stone and riotous growth. The Protectors seemed to make no use of the remaining enclosures, whether to avoid desecration or from practical concern they might cave in at any moment. Instead they wove their huts in among them. These, too, were cunningly worked, incorporating living limbs and vines in the roofs and very walls, so that they were hard to spot until you were right on them. The villagers lived off fruit and small animals, and by working hundreds of dispersed garden plots so tiny and irregular that even from the air they wouldn't scream out *cultivation*.

Obviously avoiding aerial detection hadn't been part of the original intent, although the Protectors' practices worked to an extent against it. After a century of aviation, though, Annja suspected the villagers had adapted to improve their overhead security. They struck her as smart, resourceful folk. Though she was no social anthropologist, she knew the study of these people and their society would be as fascinating and fruitful in its way as exploring the entire vast complex of ruins.

Enthralled at hearing their own story, the villagers seemed to have forgotten the outsiders. Easy sat beside Annja. The younger woman was smiling and shaking her head.

"It's ironic, you know," Easy said.

"How's that?"

"These people aren't warriors, or at least, their ancestors weren't," Easy said. The bonfire, head high to Annja, gilded her face with ever-shifting highlights. "They're descended from the builders of the temple complex."

"I see."

"Do you?" Easy said with a slight, infuriating smile. She had a tendency to show off, Annja thought.

Still, she's smart and she's spent time here. I'd better sit on my own ego, bite my tongue and listen up.

"They aren't descended from the princes and priests," Easy explained. "But rather, the architects and the master masons. The people who designed and physically built these enormous structures."

"Oh." It put an interesting spin on the story.

"They made the perfect caretakers, of course. Over time the other people who hadn't run off to join the army or fled the Mongols probably wandered away or simply starved—this mesa won't support a large population. These folks are just barely at the point of maintaining sufficient genetic diversity, although there's intermarriage with tribes from the surrounding plateau. And people from here often go into the outside world, sometimes returning with spouses or at least children. They and their culture, and the whole wat complex, aren't lost so much as hidden."

Annja nodded. She'd experienced that before with the hidden Amazon city of Promise. But the Promessans had retreated from the world deliberately. Whereas they built a hidden civilization that was palpably more technologically advanced than the outside world, the Protectors seemed content to maintain traditional lifestyles.

"Don't they have trouble when some want to leave?" Annja asked.

"Surprisingly, no," Easy said. "They lose some that way, of course. But their culture keeps alive a sense of mission. I believe they're awaiting the return of Gautama, or reincarnation of Vishnu, as Maitreya. Like a lot of Buddhists in this part of the world they mix their faith up with the mother religion pretty liberally."

THROUGH THE COMPACT BINOCULARS Easy Ngwenya had handed Annja, the men in the dark green not-quite-uniforms and blue turbans looked like roaches climbing the cliff's red face with the aid of piton-anchored ropes. The two women lay on their stomachs on a high point on the cliff 150 yards or so to the west. The invaders had found a groove worn through the rock so that they were able to climb at an easier angle. It was still a risky business.

But the Grand Shan State Army had no idea how risky it really was. Out of sight beyond the head of the cut a trio of small, wiry Protectors, wearing drab sarongs and headcloths, worked diligently at a tilted slab with pry bars and chisels. The red sandstone was prone to fracture along a plane—the same phenomenon that killed Patty Ruhle.

As Annja watched a flat piece of rock the size of a Volkswagen chassis suddenly shifted and broke free with a grinding sound. The Shans raised their turbaned heads to see doom accelerating down at them.

It smashed the top two men outright. The man right below turned and jumped down reflexively—a bad move, given that he was about sixty feet up. He bought himself about a second more of life. The stone slab was constrained in the channel the men had been climbing up. Banging off the sides in pink sprays of rock dust, it smashed two more men off. Then it struck an outcrop, bounced, went end over end away from the cliff.

That spared the half dozen men below it in the chute. However, it landed on two more waiting their turn to climb from the ground below. The more prudent turned and ran.

The Protectors, for their part, acted like pros. Reminding Annja of the football coach's admonition to his players to "act like you've been there before" when scoring touchdowns, they didn't indulge in any boastful triumphant display. They just turned to make their escape.

A Shan militiaman on the ground shouldered an RPG and launched a grenade toward the head of the narrow cut running down the cliff where the rock had tumbled. More by luck than wizard aim his rocket-propelled grenade struck near the top of the outcrop from which the defenders had levered the boulder. It went off with a white flash and a vicious crash that went like needles through Annja's eardrums into her brain.

Vaporized copper from the shaped-charge head and a shotgunlike spray of shattered rock blasted the nearest Protector in the back. He fell on his face thrashing. His comrades grabbed his arms to pull him away. The right one came off in his companion's hand.

Annja jerked back from the binoculars. Beside her Easy grimaced.

"Hard luck, that," she said.

"Maybe we'd better shift out of here, too," Annja said. Although they'd been careful she realized with a sick shock she couldn't be sure she hadn't been spotted from the ground, although with the sun over their left shoulders there was little chance of a lens glint giving their position away. She also did not feel like betting her life that had just been a lucky shot.

"These aren't helpless farmers, you see," Easy said as they trotted back away from the cliff.

"No," Annja said.

"But here's the rub," Easy said, "the cold equations. The Protectors have about a hundred effective fighters, including some pretty young and pretty old. The Lord's Wa Army is bringing four times that number against them, the GSSA almost five.

"Our friends had every advantage in that ambush. Granted, that shows their skill—it's part of the art of ambush, after all, knowing how to stack the deck in one's favor. And a lucky shot by a Shan militiaman did greater hurt to our side than a well-conceived and executed ambush from the heights did theirs."

Annja felt the corners of her mouth draw back in dismay. She had felt nothing but exultation over their victory, then grief for the loss of a brave man whom she didn't actually know. What Easy told her now sat in her stomach like badly curdled milk.

"If they had modern weapons—and the sort of near infinite resupply it takes to use them in battle—the Protectors could dig in along the heights and stand

both armies off forever. They lack such weapons—
don't like them, actually. They fear to use them lest
they become dependent upon them to fight effectively."

"And you agree with that?" Annja asked in surprise.
Easy was well-known as a technophile.

Easy laughed. "Oh, yes. In this instance. They lack
the resources to support that kind of war, having no
income from the ever-lucrative drug trade, nor the
support of wealthy and delusional American funda-
mentalists—nor the likely support of shadowy U.S.
government agencies.

"And anyway that kind of Gallipoli-style stand
would work an even greater disaster on them. They
could withstand anything short of a heavy artillery
bombardment. Neither the Shan nor the Wa have such
artillery. The Tatmadaw Kyee does in abundance. And
the noise of protracted firepower-intensive battle would
surely attract their attention. And I doubt I need to tell
you what would follow then."

"No," Annja said. She looked at her companion.
"So why the sudden interest in this place, anyway?"

Easy shrugged. "Coincidence, it appears. Truly.
Marshal Qiangsha, the GSSA supremo, has taken it
into his head that this would make an ideal base of operations for his drugs concern, as well as his war with
Yangon. Unfortunately, Jerry Cromwell and his Wa
have got the same notion. Of course, Cromwell has to
have an additional bee in his bonnet—he's declared the
temples and all the relics within them are abominations
in the eyes of the Lord and must be expunged."

"Even though they're mostly ruins?"

"Apparently they're not ruined enough. Too impressive by half. So he wants to dynamite the lot and then use the mesa as a base to spread his brand of righteousness across the Shan Plateau and, presumably, all of Southeast Asia."

"So he wants to do for this archaeological treasure what the Taliban did for the statues of Buddha at Bamiyan?" Annja asked, horrified.

"The very thing. A bit of an irony, that, really. He gets financial support from certain right-wing fundamentalist groups stateside because he claims to be battling Islamic terror," Easy said.

"You mean he doesn't fund his operations through drugs the way Qiangsha does?"

"I didn't say that. Truth to tell, I don't know. Still, one thing I've noticed about true believers of every stripe—being utterly and inalterably convinced that you know the real truth, the only truth and nothing but the truth doesn't translate to decent behavior the way everybody thinks it does. Rather, once you start from the standpoint of unassailable righteousness, it's no trick to rationalize any atrocity whatever, so long as you claim it's directed against the wicked."

Easy shrugged. "It's even possible both commanders believe the mesa will provide them a stronghold secure against the full might of the Myanmar armed forces. I think that's a faint hope myself, but they'd not be the first to think that way."

Annja remembered the heat-lightning flicker and

the rumble of distant rocket artillery vibrating right up through her bones into her belly. "I don't think there's much hope at all."

Easy laughed without joy.

"What about the Protectors?" Annja asked. "What're the invaders' plans for them?"

"Qiangsha is looking to enslave them, I gather, based on past performance. Basically force them to provide food and labor to his merry men. Cromwell feels that Protectors of pagan abominations—in this case, in more ways than one, 'Pagan' is the old spelling of the kingdom now known as Bagan—are themselves abominations in the eyes of the Lord, hence worthy of extirpation."

Annja made a sour face. "Chalk up another moral victory for religion."

"Oh, yes," Easy said sweetly. "Militant atheists like Pol Pot and Mao Tse-tung would never get up to large-scale mischief such as genocide."

Annja's expression got sourer. "Do you ever get tired of being right all the time?"

The younger woman laughed. "Oddly, my father used to say that, too."

"I'm beginning to empathize with him," Annja said.

They walked a time in silence. Monkeys scolded them from the trees. Birds called. Bugs trilled.

As they walked Easy regarded the taller woman sidelong. "There's not really anything keeping us here," she said in a leading way.

"Do you feel like abandoning these people to their fate?" Annja asked.

"No. But then I have what might be seen as an overly sentimental fondness for tribal peoples—especially inasmuch as I come from one myself. Then, too, I have a reflex hatred of injustice. I don't care to see these brave people crushed."

"Hatred of injustice?" Annja said, legitimately surprised. "But what about your disregard for the law?"

"Do you really believe law and justice are the same thing? Do you believe there's any necessary connection between them? And as I've asked before—if you really believe so strongly in hewing to the letter of the law, where's your permission slip from the SPDC?"

"All right, all right," Annja said. "It's just that your activities—"

"My tomb robbing, as you'd call it? My pot hunting? All those other flip pejorative phrases you academic archaeologists use to reassure yourselves that you're righteous grave robbers, while those whose methods differ are not?"

Annja winced. That's not fair! she wanted to protest reflexively. Yet she had to admit there was truth in what the younger woman said. At least a little.

"We have a different conception of what's right, perhaps," Easy said. "But am I wrong in believing you possess a strong urge to defend what you feel is right? And are our differences really that wide, at least where human decency is concerned?"

"No," Annja said deliberately. "No, I guess not. But should we let ourselves lose track of why we're both here?"

"What do you mean?" Easy asked.

Annja stopped and faced the shorter woman. "You came to seize the Golden Elephant, didn't you?"

Easy looked at her calmly. "Yes. Didn't you?"

It hit Annja like a sucker punch. *I did.* She had gotten so wrapped up in her conviction that her race with Easy to the Temple of the Elephant was a primal contest between good and evil, that she was trying to preserve an ageless archaeological treasure from the bloody claws of a soulless murderess that she forgot she was trying to grab the idol, too. For profit. To sell to the mysterious private collector who had contacted Roux.

Of course, now that the secret seemed to have gotten out, she could say she was only trying to keep it out of the clutches of the Yangon government. But didn't she believe national governments were the righteous protectors of their people's heritage? And how about the near-total certainty that the State Peace and Development Council would melt the idol down, the Bamar people and their heritage be damned?

"Are you all right, Annja?" Easy asked with what sounded like genuine concern. "You've gone rather ashen, and your breathing is shallow."

"An acute attack of conscience," Annja said. "Never mind. We do need to know where we stand, though."

"Relative to—?"

"Each other," Annja said grimly. "And the idol."

Easy nodded. "Fair enough. I'm willing to bind myself to do nothing toward recovering the idol until the people of the mesa are safe—or until I've died trying to keep them that way. As for the idol…there's time enough to settle that when this thing's resolved and we both stand before it. And I am also willing, if you are, to give my word to do my best to make sure we both come to stand before the idol, of our own free will on our own two feet."

"Why should I believe that?" Annja said.

Easy shrugged. "Why believe the other, then? We can do this the Easy way, or—"

She let it trail away with a little smile. Annja frowned.

Easy's protestations rang true to Annja. The Zulu princess's motivations might differ radically from her own. Yet nothing she knew or had seen of Easy's actions indicated that she did things without reason. And once her rival had spoken to Sir Sidney or even if, despite her denials, she'd talked to Isabelle, what point would there be in killing them? Annja wasn't sure what the point would be for anyone to do so—and that was a loose end that bothered her.

But the fact was, having met Easy, listened to her voice, seen her body language, looked into her eyes— Annja believed her.

Perhaps the woman was that good an actress. And then again, if she was really that sociopathically ruthless, she'd had plenty of opportunity to finish off her rival. She could then have made her own way to the Temple of the Elephant while the Protectors were distracted with the unprecedented double threat to their holy mission and very way of life. She could have made away with the idol, leaving all concerned to their fates. Surely the person who beat a harmless old man to death, and shot an innocent woman, wouldn't hesitate to do exactly that.

"All right," Annja said. "I'll swear. How do guys handle this kind of thing?"

"Customarily with some ridiculous, unacknowledgedly homoerotic ritual," Easy said. "While I've no aversion to that sort of thing, I suspect you're much too straitlaced to be comfortable with it. So why not just shake hands? Or would you Americans cross your hearts?"

Annja looked at her a moment. Then, solemnly, she crossed her heart.

Easy did likewise. Then they broke out laughing and hugged each other.

As they walked on toward the village, Easy said, "Well, now that we've got the awkward bits out of the way, there's a very real question of what we can do to help the villagers except die futilely and bravely at their sides. Which, while satisfying on a certain teen-angst level, is hardly useful."

"Wait," Annja said. "The Protectors seem to base their whole strategy on hit-and-run attacks, traps and ambushes."

"The classic resource of the weaker defender against the stronger invader," Easy said. She shrugged. "Also, they work."

"And they have," Annja said, "for almost a thousand years. But what if that's too long?"

"For success—" Easy began. Then she stopped and grinned and once again looked even younger than she was. "Oh. A light begins to dawn."

"We can let go of the comforting neocolonial illusion of being superior minds from the West come to save the savages through enlightenment," Annja said.

"Ouch," Easy said. "Especially since I really do fear I resemble that remark."

"But what we can bring," Annja said, "is a fresh perspective, yes?"

"After almost a millennium," Easy said, " a habit of thinking can be tough to break."

"My point exactly. Never before have the Protectors faced two powerful and determined foes at the same time. And I think their long strings of successes may just be blinding them to the obvious."

Easy stopped and looked at her. "I have to admit I was blind to it, too," Easy said. "But now that you rub my nose in it…"

"It's pretty obvious, isn't it?" Annja asked. "To an outsider."

Easy nodded decisively. "Yes," she said. "So it is."

"The only problem," Annja said, "is selling it to the Protectors."

Easy's grin came back wider than before. "Oh, don't forget the Protectors are well aware of the modern world. Some have even lived in the United States. They may disdain modernity, but on the other hand, if anything I think they overestimate its abilities and powers. A fact we can shamelessly exploit—to their advantage, of course."

"Isn't that a classic Western-colonialist attitude?" Annja asked.

"Did I ever claim to be perfect? Come on, Annja. Are you in or out?"

Annja laughed. She couldn't help liking the woman, despite their differences.

"You know I'm in," she said. "I guess I'm not perfect, either."

26

Sometimes I have to admit, Annja thought, the old ways are the best ways. Which was hardly a radical thought for a professional antiquarian such as herself.

The Lord's Wa Army carried mostly American-made equipment, prominently M-16 automatic rifles. Annja suspected they had been funded, at least, by the CIA. The grenades that dangled like heavy metal fruit from their web gear had a made-in-America look to her, as well, although she knew much less about grenades than she did guns. However they got that way, they were frighteningly well armed.

Given the fearful reputation the mesa enjoyed among the surrounding tribesfolk, according to Easy, the Wa patrol seemed ridiculously incautious. Maybe they believed God was keeping a special eye out for them.

In which case He was just about to blink.

Annja didn't see the hidden trigger. Then again, neither did the point man. He was walking along, his long black rifle held in patrol position in front of him, when with no warning, a four-inch-thick sapling that had been bent until its top touched the ground snapped upright into his face and body.

The trunk had eighteen-inch wood spikes jutting from it.

The point man, massively and multiply impaled, didn't even have time to scream. He emitted a brief squealing grunt, then hung limply from the blood-tipped spikes. His comrades dived off to both sides of the narrow game trail they'd been following.

Some of them screamed, though, and very loudly, as hands and feet plunged into small concealed pits, themselves dug no more than a foot or two into the jungle clay, to be pierced by needle-sharp slivers of bamboo.

The patrol's undamaged members opened fire. The poorly trained, panicked men shot high. As Annja and her escort of four grinning Protectors slipped away through the brush, a burst clipped branches ten feet over their heads.

No one else came close.

THE LAST MAN IN the line stopped and slapped a tattooed hand to his neck. He looked annoyed by the forest insect that had just bitten him. The rest of the eight-man GSSA patrol moved out of sight, hardly more noisily than a herd of water buffalo, around a curve in the trail through tall grass.

The last man blinked. A curious expression crossed his mustached face.

He then pitched over in the grass and lay still.

"Neat," Easy Ngwenya said softly to her companion.

Although it wasn't common on the Shan Plateau, the Protectors had somehow acquired the art of the blow-pipe. For its ever-necessary complement—fast-acting poison—they used some manner of secret decoction whose effects, on the visual evidence, bore a striking resemblance to curare.

Dr. Philip Kennedy, whose work Easy rather admired, would've been quite fascinated at the intersection of sociology and biochemistry. It was a pity Annja Creed had gone and mislaid him, she thought. Although from her own account, despite her best efforts to claim all responsibility, it was clear to Easy that the silly self-important sod had gone and mislaid himself. Self-importance seemed an occupational hazard among cultural anthropologists, she had noted, and ethnobotany wonks in particular.

"Come on," said her companion in piping, urgent English.

Easy looked down. Short as she was she saw eye to eye with most of the Protectors. The adults, that is. Her guide was a young man who had spent two years in America. He insisted on being called Tony.

The rest of the party, the actual blow-pipe men and

their guards, were armed with spears and singe-edged bladed weapons like swords with hilts at ninety degrees to the blades, which they held along their forearms. They had already moved out toward the preselected position from which they'd pick off the next Grand Shan State Army man to be last in line. They'd keep up the game until they were discovered. Or until they ran out of intruders.

Either outcome was satisfactory. The survivors would bear back to Marshal Qiangsha with tales of silent death from the bush; or the lot would vanish. In either case, the marshal would find his men unwilling to come this way again, no matter how he might threaten and bluster.

And if they did, of course, the Protectors would ring in more fiendish surprises on them. They had a wonderful selection, really, Easy thought. They had been collecting them for centuries, it seemed, like avid little hobbyists.

Impatient, her guide started off through the bush. Like his older fellows, he glided through the thick undergrowth as noiselessly as a shadow. Easy's bush craft was good and she knew it. But she envied these people their skills.

She concentrated keenly on what the boy was doing as she made to follow him. A true professional was always learning.

"HOW GOES THE WAR?"

Despite herself Annja smiled. They had rendezvoused amid especially high walls of stone, where monkeys capered and screeched as they leaped among the lianas in the velvet lengthening shadows of late afternoon. Like their Protector allies Easy was bright eyed and practically vibrating with excitement.

Annja was, too.

"Goes pretty well so far," she told her ally who had so recently been her enemy. "We didn't inflict too many casualties. But we've definitely got them moving in the right direction."

"Ah, but that's the whole point of the exercise, isn't it?" Easy said.

"Best of all," Annja said, nodding, "is that we didn't take any ourselves."

"We, neither," Easy said with an answering grin. It quickly faded.

"But that can't last," she said.

"I know," Annja said, frowning.

ANNJA CROUCHED BEHIND a waist-high rampart of crumbling red brick. Some freshly cut brush, arranged on top of the wall, hid her neatly from observation by the Shan patrol noisily crunching its way through the woods toward them. Thermal imaging, she knew, would show the cut foliage. But the Shans didn't have any.

Tony crouched at her side, ready for anything. He said nothing.

A dozen adult warriors crouched behind the varying-height wall to either side of her, and behind stumps or in depressions in the uneven ground. They were very careful not to walk or hunker down behind Annja.

The first members of the GSSA patrol came into view across a clearing fifty yards wide. The blue-turbaned men in their dark-green battledress, some solid colored, some jungle camouflage, were smoking and joking. Loose and easy.

They thought they'd found a route delightfully free of booby traps, or ambushers who struck silently and fled, often before the survivors knew they had been attacked.

Annja raised an RPG to her shoulder and peered through the low-power optical sight.

The RPG was part of the booty scavenged by Protector scouts from their victims of the actions the day before. As were the AKMs and ancient AK-47s Annja's companions held.

As she sighted, instinct took over. Slipping her finger inside the trigger guard, she drew in a deep breath. The weapon felt lightweight and cheap, in contrast to the chunky solidity of a Kalashnikov rifle. But then, the launcher only had to shoot once.

She snugged the weapon in, let out half the intaken breath and squeezed.

With a great whoosh the rocket-propelled grenade streaked from the launcher, surrounding Annja with nasty, acrid, dirty-white propellant smoke. It also sent a long jet of flame out the rear end of the tube.

The rocket motors made a loud, furious buzzing as

they sent the missile spiraling toward the target. It struck with a silver-white flash and the hideous high-frequency crack of its shaped-charge warhead that was so hatefully familiar to her.

She still didn't care for it much. Even from the other side.

The grenade blew a great yellow wound in the tree's hard wood a dozen feet above the turbaned heads of the patrol. Long splinters flew in all directions. To either side of her the Protectors held their Kalashnikovs over their heads and, whooping enthusiastically, blasted away with them.

Lowering the spent launcher, Annja took her eye from the scope. She had to fight to control the trembling of her hands and even remember to breathe.

Three of the Shan militiamen had fallen to the ground right below the grenade's impact point. Two of them flopped around vigorously and screamed shrilly. That pleased Annja in a grim way. The point was to sting the Shans enough to anger them, without hurting them badly enough to rout them or even send them to ground.

At once the Shans did what most other troops in the world, trained or not, did when unexpectedly taken under fire—they dumped their whole magazines as fast as their full-auto actions would cycle in what they hoped was their enemy's direction. As far as Annja could tell they came no closer to hitting her hidden comrades than the Protectors did to them. And the Protectors were trying to miss.

A terrible agonized scream pealed from right beside Annja's right elbow. It was loud enough not just to be audible but painful even above the ear-punishing racket of assault rifles cracking off close on either side.

Annja threw the empty launcher away from her as if it were hot and spun.

Tony squatted at her side. He had his hands cupped around his mouth, which was wide open. He rolled his eyes at her.

"How'd I do?" he asked.

"Great," Annja said, a little unsteadily. A beat late she realized his unearthly shriek was intended to convince the enemy their ridiculously poorly aimed fusillade was having lethal effects. The kid was a natural, no question. "Now yell what I told you to," she said.

His inhalation seemed to swell his skinny body to twice its normal size. "Run away!" he screamed.

Laughing, the Protectors threw away their emptied weapons. They refused to fight with them, both for the cogent reasons they expressed and also, Annja suspected, because they thought them unmanly.

But the Protectors loved a good ruse. The sneakier and more underhanded the better. They were only too happy to fire the captured firearms once Easy persuaded them they were only noisemakers, to bait the trap. There was something seemingly universal in the human animal that absolutely loved making loud noises, especially when accompanied by big flashes of fire. She wondered what Phil Kennedy would make of that.

Wish I could ask him, she thought with a twinge.

She joined her companions racing into the jungle. Behind them the Shans, shouting in triumph, began to advance in cautious pursuit.

"ALL RIGHT, EASY," the young woman said softly to herself. "Piece of cake."

In each strong hand she held the pistol grip of an American-made M-16, recovered from Wa Army men unexpectedly recalled to their Lord. Each had a full 30-round magazine in the well. She carried no reloads. If all went well, she wouldn't need them.

And if things went poorly…she wouldn't need them, either.

The plans were all laid out for a faux ambush similar to the one she knew Annja Creed should be stage-managing scarcely half a mile away that same moment. Even as she thought that, firing broke out furiously from not very far behind her. She smiled.

Easy had tossed the plans promptly in the dustbin when her Protector scouts, slipping from the jungle as effortlessly and undetectably as wraiths, announced that the Wa patrol they were shadowing was just about to pass within thirty yards of a dead bold— or dismally lost—Shan patrol on a roughly recipro-cal heading.

It was too good an opportunity to pass up.

She had shucked off her pack, all her gear except the lightweight tropical-pattern shoulder holsters that held her custom-made Sphinxes, sent them off with her escorts scampering for what should be relative safety a quarter mile deeper into the ruined temple complex.

Now she crouched clad only in black sports bra, cargo shorts and hiking boots, taking deep abdominal breaths to calm herself. To either side she heard the sounds of the mutually hostile patrols—boots crunching leaf litter, branches crashing, voices laughing or cursing, depending on whether the speaker was the man who got hit in the face by a branch or an amused bystander. The only thing that kept each column of twenty or so men from hearing the other was their own noise.

She drew in one last breath. Then, crossing her arms beneath her breasts to point the two black rifles to right and left, she launched herself in a dead run right between the passing enemy patrols.

27

As she ran flat out Easy Ngwenya ripped short bursts from both rifles. To her left ran a low course of ruined wall, with one full window arch, thoroughly entwined in vines, intact. To her right nothing but a thin screen of vegetation stood between her and a score of hostile heavily armed intruders.

She didn't aim. That wasn't possible. Nonetheless, from the corner of her eye she saw the dark-uniformed Shan point man on her left crumple like an empty sack without so much as twitching his Kalashnikov. She felt the old hunter's exultation at drawing blood.

Just run! she ordered herself, and did.

Gunfire rattled in her wake as if she were a running fuse lighting off strings of firecrackers in passing. These were not troops disciplined enough to aim under the best of circumstances. They fired not at her but at the flash of motion and flickering fire that tore at the edges of their peripheral vision. By that time they were too late—except for hosing their equally astonished opposite numbers thirty yards away through the bush. Easy was in no danger from the men she passed beyond the usual stray-round risk.

The problem was the tumult inevitably alerted the men in front of her, as well.

Well, the Easy way wasn't always the *easy* way. Not for E.C.

The air before her was suddenly ripped by muzzle-flames and blasts so terribly loud and powerful that the air itself seemed to shake. She unwound her arms. Her lightweight assault rifles were almost empty.

Her head snapped right. She caught a flash picture across the right-hand weapon's open sights on the mass of a man's chest. She held down the trigger, knowing the well was nearly dry.

Two shots snapped out before the bolt locked back. One must've hit. He started down.

She was already whipping her head the other way, lining up a second quick sight picture on a Shan fighter, trying to will her vision past the huge yellow flame billowing from his Kalashnikov's muzzle brake. She fired high.

The last round in her left-hand magazine snapped his head back. He toppled backward, dropping his heavy Russian-made gun.

She dived forward, letting the empty rifles fall. She landed in a forward roll but instead of snapping upright into the crossfire of the last elements of both patrols she came up on all fours and scuttled through the grass like a lithe lizard.

The near-panicked militiamen shot high. She made it to the comforting green embrace of the undergrowth unscathed. Ignoring thorns that raked her cheeks, arms and thighs, she slipped inside and was gone before the patrols even knew what had hit them.

"I FAILED," EASY SAID.

"We didn't fail," Annja said, hunkering down beside her in the plaza among the great stone ruins. Evening gloom gathered particle by mauve particle. It suited the mood. "*You* didn't fail."

"Tell that to them," Easy said, gesturing.

Five dead tribesmen lay under woven reed mats. Half a dozen wounded men moaned in the huts. The Protector women had gently but firmly chased Annja away when she tried to help care for them. Belatedly it struck her the Protectors probably had experience dealing with battle trauma. In fact, given the way their world was changing, she realized they probably knew quite a bit about bullet and high-speed fragment injuries, as well.

They had accepted with smiles of gratitude when Annja turned over her meager stock of medical supplies to them. These weren't as meager as they might have been—the Protectors had recovered Eddie Chen's body and backpack after sunset the first night here.

"Look," Annja said. "Your tactic worked—we got the two armies to fight."

"But it isn't stopping them," Easy said. She hunkered down with her arms draped over her bare thighs and her head hanging. "They just keep pushing toward the center of the mesa trying to get around one another's flanks."

Annja sat back on her own heels. It was true enough. That was where their plan, admittedly, had gone awry. Rather than simply going for each other, the two sets of invaders kept driving inward, dogfighting as they went. In the process they brought more force to bear than the sparse Protector warriors could handle, even with booby traps for force multipliers.

"We couldn't foresee that," Annja said. "It is delaying them. The Protectors are delaying them some, too."

Easy looked at her. "Do you really think that's going to be enough?"

No, Annja thought. No, I don't. She refused to say it. But she couldn't deny it.

The Protectors only maintained live booby traps in a zone around the perimeter of the mesa itself. With a millennium to work on their techniques they clearly had means of keeping track of where the traps were laid, but it was simply too hazardous leaving them all over the place where the drunk or merely inattentive might stumble into them. Or children at play. Also it took work; the Shan Plateau was dry by the standards of lowland Southeast Asia, but that still made it pretty wet by the standards of most other places. Things rotted quickly in the jungle.

The Protectors had displayed remarkable speed and efficiency setting traps to guide the rival ethnic armies into colliding. But that was in a very limited area. They didn't have time to set enough to halt the progress of the rolling gunfight that threatened the heart of their tiny nation.

Ironically, once caught up in a running gunfight, the invaders were less inclined to be slowed by threat of booby traps or ambush, rather than more. Walking cold-bloodedly into a mysterious, unfamiliar jungle, knowing some awful fate might take you at any minute, would grind down anybody's nerves. And when somebody did trip a deadfall—or vanished from the rear of a marching file, never to be seen again—what was bad enough in fact was magnified tenfold in emotional impact.

But when blood was hot, and spilling freely, and caps were being busted all around—it was war and men would face ridiculous threats without a second thought.

If nothing else, by dint of Easy hopping and expostulating in energetic Chinese, the Protectors had allowed themselves to be talked out of their taboo against using modern weapons pretty quickly, once it became lethally obvious that blow darts and bows were decisively overmatched in the situation. The Zulu woman struck Annja as remarkably persuasive.

For her part Annja felt vaguely like the serpent in the Garden of Eden for helping introduce them to firearms.

Some village men came in with AK-47s. Their famed ease of use had come in handy, and there were fairly abundant numbers available to be scavenged by people adept at sneaking through the woods.

Easy roused herself to go listen to their report. Exhausted by her own part in the day's strenuous events, Annja sat below a crumbling edifice and rested. In a couple minutes Easy returned.

"They say both sides have stopped for the night," she reported. "They don't like doing anything in the dark. Especially with all the danger from traps and ambushes. But they're already a quarter of the way here."

Annja grimaced. There were, as she appreciated even more keenly now than she had this morning, infinite ways a battle could shape up. The way this one had the only issue was whether the Protectors, and the timeless treasure they guarded with their lives, got overrun tomorrow or in a week. In either case the outcome looked inevitable.

"Quite," Easy said. Annja looked up at her. "Unless the Tatmadaw notices all the noise up here and decides to join in. Won't that be fun?"

"You have ESP, too," Annja said.

"I do," Easy said, with a tired little laugh, "but it's hardly necessary. Your thoughts show as clearly as if your forehead was an LCD screen. Under the circumstances, they're pretty inevitable thoughts, really."

"Maybe." Annja stood up. "But we aren't dead yet.

And while there's life, there's—well, not hope, maybe. But there's always something we can do!"

"Like what?" Easy said.

Annja sucked in a deep breath and let it out. Her head sagged; it felt like lead. But she would not let herself slump.

"I don't know," she said. "But there's one rule I live by."

"And that is?"

"When in doubt, bust stuff up."

ANNJA HEARD THE SOBBING from several feet away.

The woman sat just inside the brush that surrounded the central plaza. She had her knees drawn up and her arms clasped tightly about them. A huge, nearly intact structure rose to her right. The moon came up over the forest to the east.

Annja sat down by her side. She said nothing. Only waited.

"I'm afraid," Easy said in a broken voice.

Annja looked at her. Her normal impudent—arrogant—poise had deserted her. Its departure deflated her, left her looking like a small adolescent girl.

"Why?" Annja asked. "You don't seem to be afraid of death."

"Oh, I am," Easy said. Strangely, saying that seemed to calm her. If only slightly. "But that's not what really scares me."

Annja herself felt terrified. In action she settled into a sort of mindful trance—maintaining the invaluable presence of mind that was life in combat or any kind of blood crisis. Some of her combat instructors, like ex-SAS operator Angus, had remarked upon her gift. It was rare, naturally possessed by one in a thousand, or ten thousand, or even a million. All of special-operations training was designed to impart that ability. And even then it succeeded only part of the time.

But nothing made danger's imminence any easier to take.

Easy uttered a bitter laugh. "Death seems the easy way out right now."

"Correct me if I'm wrong, but I get the feeling that where you're concerned, the Easy way is really the hard way," Annja said.

"Found out for the fraud I am!" This time her laugh sounded more genuine. Annja felt a quick rush of relief. Maybe I'm getting through.

It was strange. We started as rivals, she thought. Adversaries on opposite sides of law—and right, she still believed, although she had long recognized those as two very different things. Then I hated her, as much as I've ever hated anyone.

Now I feel like her big sister.

She reached out an arm and hugged the woman to her. Easy almost melted into her. Annja held her for several minutes while she clung and sobbed as if her heart were broken.

At last the passion of grief and fear passed. Easy pulled away and smiled feebly. "I'm acting quite the fearless action heroine, aren't I?"

"You're acting human," Annja said. "Unfortunately, what we all need—me, the Protectors, even you—is the action heroine back."

Easy shook her head. "If only that were really me. And not just a pose."

"You feel like a phony?" Annja asked.

Easy nodded. "Just a little girl trying to get her daddy's attention. Maybe, if I am very, very good, his approval. Yet when I well and truly caught the attention of the parental unit the resulting explosion launched me an entire continent away."

"Welcome to the world, Princess," Annja said, surprised her own tone sounded bitter, and slightly embarrassed by it. "Everybody feels like a phony. Everybody lives in fear of being found out." She laughed, a little too sharply. "Heck, I thought you might be the exception."

"Not me," Easy said. "Overcompensation is my middle name."

"I thought it was Calf."

Easy goggled at her a moment. This time her laugh was free and clear.

But she clouded over again almost at once, huddled back over herself. "I thought I was so clever. Let's get the red ants and the black ants to fight. I thought it was the answer to all our problems."

"So did I," Annja said. "So did the Protectors. It wasn't just our best shot, Easy. It was a good idea."

"But it didn't work."

Annja shrugged. "Well, good ideas don't always.

And sometimes bad ones do. The best we can do is the best we can do."

Easy sniffled loudly twice. Then she sighed. "You're not going to allow me to indulge in self-pity, are you?" she asked.

"Nope," Annja said. "Not now. Maybe later. If we, you know, live."

Easy lifted her head and smiled at her. "You give me so much to look forward to."

Annja shrugged.

They sat in silence. Fifty yards away the villagers sat and talked or played soft music on reed flutes, among the firelit faces of the ancient walls of stone they had protected for a millennium from all enemies except the one no human wit nor valor could overcome— time. Around it all the nocturnal noise of the jungle wrapped like a membrane of noise, reassuring some- how.

"Did you really kill a lion with a spear?" Annja asked.

"Oh, yes. And somehow managed not to get disem- boweled in the process. Frightfully silly thing to do. Daddy was fearfully angry with Old Tom. He was his chief conservation officer. Which really meant *hunts- man*. Only it's shocking bad publicity to call it that."

Annja shook her head more in wonder than disbe- lief. "What on earth made you do a thing like that?"

"Bravado. I was raised to a warrior tradition. Also I had a need to prove I was the equal of any man, and then some. My father, you'll doubtless be shocked speechless to learn, was always disappointed his first-born, and as things turned out his only born, wasn't male. So I tried to show him I was good enough."

"But a spear?"

Easy shrugged. "Hunting lion with a rifle didn't seem much of a challenge. All you need to do is keep your wits about you to place your shot properly, and the poor beast rolls up at your feet dead as a stone. I never really understood how some people managed to panic and get themselves killed."

Easy cocked her head. Then she grinned. "Ah, yes. The ability to keep one's head in danger. A gift we share, I take it. Given that we've both survived our respective follies."

Annja managed to bite down on the words *so far.*

"I read about the Masai rite of passage," Easy went on, "where young boys proved themselves by killing a lion with a spear. Or proved their unfitness, and got out of the gene pool at the same time. I must admit a certain adolescent ethnic pride came into play—a tribal princess was not going to be outdone by a bunch of primitive gawks who wear caps made of red clay and cow crap on their heads."

Annja laughed.

"We're similar, Annja Creed," Easy said. "We're both rather too smart for our own good, with a tendency to overintellectualize. What saves us from the sterile ivory tower lives that most of our fellow intellectuals lead is a tendency to put our heads down and charge in straightaway, trusting to our improvisational skills to take us through. And a little bit of luck. Or am I mistaken?"

"No," Annja said, drawing it out, shaking her head. "I'd call it a pretty spot-on assessment. Even if a little uncomfortable."

"We can never be a great team," Easy went on earnestly, "precisely because we're so much alike. Our strengths and weaknesses overlap, rather than complement each other. In the present case, however, two women who are our precise kind of crazy may be exactly what's needed."

"And if it's not," Annja said, "we probably won't live long enough to worry about it much."

"Here, now!" Easy said sternly. "I thought you were in charge of positive thinking."

"Me? I thought it was *your* job!" Annja exclaimed.

They laughed. Probably, more than it was worth. But it kept them from breaking…

28

"The neighbors mocked him." Jerry Cromwell's voice rang through the camp of the Lord's Wa Army, pitched in the middle of an ancient plaza. He had sworn to eradicate it as an abomination in the eyes of the Lord. "Lord, how they mocked! But Noah worked on. He trusted in the Lord! The Lord of Israel, the Lord of Hosts!"

His voice, which sounded to Easy—lying on her belly in the underbrush—at once strained and over-enunciated, had electronic assistance. Dragging a generator up here made at least some sense. But who knew what possessed Cromwell to lug along speakers and microphones for a public-address system.

Apparently his followers felt reverence for his strident voice as it echoed among the crumbled massive cliffs of stone. In any event his actual sermon had to be translated by Wa translators with their faces hard beneath their distinctive yellow head wraps.

Their painfully young faces. Easy guessed the fallen preacher's translators, like the dozen bodyguards who stood flanking him with M-16s leveled at their own fellows, ranged from twelve to fourteen. It didn't make them any less dangerous, she knew—her own continent's recent history bore ample witness to that.

Easy lay scarcely fifty yards from the nearest of them. Sixty from their gangly, pasty-white messiah.

It isn't the marksmanship that makes the hunter, you see, she thought. It's the stalk.

Elephant Calf Ngwenya had been born into a culture which, for all its pride in its modernity, was very different from the one in which Annja had been brought up. Although an upbringing in a Catholic orphanage in New Orleans, Easy reckoned, was likely to be considerably more Darwinian than girls of Annja's race and class usually underwent. To Easy's mind that probably accounted much for the fact that Annja was a heroine, and not another ineffectual, overeducated wimp.

Warrior-princess though she was—she had always tried, not always successfully, not to be too smug about that—Easy harbored strong ethical standards when it came to killing people. It was not all right unless they were actively committing aggression. Then they became not only legitimate targets, but it was also an act of virtue to kill them.

Jerry Cromwell and his fanatics fell into that category as far as she was concerned. Easy still felt bad about the lion after all these years. He was mighty, a truly impressive beast, guilty of nothing more than doing what was natural for him.

She would dampen her pillow not at all over Jerry Cromwell. In the unlikely event she survived, of course.

She ignored the insects crawling over her exposed skin, and the long, gleaming, diamond-patterned serpent coiled on a branch above her, which she had quickly determined was a constrictor, unlikely to bite unless she grabbed it, and not in the least venomous.

Every day at noon, rain, shine or war, Cromwell gathered his followers about him to preach to them. He wasn't sufficiently crazy to pull fighters off the battle line to harangue them, though.

The Protectors were well aware of the Lord's Wa Army. The people of the temple routinely scouted potential foes wandering into their district. They had told Easy, laughingly, about Cromwell's preaching well before Annja arrived.

She understood his rationale—fanaticism was a flame that needed constant stoking. But any habit is a weapon to your enemies. One a huntress as skilled as Princess Easy planned to exploit.

She'd heard said of assassinations that anyone can be gotten at, no matter how well protected, as long as his or her would-be killer doesn't care about getting away alive.

Easy fully intended to escape. Of course, she reminded herself silently as she wriggled a few inches forward beneath the boughs of a bush, noiselessly as the snake who watched unblinkingly from above, between the thought and the action falls the shadow.

But the key thing was she would take her shot. She would make her shot. And then the chips would fall where they might.

"And so the rains came," Cromwell said. "And they fell and fell and fell—for forty days. And forty nights. Forty days!"

Easy could hear the way he used his tone of voice, his cadence, to stir the blood like a marching drumbeat.

The smell of the vegetation in which she hid was unfamiliar yet by no means strange. She felt a touch and froze. A lesser snake slithered across her left calf, then her right. She lay on her belly unmoving. She did not look back.

Best not to.

The serpent moved on. She couldn't hear its rustling for the preacher's declamations and the fervent responses of his congregation. Within a few heartbeats she forgot it. She focused her thought, her intent, her entire being on her stalk and its target.

She had penetrated well inside the Wa main camp. In itself that was small challenge, especially since she crossed the perimeter in the twilight half an hour before dawn, when human metabolism ebbed lowest and the guards were likely to be least attentive. The camp had been laid out without conspicuous regard to security. Apparently the great man believed his God would provide, or at least make up any shortfalls in his arrangements. Probably he couldn't take seriously that anyone might dare to threaten him here, in the midst of his bloodthirsty flock.

She was close as she cared to get now. She had a clear shot of under sixty yards—a simple shot, she considered, for a true marksman, even over open sights. She had the most accurate of the captured rifles, which she had tested and sighted in the previous afternoon.

A clump of brush lay even nearer the ancient stone stairway to nowhere Cromwell used as his podium. She felt confident she could reach it but she wouldn't. It was too obvious a lie-up for a sniper. The guards'd be on her in an instant like terriers on a rat.

Cromwell was working himself into a frenzy.

Wrapping the sling snugly about her left forearm, Easy propped herself on her elbows. She pulled the lightweight synthetic stock's steel buttplate firmly against her right shoulder. Keeping both eyes open, she sighted. She drew a deep breath, let half of it go.

The trigger surprised her when it broke. It surprised others even more.

The front of Cromwell's big oblong forehead blew out in a spray of blood and bone.

Easy let go of the rifle. It would serve no purpose now save to encumber her, for all its lightness. Instead she slid backward as quickly as she could and still remain relatively quiet. It was time to go. If she could.

Not that the noise she made particularly mattered. After a moment of staring in stunned silence at their living prophet, struggling to absorb the shocking fact of what they'd witnessed, the Wa faithful began to babble in terrified excitement.

The surrounding stone walls' amphitheatric effect abetted the already poor directionality of human hearing. Unable to tell exactly where the killshot had come from, the martyred prophet's bodyguards reflexively opened up with their assault rifles on the most obvious threat—Cromwell's own congregation.

29

The captor behind Annja's left shoulder gave her a rough shove. She stumbled. It was difficult to keep her balance with her hands tied behind her back. She went down hard, scraping her bare knees on eroded but still abrasive red paving stone.

The man who stood at the top of a brief broad flight of time-crumbled steps looked down on her with an expression she could only describe as quizzical on his mustached face. Behind him rose a largely intact building about the size of a suburban ranch-style house. Its doorway was an oblong of shadow. The self-styled Marshal Qiangsha, unquestioned commander of the outlaw Grand Shan State Army, looked younger than Annja expected.

When he spoke his own dialect, his voice was a well-modulated baritone. His tone was low but penetrating.

His voice gave the impression of being held in tight control.

I could be in trouble, she thought, if he turns out not to be the impulsive Third-World warlord type.

But then, she was neck deep in trouble anyway.

They had caught her that morning. Though she wasn't the skilled tracker and woodswoman Easy Ngwenya was, she had skills of her own. She had infiltrated past the Shan patrols circling outside the perimeter of their central encampment with relative ease. The Shan militiamen seemed preoccupied with not stepping into any *punji* traps, being crushed and impaled simultaneously by diabolical deadfalls or getting picked off with silent darts.

But the guards closer in to the great man's headquarters were more alert.

The first guttural shout from behind her confirmed she'd been caught by Shans. Surprisingly, the militiaman followed his challenge with, "Stop! You! Hands on head now!"

Kneeling, Annja straightened and clasped her hands obediently behind her neck. She had been crouching in what she thought was pretty good concealment, actually, a minivan-size clump of vegetation growing beside a roughly triangular, free-standing fragment of wall, eight feet tall and made of weathered three-foot blocks. All around her ruined stones rose like a Cubist rock garden. The marshal had chosen one of the more intact concentrations of ancient structures in the area, a mile or two from the central complex, as his current base of operations.

"Come out now," the Shan commanded. Annja stepped gingerly from the brush.

She found herself surrounded by the muzzle brakes of at least four AKMs. Annja wasn't the tactician Easy was. But she knew face-up fighting—and firearms handling. She knew perfectly well that if she simply dropped down flat on her face her captors would immediate cross-fire each other, dumping their entire magazines basically into one another at point-blank range.

She also knew the odds were pretty good at least one of them would be left functional. The thought of what he'd do to her for pulling a stunt like that drove the notion right out of her mind.

"You spy," her interlocutor said in his rough-and-ready English. "CIA." He grinned at her.

"I'm a photographer," she said. She used as thick a French accent as she thought might be understood by a guy whose English comprehension probably wasn't the greatest, and who was almost certainly used to hearing it spoken exclusively with an American accent. Burma's British colonizers had left a long time ago; the Americans had played in this particular murky pool way more recently, not to mention their culture covering the world like an old-time paint ad.

As for playing French, she guessed it was a fifty-fifty split whether the GSSA currently hated Americans or loved them.

She nodded toward the camera hanging on a strap around her neck. "I am a photographer," she said. *Une journaliste.*

The guy grinned and nodded. He was short a front incisor. The beard that fringed his mouth was scraggly.

"You spy," he affirmed cheerily.

A hand grabbed her arm. By reflex she pulled back.

It was a bad move. She knew that even before a Kalashnikov buttplate slammed into her right cheek. The stroke blindsided her, caught her totally off balance. A fat yellow-white electric spark flashed through her skull, behind her eyes but dazzling her like lightning hitting twenty feet away. She went down hard. She hardly felt the jar on her tailbone.

As she sat there shaking her head slowly and trying not to vomit from the nausea that roiled like a storm-tossed sea in her belly, she became vaguely aware, above the ringing of her ears, of somebody shouting in Shan. She couldn't be sure but it sounded like abuse. Apparently the English-speaker was the patrol leader, and giving the man who'd unloaded on her a good ranking-out.

That encouraged her. Reputedly Marshal Qiangsha had an eye for long-stemmed Western roses. The squad leader's fury suggested she was going to live a bit longer—be marched into camp, probably into the presence of the man himself. Instead of being marched fifty yards or so into the jungle and shot.

Hands caught her arms, hauling her to her feet. This time she was ready, more or less. She wouldn't have fought them even if she could. But the way her head reeled, it was all she could do not to pitch straight forward.

Her captors held on firmly, pressing their hips against hers to keep her upright. They jerked her hands behind her back. Something hard and narrow was looped around her wrists and yanked painfully tight. By the way it bit her flesh, thin on the bone there, she guessed it was a nylon tie.

THE MARSHAL EXCHANGED clipped phrases with the men who had captured Annja.

Given the way the man's shoulders slumped, the big boss was taking his turn dressing down the guy who'd hit her with his rifle. It wasn't very satisfying as moral victories went. She feared she'd gotten concussed. And she doubted Qiangsha was going to let her go by way of compensation for the abuse she'd suffered at his minion's hands.

He turned to look at her. He was actually somewhat handsome, in a lean and hungry way. His head was bare. His olive-drab uniform was crisp and clean and pressed to knife-edge creases. Apparently the job description of marshal of the Grand Shan State Army did not include belly-crawling through the jungle.

"You are American?" he asked, in clear English.

She made a snap decision. "Yes," she said. Disoriented as she was, she hoped that was the right thing to say. Clearly he wasn't an illiterate bandit toting ten pounds of wood and stamped Russian steel in lieu of a spear like the goon who'd hit her, or even the English-speaking squad leader. She didn't trust herself to match wits with him just this moment.

His high brow furrowed as he studied her. The whole right side of her face felt numb, as if she'd had a shot of dentist's Novocain. All too soon that would give way to a headache like a wedge being driven into her skull. She suspected half her face was puffed like a blowfish's.

Still, the marshal seemed to like what he saw. A spill of her hair had come loose and hung down over her left shoulder. She wore a lightweight and light-colored blouse, its floral pattern serving as minor camouflage in the brush, breaking up her silhouette a bit. It was tied up to bare her flat midriff and a generous expanse of lime-green sports bra. Cargo shorts left her long legs mostly bare.

Though she usually preferred to wear short pants and sleeves in the bush anyway, she was dressed that way on purpose.

Qiangsha weighed the camera in his hand. "Nice," he said. "I haven't yet seen this model. I'm an amateur photographer myself."

"I'm not a spy," she said. "I'm a photojournalist. Uh, freelance."

For a moment she thought he might smash Patty's camera. Instead he handed it to a subordinate. He had just acquired a new tool for his hobby.

"And the difference between that and a spy is what?" he enquired.

Annja's normally quick wits now seemed to have their feet stuck to flypaper. She had no answer.

"What's your name?" he asked.

Again, the risk of a lie didn't seem worth the downside if he caught her. "Annja Creed. I work for the Knowledge Channel."

He smiled warmly, almost welcomingly. Her heart rose.

"Outstanding," he said. "They'll doubtless be willing to come up with a most handsome ransom. In the meantime—"

A shout brought his head around. His face clouded. Annja turned her own head, at the risk of both a clout from one of the guards still hovering near to her.

A party of eight or ten men had swung into view around the corner of a structure wholly overtaken by the forest. They were led by a small man, even for a Shan, with a large head, who wore a simple blue band instead of a turban. From the way he swaggered, and the fact he wore a handgun holstered at his hip the way the marshal himself did, Annja guessed he had more than just a small-man's complex going on. Nor was he a mere noncom like the man in charge of the group that captured Annja. Such would never dare carry himself that way for fear of being swatted down hard. He had to be one of Qiangsha's chief lieutenants. Not the best beloved of them, by the look he exchanged with his leader.

The newcomer gave her a quick glance. For all its swiftness she had the feeling it had totally undressed her. He spoke to his nominal master in Tai Shan.

Qiangsha's answering tone sounded pleased. They exchanged a few more words. The lieutenant and his entourage wheeled smartly and strutted away.

Despite what even a befuddled Annja thought was a pretty impertinent departure, Qiangsha now was smiling.

"It seems, Ms. Creed, your countryman, that nitwit Cromwell, has met with sudden misfortune," Qiangsha said. "It's given me the chance to see off those head-hunting little Wa bastards once and for all. Then we'll settle with the local savages who have been giving us fits, and finally get settled in."

He looked past Annja to her guards. "Put her in my quarters," he commanded, still in English. "Guard her well. If anything happens to her, or she escapes—"

He continued his instructions in his own tongue. The stained-oak face of the man at Annja's side went ashen.

Qiangsha nodded briskly and strode off down the steps. The guards seized Annja's upper arms and thrust her up time-eroded stone steps and into cool darkness.

30

The rectangle of light that was the doorway was no longer the blinding white glare it had been for what felt to Annja like days. Evening had settled onto the cluster of semipreserved buildings where Marshal Qiangsha had set up his headquarters. The sky through the opening was dark blue brushed with pink and yellow.

Lying on her side on a woven rice-straw mat, which offered no more cushion from the cold, hard stone beneath than a sheet of paper, Annja had drifted in and out of consciousness all day. Her eyes had grown accustomed to the cavern gloom. She knew she shared the chamber with the marshal's surprisingly Spartan personal furnishings—a cot with a footlocker beside it, a folding table that evidently served as a desk, with a folding chair next to it. A low table next to the cot held a Coleman lantern, currently unlit, and what looked like a couple of paperback novels.

A second door led through the rear wall against which she lay. It was a blank square of blackness. She thought she felt a slight draft, indicating it led to another opening to the outside. She had writhed around earlier to peer down it, but had only seen the dark.

Annja might have gotten to her feet, explored where it led, searched Qiangsha's trunk, the papers on his desk. No one had so much as peeped in at her since she was hustled inside, although she had heard voices off and on throughout the endless afternoon, and smelled periodic cigarette smoke.

But movement still made her dizzy. She saw no reason to take either the effort or the risk. She wasn't here on an intelligence mission.

Whether it turned out to be an intelligent mission was a different question entirely. Right now it looked... not so much.

Marshal Qiangsha had commanded a sizable and relatively effective fighting formation for over ten years, according to Easy. Moreover, he had survived under the most intensely Darwinian conditions, facing constant threats from rivals—Karens, enemy Shan formations, the Tatmadaw Kyee, even the American DEA, which Annja gathered the common folk of Thailand and Burma regarded as just another ruthless ethnic army, no better than any other—and potential challenges from his own subchiefs. Like the cocky low-rent Napoleon who'd brought the news of Jerry Cromwell's sudden fall from grace. Qiangsha had to be smart to have survived. And he was clearly a thoroughgoing professional, in his way.

Historian that she was, Annja knew disease killed far more soldiers than bullets or shells did. Even though they were natives, relatively inured to local contagion, plague would have winnowed the GSSA ranks if Qiangsha had not clamped an iron hygiene discipline on his troops. Whether he'd known it at the outset or had to learn it, Qiangsha clearly understood that.

He understood way too much, Annja feared.

She had taken a calculated risk coming here. Now she wondered in her aching head if she'd calculated well at all. Easy said they were much alike. Which, aside from strongly differing views on professional ethics and even more wildly divergent backgrounds, increasingly struck her as true.

And maybe that means I share Easy's propensity for intellectual arrogance, just a wee little bit, she thought. Or was it some kind of smug subconscious racism that made me underestimate Qiangsha?

One thing was clear to her—if she did not see, and seize, some opportunity soon, she was lost. And so too were the Protectors. And the vast, untold trove of cultural heritage that was the temple complex. And the priceless Golden Elephant.

Overwhelmed, she lost consciousness again.

THE SOUND OF A BOOT crunching on stone roused her. Annja rolled over from facing the stone wall.

Light flared orange, then yellow, then white. Marshal Qiangsha straightened up from where he had just lit the lantern beside his bed. He smiled.

"It has been a good day," he said. A flare of orange light from the doorway caught her eye. She glanced out to see a bonfire blaze up before the building he had chosen as his personal billet. Voices shouted and laughed to one another outside. "The Wa barbarians have been routed. We've won," he proclaimed.

From the slight overprecision with which he spoke, Annja guessed he was drunk. That could be very good for her. Or very bad. Like, basically, everything here and now, she thought.

She forced herself to sit up. Though her head had mostly cleared, the exertion drained her; she slumped back against the wall.

Her shirt was untied and fell open. She still had the green sports bra on, and it was a pretty effective sight barrier. Still, she arched her back to thrust her cleavage, such as it was, toward her captor.

"I know where I stand," she told the startled-looking marshal. "I'm completely at your mercy here. If I just vanish, who'd ever know?"

He blinked at her owlishly. "This is true. But why tell me this? Isn't it against your interests?"

She smiled as seductively as she knew how. Given her track record, that wasn't very. "I figure my best chance is to earn your goodwill. So I want to show you a victory celebration you'll never forget," she said.

Cross my heart and hope not to die.

"Ah," he said.

"Do you want me tied?" She tossed back her hair. "I can do much better for you if my hands are free."

He stared at her with one brow arched.

Did I overplay my hand? she wondered as the moment stretched toward infinity.

Then inspiration hit. "Or are you afraid? You can't take us Western women lightly, you know," she said, challenging him.

He glared at her. Now Annja feared she had pushed too hard. Then he laughed. His laughter had a ragged edge to it. An ugly edge.

"You Western women," he said, swaggering toward her, "are arrogant and spoiled. You always overestimate yourselves. As you underestimate us Asians."

He grabbed her by the arm and hauled her to her feet. "Ow," she complained. "That hurts."

He laughed. "See? You're just a woman after all. And my men are right outside."

He brought his hand up. With a snick he opened a lock-back folder. It was a good knife, she saw, a Spyderco. Or at least a pretty convincing knockoff.

"Really," he said, reaching behind her, "what choice have you got, other than to do your best to make me happy?"

She gasped as the keen blade sliced her skin. The plastic restraint parted. Blood rushed back into her hands. It felt as if she had plunged them into red-hot sand.

She had been wondering if she could do this thing.

It seemed so cold-blooded. But knowing his plans, it had to be done.

He was armed—he held a knife with a four-inch blade. She knew it would certainly serve to slit her helpless female throat when he was done with her.

She put her face to his ear. "What choice have I got?" she asked throatily.

He grabbed her hair with his left hand. And stiffened.

She stepped back. To give him a good look at the sword that had appeared from thin air an eye blink before she rammed it through his belly.

He opened his mouth. All that came out was a voiceless squeal. And blood.

She tore the sword free with both hands. Marshal Qiangsha fell to the stone floor.

The quick flurry of motion had apparently caught eyes outside. She heard voices coming closer. A shadow fell across the doorway.

Annja turned and bolted through the back door. She prayed it indeed led out into the night.

UNSEEN, THE ROOT ARCHED up out of the red clay earth and caught Annja's right instep as if it had deliberately reached to trip her. Winded from her desperate broken-field run, still dizzy from aftereffects of the blow to the head hours before, she couldn't prevent herself pitching into a bush. Another tree root sticking up from the ground gave her a savage crack on the forehead as she hit, causing a white flash behind her eyes.

If she had gotten a concussion earlier, it might have a friend to keep it company now, she thought.

She lay still. She had used up all her energy fleeing the tumult of the GSSA camp—and the angry pursuit hounding after her. Her last molecules of strength had been knocked out of her by the fall. For endless, horrific moments it was all she could do to lie there and breathe.

In the distance she heard the sporadic clatter of gunfire from the direction of the late Marshal Qiangsha's camp. As she fought to stifle trapped-animal moans of pain and desperation, she heard the distance-dulled thump of a grenade. The issue of who should succeed as marshal of the Grand Shan State Army was still being vigorously debated.

For all his apparent executive ability, Qiangsha had in the end just been the leader of a bandit gang. Like most such groups, the GSSA ultimately operated by the ethics of a wolf pack—the most dangerous male ruled. Like many leaders of such human packs, Qiangsha apparently had secured his own position in part by keeping his chief lieutenants in constant rivalry with one another. The theory was they'd be so occupied trying to pull one another down, and to prevent themselves being torn apart by ever-hungry rivals, they would leave the alpha in relative safety. Among others Adolf Hitler had practiced the technique, successfully enough, so far as it went.

But it meant that when the alpha was removed from the scene, no subordinate held a strong enough position to assert dominance and make it stick.

But dominance wars hadn't stopped a smaller wolf pack from baying after Annja.

She knew she could not have run far. It was less than two miles from the middle of Qiangsha's camp to the middle of the Protector village. But Annja had dodged and backtracked as she ran through the jungle, trying to lose her pursuers in the humid night.

She had failed. She had, however, succeeded in losing herself.

She had managed to bushwhack three of her pursuers and kill them with her sword. But always their comrades had been on her like rabid dogs, driving her away before she could scavenge a firearm. The calculus was inescapable—sooner or later they'd hem her in and finish her with gunfire. Or she'd simply catch a stray bullet from one of the random bursts the pursuers loosed periodically, in hope of just such a lucky hit on their prey.

"Move, damn you," she gasped to herself. She got her hands beneath her, pushed herself upward from the warm, moist, fragrant earth.

Vegetation rustled behind her. She turned her head to look back over her shoulder.

A Shan stood eight feet away. He grinned as he raised his big rifle to aim at her.

His head suddenly jerked to the right. Dark fluid jetted from his right temple. He slumped straight down to the ground like an imploded building collapsing.

Annja heard the high sharp crack of the handgun shot that had killed him. Another man burst into the moonlight several paces behind, thrusting his Kalashnikov before him. Before he could spray the prone and still-helpless Annja he dropped the heavy weapon, clapped a hand to his left eye and uttered a shrill scream. A wood sliver, doubtless tipped with poison, that had just been blown into his eye from a bamboo pipe.

Gunfire crashed out to either side of her. She had already heard someone walking toward her from the direction she had been running. She looked around.

A small, emphatically female form strode toward her. Gunfire flashed from its right hand, then its left.

Easy Ngwenya knelt by Annja's side. "Lord, girl, you look a fright. Are you all right?"

"Never…better," Annja croaked. She sensed Protectors slipping past like shadows. Shadows that occasionally paused to reveal themselves in shattering blasts and jumping flares of full-auto gunfire. Few shots came back in reply. The surviving pursuers had already turned and fled back the way they had come.

"What…took you?" Annja said. "Couldn't find me?"

"My dear girl, neither the Shans nor the Wa answer nature's call without the Protectors knowing within moments what they had for breakfast, to be perfectly crude. And anyway, you and your fan club were about as subtle as water buffalo stampeding."

"I thought speed was more important than stealth," Annja said, sitting up. The African woman had holstered her left-hand piece and offered her a canteen. She accepted and drank desperately.

"Wise choice," Easy said. "But therein lay our problem—we had the devil's own time intercepting you. When you were keeping away from the Shans, you also kept away from us."

Annja spit. Her mouth felt like an old gym shoe. "Qiangsha said Jerry Cromwell's dead."

"Oh, yes." Easy smiled and nodded. "Curiously enough, the wound proved instantly fatal. I rather feared he'd live on for days without his head, like a roach."

Annja shook her head. "And the Wa?"

"Gone with the proverbial wind. Apparently they took their prophet being struck down in their midst as a sign the Lord had withdrawn his favor from them. The GSSA did their brutal best to reinforce the impression. The last living Wa was off the mesa by sunset."

"Last living?"

"A few were unwise enough to straggle. The Protectors can be remarkably vindictive. They aren't given to torture. Inflicting sudden death—that's another thing."

She stooped to wind Annja's arm over her shoulder. "And now we'd best be getting back. While our Shan friends are occupied killing each other, the Protectors are going to encourage them to move their dispute elsewhere."

"But they still outnumber the Protectors!" Annja said.

"To be sure," Easy said. With surprising strength she pushed off, hoisting Annja to her feet with little help from the larger woman. "But with them split into multiple factions, demoralized by recent events, and with the Protectors fighting the sort of battle they know best—sniping from the trees and the like—I doubt they'll have much stomach for staying where they're so obviously unwanted."

31

"Seriously, Easy," Annja said. "We need to work this out."

"Well," Easy said. Was the lightness in her voice real or feigned? "The villagers did give us free rein to do as we will up here."

It had been a brisk climb through stinging morning sun up the sheer face of the red pinnacle to the Temple of the Elephant. Despite their bruises and residual exhaustion from their recent adventures, the two young women had climbed with vigor. We're nothing if not resilient, Annja reflected.

"I doubt that means they'll let us steal their priceless idol," Annja said. It gave her a jolt to recall that she had come here at great personal cost—and as she could never forget, far greater cost to her companions—to do exactly that. But I didn't know about the Protectors then, she thought.

It sounded lame even inside her head.

"We agreed, did we not," Easy said, "that we'd get up here and then see what we might see? After all—"

She started to say more. But then they mounted high enough on the steps inside the temple's spacious foyer to behold the Golden Elephant itself, its golden glory brilliantly lit by a ray of morning sun through the arched entryway.

Annja stopped. She couldn't seem to breathe.

"Oh, my God," Easy said.

"This changes things," Annja managed to say.

"Quite."

"Ladies," a male voice said in musically accented English from behind them, "there's no need to fight. As entertaining as that would be to watch, I'm afraid I cannot take the risk."

The two young women spun in place.

"Giancarlo?" Easy said in a breathless schoolgirl gasp.

"Giancarlo?" Annja said in shock.

The archaeologist smiled a smile as radiant as the idol itself—still out of his view beyond the high temple steps.

He stood limned against electric morning dazzle. He was flanked by pairs of burly men in expensive expedition wear. They pointed handguns at Easy and Annja.

"You son of a bitch," both women said at once.

He spread his hands innocently. "Ah. Harsh language does nothing to help us here."

Annja's throat was suddenly so dry she had to work

her mouth to summon saliva and swallow before she could force words out. "So you're behind this," she said angrily.

"Not exactly," he said, still smiling benignly. He wore no pack, but his normally svelte figure looked oddly bulky beneath the lightweight tan jacket he wore. Despite a bit of a breeze it was hot as hell out there in the morning; Annja and Easy alike were sheened with sweat from their own exertion scaling the seventy-foot sheer precipice. Giancarlo looked as cool as if he lounged in an air-conditioned private club in Buenos Aires. "Let's say I accepted a commission similar to the one that propelled you both here."

"So you set us up," Annja said as mental tumblers fell into place with clicks she thought Easy ought to be able to hear beside her. "You…got the red ants and the black to fight."

"Competition, the current wisdom avers, works wonders. And in any event, by the time I was offered the commission you both had attained a substantial lead. So I thought—" he shrugged "—why wastefully duplicate effort myself, when not just one but two brilliant and ingenious young women were already on the trail? Simpler to let you do what you did so well, and follow in your tracks."

"But I slept with you!" Easy wailed.

Annja shifted her weight uncomfortably. "You, too?" Easy asked her.

"No," Annja stated emphatically, relieved it was the truth.

Giancarlo cleared his throat. "Ladies," he said, raising his voice only slightly. It echoed within the high arched foyer of the Temple.

The professional-archaeologist part of her mind, still working below surging tidal layers of despair, outrage and fury, told Annja that must be a mark of sophisticated acoustic design.

"I fear we've no time for recriminations. Or rather, you've no time for recriminations."

"Not so fast, pal," Annja said. "You killed Sir Sidney. And poor Isabelle!"

"And set those dogs on me in Montmartre," Easy added.

"Whom you dispatched with admirable ruthlessness, my dear," Scarlatti said. "As for Professor Hazelton, do these look like hands that could beat a gentle old man to death? No, it was Luigi, here, who did in the ridiculous old blatherer." His head flip indicated a goon on his right, who had a slab jaw and a black-browed scowl.

"And a fearful mess he made, although I scarcely blame him. An unavoidable by-product of such work. As for Professor Gendron, though, I admit I pulled the trigger on her. An occupation at least marginally more suited for a gentleman."

He shrugged. "You must admit, it proved an admirable goad. You in particular acted like one obsessed, Annja Creed. You drove your expedition furiously enough to shed all three of your companions without requiring my assistance at all."

Her eyes narrowed with fury. Not content with using her—and Easy, too, a vulnerable child still in so many ways for all her erudition and lethality—he was now sticking his finger in her rawest emotional wound and twisting. Clearly he was a master psychologist. And a sociopath.

"You're a dead man, Giancarlo," Easy growled. Her tone suggested an angry cat. Her eyes had grown red.

He laughed. "So we've progressed to the threats stage. Obviously, the fact that my quartet of multinational stalwarts have the drop on you fails to make the slightest impression.

"And well it might, seeing the deft way in which you saw off heavily armed and bloodthirsty foes in just a few days. Did you know both the Lord's Wa Army and the remnants of the GSSA have dragged their pathetic tails entirely out of the district? They must have thought the temple was guarded by demons in all fact."

Annja glanced at Easy. She had taken for granted the woman was no more inclined than her to go down without a fight. Unfortunately it was looking as if Giancarlo had, too. Cagey bastard.

"Of course, with the indigenous defenders scattered to shadow their defeated foes, and weary from their battle, it proved relatively easy for my men and I to make our way here undetected. However, as you'll appreciate, our time here is limited. So I've resorted to a traditionally invaluable adjunct of what we might call the more informal brand of archaeology—dynamite."

Annja gasped.

"You wouldn't!" Easy exclaimed. Annja's eyes flickered toward her in surprise. She would've expected a pot hunter to embrace the use of dynamite to get at the goods.

Then again she realized she had never seen any evidence that Easy used destructive means in her activities, pot hunting though they were.

"Spoken like a true academic, my dear," Giancarlo said, allowing his tone to taunt. "I've murdered two innocents, that you know of, contrived the murder of heaven knows how many more. And you think I'm going to shrink from blowing up some half-rotted ancient public works project to get what I want?"

He held open his jacket. He wore a nylon vest with dynamite sticks tucked neatly into special loops, like cartridges on an old-fashioned bandolier.

"Where'd you get that?" Annja asked, "Safari Outfitters' special suicide-bomber shop?"

"Whistling past the graveyard, Annja," he said. "Admirable spirit—execrable judgment."

"You wouldn't actually kill yourself," Easy said. Her tone belied her words.

He shrugged again. "As you may have inferred, bright young women that you are, I am a most results-oriented man, as opposed to a process-oriented one. Failure is unthinkable to me in anything I set my mind to.

"I am also, I pride myself to say, a consummate realist. You are both dangerous as vipers. You are highly resourceful. And you are scarcely more encumbered by conventional morality concerning the employment of violent means than I am myself. I take for granted that you will try to turn the tables on me. Likewise I take for granted that should you succeed, my own life span will be measurable in milliseconds."

He reached in a pocket, brought out something roughly the size of a cell phone and clicked a button with his thumb. "This is, please take my word for it, what is quaintly yet accurately termed a dead man's switch. Should you ladies contrive to spring some lethal reverse upon us, then you, and I, and this temple with all its priceless archaeology and culture will be blown to rubble. See how I respect your personhood?"

He looked left and right and nodded his head briskly. "Now, gentlemen."

A pair of husky goons each advanced upon Annja and Easy. They held guns before them, one arm locked out, the other bent for support, and moved with little crab steps in approved counterterrorist style. Annja almost laughed out loud.

"Rather pretentious for hired thugs, wouldn't you say?" Easy muttered sidelong to her.

"Spirited to the end, I say!" Giancarlo called out. He seemed a little miffed at losing his stage for a moment. "And now, since you've been doing as much of the talking as I—"

"Another lie," Easy said.

"I can't be convicted of monologuing if I go ahead and acknowledge what I'm sure is obvious to you both—once the treasure, and we, have flown, you two will be found here. Apparently a classic battle between archaeological good and evil will have been resolved by the tragic deaths of both comely young contestants. So sad."

While one goon held down on Easy with a 9 mm Beretta his partner relieved her of her two Sphinxes. She only smiled a cool smile.

She glanced at Annja. Easy was clearly not giving up.

Nor would Annja.

If Giancarlo had his way with this site, as he had with Easy—and thankfully not Annja, although she felt a weird chill sickness in her stomach at how close she had come, and bitterly resented every second she had spent longing to be reunited with him—the treasure and its priceless context were done anyway. So, obviously, were Easy and Annja. And he was right that his announcing his plans to them didn't matter much, since they'd worked them out for themselves already, thank you very much, she thought bitterly.

Annja carried no obvious weapon. So while one thug, a little shamefacedly, pointed his Glock at her, his partner grabbed her upper arm.

"You gentlemen have things well in hand," Giancarlo said. "Now let's see what prize awaits us behind door number one."

He swept confidently up the steps past Annja and Easy.

Then he stopped. And stared. *"Dios mio!"* he all but shrieked.

"Boss?" the man with the Glock said in English. His eyes flicked to Giancarlo.

The sword flashed into existence. Blood spurted from the stumps of the gunman's wrists. His piece, still clasped in both scarred hands, clattered on the worn ancient stone steps.

Easy Ngwenya's right hand whipped up over her head. Silver flashed. The gunman holding her grunted as the chromed hilt of a specialized throwing danger suddenly protruded from the juncture of jaw and throat. Easy was just jam-packed with surprises, it seemed.

As his lifeblood spurted past the left hand he had clasped immediately to the wound, his right pumped out two shots, even their echoes shatteringly loud in the entryway.

The bullets slammed into his partner, above the body of Easy Ngwenya, who had twisted free of the second man and dropped prone.

Annja turned away from the screaming, spurting man. The other had released her arm in astonishment. Now he tried to bring up his gun to shoot her.

It was Luigi, she noted, in the split second before she split the heavy, brutal face to the chin with a downward stroke.

Annja heard more shots. Giancarlo ducked an end-the-world slash of her sword and scampered back down the stairs. He held the dead man's switch out at the two women like a talisman.

"Don't forget!" he screamed. "I have this! I'll use it!"

Annja looked around. Both of Easy's opponents lay

facedown in widening pools of blood and she had her Sphinxes in her hands. She was an efficient little creature when it all came down, Annja had to admit.

"But you haven't, Giani," Easy said in contemptuous tones. "Because you still have hope. And because it's so unthinkable to you that you should lose you're not ready to admit defeat by ending your worthless life."

Fury blazed in his wide eyes. He pushed the switch toward her.

Easy shot him.

Annja braced for instant immolation. Then as the thump of the bullet hitting soft flesh—not dynamite—reached her ears even beneath the cracking and ringing of the gunshot she saw blood appear on the fine fawn-colored designer fabric over his flat abdomen. He grunted and bent over in terrible agony.

"The pain reflex has caused your muscles to contract," Easy said. "It won't be so easy to let go of the button, now—"

Annja was already in motion. A skipping, spinning back kick took Giancarlo in his injured belly. He screamed hoarsely, staggered back to the very edge of the precipice.

He raised the dead man's switch. Annja kicked him again, hard.

As he fell Annja turned and threw herself facedown on the stone. From a corner of her eye she saw Easy do the same.

The rock face directed the blast's force outward and

upward. All that came in through the yawning temple entrance was a cataclysmic roar, and a dragon's-breath puff of superheated air.

32

Annja stood on the sidewalk in front of a house whose several levels laddered down from the top of a steep black lava cliff. It stood just outside Hilo, Hawaii. This was the last stop on her current quest. It would also be the hardest.

She thought it might be the hardest task she had ever faced.

The Protectors had recovered Eddie Chen's corpse the morning after he died, contemptuously under the noses of the Grand Shan State Army, which was still scaling the mesa at that point.

After Giancarlo met his spectacular end, Annja and Easy had recovered Patty from the mesa's base where the Shans had left her. The Protectors helped—they were willing to do almost anything for the outsiders who had helped them carry out their ancient charge.

Easy's solution to the problem of transporting corpses was brutally direct—she bribed a local drug gang to smuggle them out of Myanmar. The Protectors helped her find one that would stay bribed, in process dropping a few hints that Easy had played a big part in causing the hasty departure of both the GSSA and the Lord's Wa Army, now disbanded, from the scene. Not just the ancient sanctum's defenders but the lesser predators and scavengers heaved a major sigh of relief at that.

What the Protectors weren't willing to do, even for their allies, was allow the temple complex, or the special Temple of the Elephant on its lonely peak, to be revealed to the world. They would continue to await the return of Maitreya as their ancestors had been bidden by the long-vanished princes of Bagan.

To Annja's astonishment Easy concurred readily with her decision to forgo recovery of any artifacts whatever. Even the Golden Elephant.

"Why, Annja," she said with a laugh, "it was never about the money. That's just a token to me—like points in a video game. It helps me keep track of my score. What need do I have for money? My daddy will pay literally anything to keep me from coming home.

"And anyway, once I realized there were actually people up here looking after the site—the owners, in effect—I gave over any intention I had of making off with anything. Dead people have no property, and I don't respect the claims of any government. Least of all one so thoroughly vile as the SPDC. But real, living people—them I leave alone. Unless, of course, they commit aggression. Against me or my friends."

Annja shook her head. She could not quite grasp her new friend's ethics. But she knew beyond the shadow of a doubt that Easy had ethics. A code as ironbound as her own, no matter how peculiar.

Annja would also never agree with it. At least when it came to their vision of their shared profession.

"It wasn't hard for me to let go of the idea of taking the idol," Easy said cheerfully. "It was all for the sport, all along. It always is for me. And maybe more for you than you realize."

"Perhaps," Annja said.

Easy sobered then. "And I think we both got rather more excitement than we bargained for."

Annja nodded. "I sure did."

"So, about that sword. How did you manage to get it?" Easy said.

Annja shrugged. "I always have a few tricks up my sleeve."

Easy laughed but did not push for a proper answer.

They stood together in Bangkok's Suvarnabhumi Airport, awaiting respective flights out. Despite political protests in Thailand and rising internal violence in Myanmar, travelers, foreign tourists and locals alike moved past them, as oblivious to them as to the world's turmoil.

But maybe less to them. Both continued to attract plenty of attention from male passersby. Since Annja and Easy were legal for once, fully documented under their real names and everything, they could afford to ignore the fact they made an arresting picture—the tall, slender white woman and the short, buxom black one.

"I won't say goodbye, Annja," Easy said. "I suspect our paths will cross again. And I shall keep in touch."

Annja regarded her. Cocky, impudent, a strange mixture of ageless wisdom and early-adolescent immaturity.

"You realize we're still on opposite sides of the law," she said sternly. "I'll put you out of business if I can."

"You'll try," Easy said, laughing.

She looked up. "Well, there's my flight."

She hugged Annja, as fervently as a child. Annja returned the embrace warmly, if not so tight.

Easy raised her face toward Annja's ear. To Annja's amazement the girl's huge brown eyes gleamed with moisture.

"Thank you, my sister," Easy whispered.

"Thank you, too," Annja said.

"OKAY," ANNJA SAID, returning her thoughts to the present. The morning sun warmed her face. "This won't get easier from being put off."

The first time had been hard. Though he had other children, Master Chen had lost his eldest son. His heir. The boy he had raised, sternly and lovingly, from babyhood, the man he expected to take his place in the world. He showed little emotion at hearing the news.

Annja knew he would grieve later, as any parent would who must commit the unthinkable—burying a child.

The second had been, surprisingly, not as hard. Patricia Ruhle's older sister was a Realtor in Connecticut. She had received Annja's news at a coffee shop in Mystic with a sad headshake.

"It was inevitable," she said. "We knew that all along." *We* meaning the rest of the family, whom Sarah Kingman would now have to inform. Including a young army Ranger somewhere in Afghanistan.

"Patty was an adrenaline junkie," Sarah said matter-of-factly. "She admitted it. She wouldn't have been a crisis photojournalist otherwise. And she always told us up front—she knew that one day, like any addiction, hers would kill her."

The woman looked down at her cup of green tea, untasted. "And now it has," she said quietly, and dabbed at her eyes with a napkin.

But this—

Annja supposed she shouldn't have been surprised, especially given what she had seen of the world that few others did. She already knew there existed firms, not altogether legal, that specialized in the covert recovery of loved ones from troubled developing nations. What she never realized was that some specialized in bringing back the dead. If not to life, at least to their families.

It was actually easier in a way, a few moments' reflection had told her. Nobody had to spring a corpse from a fortresslike jail guarded by trigger-happy thugs with machine guns.

It surprised her rather less that Easy knew of such companies. And quite a bit more that Easy paid to recover the remains of the late Dr. Philip Kennedy from a Shan Plateau village.

"It seems only fair," Easy had said with a shrug. "You'll do the right thing, of course. Because you're Annja Creed. But to speak practically, you're considerably out of pocket on this whole enterprise already. And these services don't come cheap."

She shrugged. "And as I said, money's not that important to me. But please don't mistake this for altruism. I feel I owe you for the pain I put you through, even though the better part was entirely unwitting. And for your help in aiding the Protectors."

"You really cared about them," Annja observed. She had smiled a little then. "Isn't that altruism?"

"Not at all," Easy said with a big grin. "As I told you, I identify to a high degree with tribal peoples. And I harbor a hatred of injustice—of unfairness. Just as you do."

"Okay. But how is that not altruistic?"

Easy laughed. "It gratifies me hugely to aid the victims of bullying," she said. "And if I get to smite the bullies in the process, so much the better!"

"All right," Annja said now, on the Hawaiian roadside with her rented car pinging at her as its engine cooled in the shade of a palm tree. "No more delay."

She had no more excuses. She had to march right up to the door, ring the bell, and then tell a little girl she would never see her father again.

She reached into a pocket of her khaki trousers and took out a piece of paper. On it was printed a digital photograph.

She gazed down at it. Taken by Easy, using Patty Ruhle's camera, it showed Annja standing beside the object of the long and bloody quest—the Golden Elephant.

The two-story-tall Golden Elephant. Even though it had been cast hollow it must, according to Easy's calculations, weigh at least ten metric tons.

An object of incalculable worth, to be sure. However, it wasn't going anywhere.

The photo was all the mystery patron who had commissioned Annja was ever going to get of the fabled treasure that so obsessed him. Given that he—or she—had seen fit to likewise commission E. C. Ngwenya and the charming, treacherous, sociopathic Giancarlo Scarlatti to compete with her in the hunt, it was more than the anonymous patron deserved. To Annja, anyway.

One thing was certain—she would not be e-mailing the image to Roux.

She wanted to be there in person to see the look on his smug, bearded, immortal face when he saw it.

Smiling, she tucked the photo back in the pocket and buttoned it again. Then, drawing a deep breath, she squared her shoulders and set off along the lava-graveled path to the door.

ROOM 59

THE HARDEST CHOICES
ARE THE MOST PERSONAL....

New recruit Jason Siku is ex-CIA, a cold, calculating
agent with black ops skills and a brilliant mind—a
loner perfect for deep espionage work. Using his Inuit
heritage and a search for his lost family as cover, he
tracks intelligence reports of a new Russian Oscar-class
submarine capable of reigniting the Cold War. But when
Jason discovers weapons smugglers and an idealistic yet
dangerous brother he never knew existed, his mission
and a secret hope collide with deadly consequences.

Look for

THE ties THAT BIND

by

cliff RYDER

GOLD
EAGLE®

Available October 2008
wherever books are sold.

GRM594

JAMES AXLER

DEATH LANDS®

Plague Lords

In a ruined world, past and future clash with terrifying force...

The sulfur-teeming Gulf of Mexico is the poisoned end of earth, but here, Ryan and the others glean rumors of whole cities deep in South America that survived the blast intact. But as the companions contemplate a course of action, a new horror approaches on the horizon. The Lords of Death are Mexican pirates raiding stockpiles with a grim vengeance. When civilization hits rock bottom, a new stone age will emerge, with its own personal day of blood reckoning.

In the Deathlands, the future could always be worse. Now it is...

Available December wherever you buy books.

If you are looking for spine-tingling action and adventure, be sure to check out all that Gold Eagle books has to offer...

Rogue Angel by **Alex Archer**
Deathlands by **James Axler**
Outlanders by **James Axler**
The Executioner by **Don Pendleton**
Mack Bolan by **Don Pendleton**
Stony Man by **Don Pendleton**
NEW **Room 59** by **Cliff Ryder**

Journey to lost worlds, experience the heat of a fierce firefight, survive in a postapocalyptic future or go deep undercover with clandestine operatives.

Look for these books wherever books are sold.

GOLD EAGLE ®

Fiction that surprises, gratifies and entertains. Real Heroes. Real Adventure.

www.readgoldeagle.blogspot.com